KILLER

DREAMS

VINCENT DONOVAN

Black Rose Writing | Texas

ISBN: 978-1-68513-255-2
PUBLISHED BY BLACK ROSE WRITING
www.blackrosewriting.com

Printed in the United States of America
Suggested Retail Price (SRP) $22.95

Killer Dreams is printed in Book Antiqua

*As a planet-friendly publisher, Black Rose Writing does its best to eliminate unnecessary waste to reduce paper usage and energy costs, while never compromising the reading experience. As a result, the final word count vs. page count may not meet common expectations.

To Mom and Dad – who led with their souls.

KILLER

DREAMS

"To sleep, perchance to dream — ay, there's the rub."
–Shakespeare, *Hamlet*

CHAPTER ONE

CASSIE MACLEAN STARED at the pool of liquid wax in the bottom of the glass candle jar and resisted the urge. For the past ten years, every candle she blew out was accompanied with a silent plea for the nightmare to end. But not today. Instead, she let the saliva pool in her mouth before hurling it at the dancing flame.

"Sometimes spit is just pissed off tears," she whispered to the insulted wick.

She turned away and began clearing the dining room table, aware how it contrasted with this morning's frenetic pace in preparing another Stuff-o-Rama-Thanksgiving. After peeling vegetables and baking pies, she painstakingly tunneled under the cellar stairs thick with spider webs and retrieved the mahogany leaf, even though the extra place settings were no longer required. After wrestling the heavy panel in place, she ironed the burgundy linen tablecloth before meticulously arranging three place settings with vintage fine china.

Surveying the remnants of the feast no one said grace over, she let a small sigh escape from her pursed lips as anticipation outweighed the experience. No matter the venue: birthday parties, exotic vacations, first dates, proms — and dare she admit after a bottle of wine, even her wedding night when James came down with the flu, all left her feeling underwhelmed. Mom's heinous surprise was the lone exception. It came like a deadly

1

earthquake, despite the bedrock foundation of their lives and wreaked devastation. The aftershocks never stopped. Every Thanksgiving since then had been another day in Numbs-Ville.

The internal referee flagged her for being ungrateful. In response, she glanced toward the family room. James and William made a beeline for the leather couch after inhaling dinner and half an apple cream pie. They pleaded with her to leave the monstrous mess and watch football with them. Her son even promised to help with the dishes afterwards, but she waved them away saying, "let me tidy up a bit." If her scripture quoting mother was not in a coma mapping all the dead ends within the giant cornfield maze of limbo, she would chime in and say her only daughter was more Martha than Mary, always busying herself with the inconsequential.

Cassie tried to outrun the self-flagellation by transporting three dinner plates to the kitchen counter. She thought of the colorful wine glass charms in the shapes of farm animals Cathy from work used at parties, but none were required for these plates. Her husband James was a deeply devoted carnivore and everyone marveled how he resembled Bamm-Bamm as a kid with long hair and super strength. His plate contained the stripped-clean bones of a turkey leg and a sizable lump of squash. William might be fifteen — and proclaim once a week he was nothing like them, but swap out the squash for mashed potatoes, and he was a Rubble too. In comparison, her plate looked stark with an unbuttered roll and a small clump of stuffing on the white plate. Normally, she would dismiss this as being brought up to not waste food, but this holiday robbed her of an appetite long ago.

To the left of the sink, she eyed the carcass of the twelve-pound bird, its warm juices long gone. "Pretty fowl," she said with half a smirk and hesitated for a second, waiting for a cymbal to clang. Picking up the carving knife, she pushed the skeleton around the grease-stained cutting board, and scrutinized the great hollow stuffed with cranberries, oranges and onions. When she took it out of the oven, the delicious aroma filled the kitchen. Now the congealed juices smelled like fat and turned her stomach. It reminded her of carefree days when she would spend hours getting ready to go out dancing, but come midnight smelled like stale beer and tobacco. Gently touching the white breastbone, she wondered was *this structure ever a bird?* She recalled a story that popped up on her news feed this morning detailing how processors butcher some forty-six million turkeys for Thanksgiving and another twenty-two million for Christmas. As she tried to wrap her head around numbers similar in size to the combined population of California and Florida, her index finger anxiously tried swiping the story away, but her eyes continued scanning most of the gruesome article, like rubbernecking an accident scene.

Cassie traded the knife for the extra wine glass she stationed next to the stove. She learned the trick from her mom, who for as long as she could remember positioned liquor stations throughout the house, just in case an earthquake hit or the Russians nuked us. If so, at least she could crawl to one of these emergency stockpiles, and enjoy last call. She took another sip and glanced again at the turkey skeleton, recalling how the giblets come nicely wrapped in a bag. But what happened to the millions of amputated heads? She recalled taking William on a field trip and learning how male turkey heads change colors throughout the day; blue if excited, bright red when stressed. She could guess what color they were when the end came. As usual, the stoic females didn't make a fuss.

She looked away. *Mom's head may still be attached to her body but who knows where she really is?* Her eyes narrowed. *And what about Dad? He's been acting like he lost his head since meeting that gold-digger after that horrible night.*

The silence suddenly made itself known and ended the dark thoughts. The quiet was puzzling, since James liked to watch football with the volume turned way up. He said it made him feel like he was in the stadium, even if the real reason was to drown out his expletive filled rants. She picked up her wine glass and headed toward the family room, expecting to find her husband and son passed out from the effects of tryptophan.

Instead, she discovered the television off, and her husband and son sitting on the floor cross-legged and wearing matching gym socks. They were sporting silly looking headsets, and she watched their fingers twitch on dual controllers as they played in some virtual reality world. She rolled her eyes and took a good swig of the Gewurztraminer, feeling beyond aggravated James broke his promise and keep this a tech free day. Technology had been a major point of contention in their marriage. Whether it be computers, video games or the latest iPhone, her husband prided himself on being an early adopter, which he also used as an escape valve when he did not want to deal with her. To be fair, his passion had been handsomely rewarded. He earned advanced degrees in computer science and interactive entertainment. This led to several interesting gigs, and he recently joined Advanced Tomorrows, which planned on taking virtual reality to a new level in gaming. As Head of R&D, he worked eighty-hour weeks, and by the time he stumbled home, had little left in the tank for her or their son. She replayed how he burst into the kitchen last night, cradling a large cardboard box.

"That's strange packaging for pizza," she snapped.

The six foot-two-frame shrunk a couple of inches, and he smacked his forehead. "I'm such an idiot," he said wincing. "I was on a conference call all the way home and totally spaced." He placed the box on the counter. "I'll call, and see if they can deliver."

"Good luck with that! No one is cooking tonight. Any order will take two hours."

He sprang forward, and wrapped his arms around her. It seemed the only time he hugged her anymore was to prevent her anger from redlining. She broke away, and smelled the musky cologne he saved for the office. The thought troubled her, and she filed it away.

"But think how much more we will enjoy the feast tomorrow after surviving on peanut butter and jelly tonight," he said pointing at a pot of peeled potatoes on the stove. He gave her a quick peck on the cheek.

It was his ability to find the silver lining in most things she found so endearing when they first met. But after twenty years together, she understood how an overused strength can become a weakness. James used his charm as a shield for his screwups. She broke away.

He pointed at the box on the counter as his blue eyes danced from either excitement or hoping to locate safer ground. "I brought home a version of our new virtual reality product. This is a game changer! It allows players to communicate without talking as new revolutionary sensors target the frontal lobe that's responsible for speech. I can't wait to show Will. We haven't spent much time together lately, and this immersive technology will blow him away. Every other product on the market looks cartoonish compared to this, and don't get me started about the sensory perception my team developed!" He motioned to her. "You'll have to try it too."

The only weapon within reach was a wooden serving spoon. She grabbed it off the counter, and pointed it at him. "Our son is at Steve's house and won't be home until nine, so I have plenty of time to beat this into you," she said pointing at the box, "and you won't need a headset to know what I'm thinking!" She waved the spoon at him. "We haven't been a family since you started that all-consuming job, and this is how you plan on spending Thanksgiving? In make-believe land?" She flung the spoon in the sink, and the clang announced the round was over.

Her husband retrieved the box, apparently afraid she might attack it next. "Let me get the pizza squared away and after we eat, I'll dig out Monopoly for after dinner tomorrow. Will loves beating us."

She took another mouthful of warm wine, remembering how her mother sought refuge in a bottle because her husband was mostly MIA too. James and William drove home the point as they were exploring some alien world while she remained marooned in a hundred-year-old house on Main Street in Salem, New Hampshire. With previous test products, James would put the display on the large screen tv, so she could at least watch their antics and admire the realistic graphics. But with this product, they sat in silence and only their fingers moved. *Didn't it occur to James to bring three headsets home?*

As she pondered how to interrupt them without ruining the rest of the evening, the back pocket of her jeans buzzed. The caller ID flashed, "Unknown." Normally, she ignored anything resembling a robocall, but realized the timely opportunity.

She turned the volume on her phone to maximum and pressed the speaker. "Hello?" she said loudly, watching the two dead men jump.

"Cassie?" a high-pitched woman asked.

The voice sounded familiar, but after dealing with a hundred people a week as a project manager, she drew a blank.

"Who's this?" she asked.

"It's Julie from Salem Long Term Care."

"Hi Julie," she replied quickly, always happy to converse with the young nurse known by a big smile with a personality that matched. "I didn't recognize your number. Is everything okay?" She heard her words and wanted them back. Nothing had been "okay" in almost ten years. She closed her eyes, and saw her beautiful mother Rose wearing a blue-checkered apron and basting a twenty-pound turkey. There was laughter around the crowded table, and the decorative candles would burn for hours.

"Since it's Thanksgiving, I didn't know if anyone would contact you." The phone went silent, and Cassie thought she could hear some sniffing. "But I had to call … because it's a miracle!"

Another hesitation followed and Cassie looked at her husband and son. They had their headsets off and looked like they were holding their breath too.

"Why? What's happened?" she asked sharply. The image of the melted candle wax mixing with her spit flowed through her thoughts.

"Well, I went into your mother's room this afternoon to change her, and she was lying there with her eyes open. It only lasted a couple minutes, but she fixated first on me and then looked out the window. I'll admit it freaked me out a bit."

Cassie could not talk, and the lump in her throat made it difficult to swallow. She thought of the missing turkey heads and suddenly felt disembodied too.

CHAPTER TWO

THE LOBBY OF THE NURSING HOME glowed with Christmas decorations, but Cassie noticed all the effort attracted no admirers. Her eyes were drawn to the strands of blinking white lights wrapped around a fake balsam tree. Instead of triggering happy holiday memories, her racing thoughts dumped her in a stuffy room filled with flashing cameras and a drone of measured statements by police and hospital staff. The vulgar earworm she kept chained in the cellar of her mind, broke loose and started singing that ugly perversion about the twelve days of Christmas. Recoiling from the ditty, she concentrated on a green wingback chair in the lobby's corner and wondered why none of the residents had claimed squatter rights. "That's where I'd set up camp, if I lived here!" she said loudly as if giving a tour. "It would be the perfect antidote for the crush of community living." Her eyes moved from the chair to the hall straight ahead, and she avoided looking at the rest of the Yuletide decorations while surmising today might be Black Friday, but the holiday season began immediately after Labor Day.

The little mind games she employed in order to reduce stress did little to counter her racing heart and the weakness in her legs. In fact, she could feel the hideous past hitching a ride on her high ponytail as she passed the first resident rooms. Strangely, the hallways were empty but smelled like pee after eating asparagus. Quickening her step, she rounded the corner and almost barreled into the dark-haired angel she was seeking. The familiar caretaker moved deftly out of the way, avoiding the near head-on collision.

"Hi Julie! I was hoping to bump into you, but not like this," she gushed.

The usual good-natured nurse gifted a weak smile, which on anyone else would go unnoticed.

Cassie read the expression and gave her a tight hug and held on. "I'm sorry if I came off as a jerk last night." She stopped and bit her lip. It would be impossible to string together the right words and describe how conflicted she felt.

The nurse gave her an extra squeeze before releasing her. "Apology not accepted. I won't insult you by saying I know how you feel, because I don't. And God willing I never will. That said, I understand your reaction." She glanced behind her. "I'd be in a lot of hot water if admin knew I called you. It wasn't my place to startle you on Thanksgiving while you were enjoying time with family."

Enjoying time with family? echoed in her ears. The image of her husband and son locked away in their VR world defined their family's holiday portrait. After Julie's call, her husband attempted to defuse the situation by asking with forced enthusiasm if she wanted to play a board game. She no sooner shook her head and they returned to make-believe. That left her alone for a long walk in the cold rain, which camouflaged the tears.

Julie touched her arm. "Are you okay?"

She pre-gamed this visit by popping a couple ibuprofen on the way, but the anti-inflammatory was outgunned for this mission. "Yes, and please don't beat yourself up about calling me because I truly appreciate it. You've been my rock for the last five years. Before you started working here, I wouldn't know anything except the stale crumbs my father fed me." She looked away for a second so the nurse wouldn't see the frown wrestling for control of her face. *From the beginning, Dad's been weird about coming here, and whenever he does, he's a bundle of nerves and barks more than usual,* she thought. *I can never tell if it's grief or anger — or maybe it's both. Either way, his visits have decreased like a battery slowly discharging, and by now his efforts so lifeless nothing could bring it back.* She pictured the hussy he was shacking up with in her tight blue jeans and clingy t-shirts she bought by the gross, which made Dad's eyes bulge like he had thyroid issues. *Why is he so gullible?* She feared that someday soon Dad's live-in would tell him in her squeaky voice to let his bitchy daughter handle the sleeping killer and forbid any more drive-by visits. After all, they had living to do!

The antidote for the brewing migraine was the young nurse standing in front of her with kind almond-shaped eyes and full lips requiring no lipstick.

"Helping you is why I'm here," Julie continued. "I remember my mother's frustration when my grandmother required long term care. That's why I went into nursing." The clang of dishes coming from the dining room nearby underscored the point. "I want the residents here to feel happy and loved. A big part of that is keeping their families informed." Her mouth moved silently for a second as if trying to find the right words. "I know many people in town have passed judgement on your mother," she began, "but I wish she would just wake up and tell her side of the story. We all deserve to be heard, and she can't defend why — " Julie stopped midsentence and shook her head.

I should be singing those words too, and did until the investigation confirmed her guilt, Cassie thought. *If word gets out that Mom is awake, there's enough anger in town to tar and feather all of us.* The asparagus scented urine suddenly spiked.

"If the situation were reversed, I don't know how I would have reacted with the news," Julie continued.

Cassie breathed through her mouth in order to escape the stench. "But I do. You would have jumped in your car, and run all the red lights to get here." The terrible song began playing in her head again and she shrugged to sum up her opposite reaction. "It took me a day to get my nerve up."

Julie finally rewarded her with a smile that orthodontists frame on their office walls. "Then let's not hesitate any longer, shall we?"

They rode the elevator up to the second floor and walked in silence toward the room at the end of the hall. Cassie had not visited in over three months and felt no guilt because she channeled the same numbness that came with her mother's vegetative state. The sixty-year-old woman lay tucked under a baby blue blanket and looked the same as she did in August, and for the preceding one hundred and twenty months since partying with a cabal of evil spirits. Sure, the strawberry-blonde curls were a few shades lighter, but her porcelain face looked remarkably plump, even with nutrition through a feeding tube. But this Rose was no Sleeping Beauty waiting on a prince.

While Julie retrieved the blood pressure cuff, Cassie recalled how her mother used to kick her butt in the Feaster Five road race— if she did not drain a couple bottles of Chardonnay the night before. She glanced at the nurse; such a sweet angel, with a husband and two-year-old son. From what she knew, Julie's life read like a storybook, and hopefully she would never know what it felt like when a sickle suddenly takes out your knees. And without knees, your back stiffens, and one cannot find the humility to beg God for relief.

She stood at the end of the bed as Julie stroked her mother's head. "Good afternoon, Rose," the nurse whispered. "It's Friday. The sun is out, and there's not a cloud in the sky. I put the window shades up so you can feel the sun's kiss." Julie looked at Cassie and gifted a smile worthy of Mother Teresa. "Your daughter is here too," she continued, "and I told her how I saw your beautiful blue eyes yesterday. She's hoping she will see them too."

The nurse backed away, and Cassie realized it was her turn at the plate. Her stomach did a headstand and she delayed stepping into the batter's box by unbuttoning her coat instead.

Julie read the procrastination perfectly. "I'll give you some privacy," she said and headed toward the hall.

Cassie walked to the window and surveyed the overcast sky. The naked branches of a birch tree shivered in the late November breeze. *There's no place to hide from the approaching winter. All you can do is hunker down.* She glanced back at the bed. *Julie is a better daughter than I've been, a loving caretaker, whispering white lies about the weather while I stand here pissed off and mute.* She looked out the window again and hoped Mother Nature would end the slow descent into darkness and quickly wield its frosting knife and bury the rotting leaves and the dead grass and all her hurt in this "Live Free or Die" state under three feet of snow. She rubbed her aching forehead, knowing no weather event this side of hell could take away from the approaching ten-year anniversary of the tragedy. The media would not miss the opportunity either to dredge up all the pain.

Cassie retreated from the window and returned to her mother's side and watched her chest rise and fall. When the ambulance transported her here, William was still in diapers — now he was signing up for driver's ed. *Time continues its forward march, and here I stand rotting from the inside out while she peacefully sleeps.* The doctors said it was possible someone in a coma can hear, but she was afraid if she did more than kiss her hello and goodbye, the levee would break. Then a violent rage infused with hot tears might have her arrested for attempted murder.

She bent over and kissed her mother on the cheek. Her skin felt soft and warm and smelled of some off brand moisturizer and triggered a waterfall of memories. *Holding hands and jumping waves at Hampton Beach and gagging every now and then on salt water. Toasting marshmallows over the firepit in the backyard — she liked them gooey, but Mom preferred hers blistered and black. Cookouts and birthday parties and trail runs all backlit by a turbocharged laugh which produced a hilarious snort that anyone within earshot enjoyed.*

Cassie took in her mother's peaceful countenance, which was an absurd feature given the consequences of her actions. *Some people do not go with their given names,* she thought, *but Mom is truly a rose and reserved her thorns for a driven husband.* She took a deep breath and realized if she could change places with her mother, William's recollections would not highlight instances of joy, but feature words like dour, dull, depressed.

She took her mother's hand. It felt warmer than hers. "When we peed our pants laughing, I never imagined we would both end up as granite roses."

The tears could only be denied by looking away, and her eyes focused on a sink across the room. When she was young, she learned to check the kitchen sink and identify what transparent devil made her mother sleep all day, or lit her up on a Sunday afternoon— wine glasses, tumblers, the curve of a martini rim.

She closed her eyes like she used to do as a child in order to block it all out. But she forgot to cover her ears, and the ditty broke free.

On the twelfth day of Christmas, the devil launched a spree
Twelve Cruisers cruisin'
Eleven Firefighters fightin'
Ten Ambulances amblin'
Nine Nurses nursin'
Eight doctors doctorin'
Seven reporters reportin'
Six swimmers swimmin'
FIVE GONE AND DEAD
Four broken arms
Three fractured legs,
Two lost limbs
And a killer in a coma, free.

"One hell of a resume, Mom," she whispered before heading for the door.

CHAPTER THREE

THERE WERE SO MANY PEOPLE in the deli, Cassie thought a celebrity must have stopped in for one of their signature sandwiches. She weaved her way through a dozen patrons, all eyeing her like she was trying to cut the line. After a tense few moments, she caught sight of her father sitting in a booth way in the back. He saw her at the same time and waved. After maneuvering around two strollers, she slid into the booth. Two Italian subs positioned in the center of the dark laminate table greeted her. The massive sandwiches could easily feed a family of four.

Her father pointed at the bursting rolls. "I got here before the rush and ordered extra hots for you."

She frowned at the spicy olive branch. "Thanks for lunch, but you're getting me confused with Mom again," she replied glancing up at him. "How can you forget I eat everything plain? I'll be popping antacids for the rest of the day."

He replied with a blank look. "Well, I'm starving, and you should thank me for not eating both sandwiches waiting for you." He picked up half a sub and took a huge bite and began chewing with his mouth open which Mom used to rail against. Cassie watched the gnashing of bread, assorted cold-cuts and vegetables for a moment before looking away and finding on the adjoining wall a mural of an Italian vineyard at harvest time. The men and women were brightly dressed and dancing around a large basket of grapes. Suddenly, the smell of onions and pickles transported her back from Tuscany, where she found her father with a thick glob of mayonnaise plastered on his chin. She held up a napkin.

He grabbed it and grunted, "Thank-you Miss Manners." After a half-hearted swipe, he rolled the paper into a tight ball. "I'm tired of all the stuffy business dinners where they have a different utensil for each dish." He pointed at his plate. "In here you can eat with your hands. Sorry it annoys you!"

She debated whether to keep her coat on for a quick exit and almost replied she saw more manners in the animals at the zoo. Instead, she watched her father take another oversized bite, clearly testing her patience. Despite the brutish manners, no one would deny he was a distinguished looking man with thick silver hair, which intensified coal-black eyes that hid his soul. Instinctively, she ran one hand through her honey-colored hair, but could not deny she inherited many of his traits, which included keeping the storm bottled up inside. Watching him inhale another mouthful made her recall how Mom said it was his broad shoulders she first noticed. She was either blind or smitten, or perhaps they did not share a meal for a while. Age had not fooled with his height, but his cheeks had taken on a red plumpness, and she noticed the short clearance now between his gut and the table.

She relented and slid off her wool coat. "I thought she had you on a diet?"

He stopped the gnashing of teeth. "Who?"

This was the sick game they played whenever they talked, which seemed less by the month. She denied giving his love interest an identity and dug her heels in deeper when they moved into a condo five years ago. *"I don't get it. You're still married to Mom, but shacking up with your girlfriend?"* she screamed after he put the family house on the market.

Their eyes locked. She learned as a rebellious teen to be still and let his anger reflect like a mirror. No wonder he was one of the top construction developers in Southern New Hampshire. Charles Owens had a triple A personality and was known as a brutal employer and negotiator, which bled into his role as husband and father. Last time they spoke, he hung up on her because she wouldn't name the hussy.

She took a bite of the sandwich and followed his lead by chewing with her mouth open, hoping to embarrass him, but the way he glared at her it was not working.

"Rachael," she replied and spit out a nail-like piece of onion. "You said she was pushing you to eat fruits and vegetables."

He sat back in the booth, and his eyes narrowed. "Do you think you're funny or just trying to get a rise out of me?"

Before she could reply, her tongue caught on fire, and she searched the table. "Where's the drinks?" she asked anxiously.

"You know I never drink with my meals. Fills me up."

"Well, thanks for thinking of me, Dad!" She grabbed her purse and skated around the queue line in the lobby and located the vending machine and purchased a bottle of water. After taking a long drink, she made her way back to the booth. He eyed her with a sly smirk as he brushed shredded lettuce off the sleeve of a starched white button-down shirt. *He probably planned all of this,* she thought.

She took another swig of water. "I saw Mom yesterday."

He nodded. "I've been meaning to get over there but the project on Lake Street has been a bear."

She cocked her head in reply. *The nursing home was only a few miles away from the worksite. When the traffic was bad, he had to drive by the place!* she thought. "Did they call you when Mom opened her eyes?"

"Yes," he replied stiffly. "They said they would let the doctor know."

She bit her lip and stared at him.

"What?"

"Didn't it occur to you I might want to know too?"

His face softened, and he sighed. "I didn't want to get your hopes up and—" He stopped and leaned in. "Wait a second! Why are you beating me up? Clearly you know." He rolled his eyes. "Let me guess, that do-gooder nurse that adopted your mother filled you in."

"Adopted sounds about right since we both avoid the place like it's full of COVID, Monkeypox and rabies. If you ask me—"

"I bet Saint Julie is the nurse that witnessed the awakening too," he said cutting her off. "She weighs your mother down with a ton of holy medals and is always saying mumbo-jumbo over her. She probably imagined the whole thing."

"Why? Because you have your heart set on seeing Mom get her ten-year coma pin?"

He pointed at her uneaten sandwich. "Look, if you want to blow off some steam, I suggest you take another bite. Otherwise, I'm leaving. I will not sit here so you can go down that rabbit hole again and insult me."

She took another sip of water but her tongue still felt raw from the hot peppers. *Change the approach, if you want anything out of this lunch,* she thought. "Are you going to speak with her doctor to see what he thinks of her opening her eyes?"

He hung his head. "Why? Even if it's true, Rose has been unconscious since plowing me into a utility pole. Given the brain damage—"

"The doctor said it was trauma!" she corrected.

"Whatever. Even if her eyes flutter every day, it doesn't change a thing. It's probably just an automatic reflex, like when you cut the head off a snake and the body continues moving."

"Are you seriously comparing my mother with a snake?" She grabbed both his hands. "Remember how we used to talk about cases on the internet where people wake up after being in a coma for years?"

He squeezed her hands to the point they hurt. "That was before the neurologist warned me to stop looking on the Web, because that's where reality goes to die."

She pulled her hands free.

"I'm sorry honey, but someone has to be the realist here. It is what it is. Frankly, I wish you would tell that nurse friend of yours to keep her mouth shut because it just stirs up trouble, and we've suffered enough." He looked around. "Plus, the last thing we need is for some reporter to get wind of this and kickoff more death threats and having our houses egged again." He flashed a devilish grin. "Whenever Rachael wants to paint a room, I tell her I'm fine with any color except for an eggshell finish."

She sat back in the booth, and shook her head. If the situation were reversed, she doubted her mother would be singing *Que Sera, Sera* and making sick jokes.

Her father reached for her hand, and she moved it away. "I know it's difficult, but we just have to keep going. You have your family and—"

"You have your girlfriend."

He blew a mouthful of onion breath her way and began to slide out of the booth and suddenly stopped. "You know I loved your mom."

"Loved? She's still alive!" she yelled and blew out all the surrounding conversations. Even the characters in the mural seemed to frown.

Her father waved his hands. "What are you doing?" he whispered, "Trying to make the evening news? You know what I mean. Of course, I still love your mother. We had a good marriage and like everyone we had our share of difficulties. Rose thought I was a hopeless heathen that worked too much. I couldn't understand how her strict faith overlooked closet drinking. But we made it work and had you, which still is a testament to our love. I will never forgive myself that I let her drive that night when neither of us were in a condition to do so.

If I had been a better husband and dealt with the situation differently, five people would be alive today not to mention all the injured." He took a deep breath. "Rose wouldn't be half-dead either."

She looked at her father's mouth quiver, and it was 3:00 a.m. again in January when the phone woke her. At first, she dismissed it as a prank call because of the heavy breathing.

"There's .... been a terrible ... accident," her father stuttered.

Her stomach dropped. "What? Where?" She could never remember what she asked first, as she bolted out of bed.

"I'm at the hospital. We were at Phil's house celebrating the Canobie project because it came in under budget and ahead of schedule," her father began flatly, but with an unusual amount of detail. "I never overdo it, but the boys kept toasting me with shots, and I didn't eat much." His voice trailed off, and she heard a man calling for him in the background. "Yes, yes, I'll be there in a minute," he replied.

"Dad what happened?" she yelled and remembered how cold the hardwood floor felt. She looked at James sitting upright in bed.

"I'm back," her father continued. "I thought your mother was fine at the party. In fact, she's been killing it for a while — eating clean, working out and taking it one day at a time. I only saw her drinking ginger ale, so I let her drive home from Phil's. Feeling hammered, I fell asleep in the back seat until I felt the car swerving all over the place. Just as I sat up, there was one thud ... then another." His voice sounded high-pitched. "I saw someone roll across the hood. I yelled at Rose to pull over and stop, but she sped up instead. It was surreal — she didn't say a word and I kept bouncing around like a pinball in the back seat because she was all over the place. The wild ride ended when we slammed into a pole."

The walls of the sandwich shop suddenly began closing in like a great vice. Grabbing her coat, she headed for the door. When she made it outside, the November sun was high in a cloudless sky.

Her father came alongside and grabbed her arm. "I didn't invite you to lunch to fight. I went through this too you know .... Hope gets stretched to the breaking point after so many years. I'll admit as time passed, I began thinking maybe it was best if she didn't come out of it. Rose is a gentle woman and couldn't face the mob waiting to hang her."

Cassie broke away. "So, what you're really saying is she's better off dead? I'm mad at her too, but I never felt that way."

"I thought she would die at the scene. Given her pathetic existence the last ten years, I wish she had."

"You think because you rip buildings down and put new ones up, that makes you the Creator? Talk about a God complex!"

"Think what you want, but I'm just trying to find some peace. What am I supposed to do? Put my life in a coma too? Rachael is a lovely woman if you will give her a chance."

"Who?" she asked.

CHAPTER FOUR

IF SHE COULD HAVE HARNESSED the heartburn from lunch, she would have set a land speed record on the way home. Instead, the cosmos intervened and made sure every traffic light turned red so she could stew in her own juices.

When she finally pulled into the driveway, she spotted William sitting on the front stairs, dressed in a t-shirt and shorts with his eyes glued to a smartphone— technology she feared would be the downfall of mankind. Not too many years ago, she would find him pacing up and down the driveway, waiting for her to get home from work so they could put up the Christmas decorations. While neighbors ran the gamut from hanging festive wreaths with strategically placed spot lights, to those preferring inflatable characters like Rudolph or Frosty, her son broke new ground by cherishing a collection they came across at an antique shop in Vermont. Hand painted on century old plywood it looked like a page out of the *Who's Who* from the dark side and featured the Abominable Snowman, the Grinch, a cadre of skeleton elves, and a life-sized Santa that looked like he spent the offseason in some honky-tonk bar chugging cheap beer. She thought it poetic justice when a mammoth icicle took out bad Santa one night.

Now William thought decorations were childish and played it cool opening presents on Christmas morning. If his heart raced at all, it was over some hi-tech paraphernalia only her husband understood. Her involvement amounted to ordering whatever link James sent and then wrapping the box. She cherished whenever her son screamed in delight— an increasingly rare occurrence, and did not miss how William's gratitude was directed solely at his father. She sometimes wondered what it must be like to have a son that got excited over simple stuff.

Cassie took a deep breath and exhaled slowly before exiting the car, hoping the crisp air would clear her head and mood.

"Hey champ," she called out still a few feet away. "There's ice on Arlington Pond, and you're dressed like July. Are you training for the polar bear plunge on New Year's Day?"

He looked up for a second before his eyes were sucked back into the iPhone. "Maybe. I had one of those stupid hot flashes again."

She looked past his mop of brown hair, and sure enough, his ear lobes were beet red. The doctor dismissed it as a hormone thing. "Well, even if it's stupid, you can still catch a cold sitting out here like this." She rubbed his arm. "Tell you what. If this keeps up, we'll convert your bedroom into a walk-in freezer so you're comfortable, and I can stock up on frozen food."

"Not funny, Mom."

Ugh! I bomb every day with him. She glanced at the open garage and empty stall. "Where's your father?"

"He had to go into work for a bit."

The words juiced her heartburn, and she clenched her teeth. James promised preserving the weekend for the three of them. They talked about tagging a Christmas tree and going out for dinner. She turned around and watched the passing cars and hoped her husband's black Jeep would appear any second. Most of her life could be charted along a three-mile stretch of Main Street. Grammar school at St. Joseph's, followed by Salem High, summer job at Hawkeyes' Ice Cream, first kiss in the mystery section of Kelley Library, college internship at Salem Cooperative Bank, wedding at St. Joseph's Church and whether by fate— or coincidence, their dream house also on this east to west road. At some point, hopefully many decades from now, Main Street would also bookmark her last chapter— wake, funeral, and internment at Pine Grove Cemetery.

The November chill interrupted the reflection, and she turned around and waved at her tech-crazy son. "What are you up to this afternoon?"

He shrugged as his fingers continued typing. "I thought Andy, Steve or Bob would come over, but they all have lame excuses."

She grabbed the phone out of his hands. "Since we've both been abandoned, let's do something fun. We could go to a movie or try that new sandwich place in the mall. I walked by it a couple weeks ago and the subs looked delicious." She couldn't remember the last time the two of them had done anything together.

William frowned and put out his hand like he was waiting for the return of an amputated body-part. "Not necessary, Mom. I'm not five years old and need a fill-in for my canceled playgroup."

The memory of her mother tickled her thoughts. They used to head for the mall in search of something specific and lose track of time and spend hours browsing all the special deals. Mom could afford anything, but loved finding a bargain and then interrogating the unlucky clerk whether there were any coupons available. By the time they got home, Dad would be furious because the shopping trips usually coincided with some social commitment. Thinking back, maybe her mother enjoyed making her husband wait for a change. She wanted similar experiences with her son and did not care about the activity.

"Hey, I have an idea," she said putting the phone behind her back.

"Look, I don't want to play Scrabble or Monopoly because it's—"

"Stupid and lame," she replied finishing his sentence. Other than food and technology, most everything else fell into those two buckets.

"How about we try something different?"

He ignored the invitation. "Can I have my phone back, please?"

"Sure, after you give me a tour of the virtual reality game your dad brought home."

He sighed. "You don't like that sort of thing."

She touched his cheek and noticed the two-day growth. "But I love you, and that's enough for me. C'mon it will be fun!"

William jumped up without moaning so she took it as a win. She followed him into the house, and did not bother to take off her coat until they reached the family room. Her son retrieved two headsets and controllers off a pine desk in the corner.

He handed her one, and she noticed it felt lighter than the other commercial sets on the market that her husband took apart and tinkered with constantly.

"Put it on so it's nice and snug, and adjust the straps to prevent a headache or motion sickness," William advised.

"This isn't my first rodeo," she replied and started making the adjustments.

"Yeah, I remember Mrs. Andrews calling 911 when she heard you scream after the virtual zombies attacked you last year."

"That was sweet. I thought for years she didn't like me none."

They both laughed and it felt good. "Do the hand controls work the same?"

William nodded. "You'll have virtual hands like before, but these are more reactive and have an increased sense of touch. But what's really cool is you don't talk to the other player, and that takes some getting used to. You think what you want to say, and the other person will hear it. You also don't have to move around the room and manage everything with the controller.

Dad says future releases will allow uploading your voice but for now you choose from a list." He fiddled with his iPhone. "I just uploaded a picture of you for your avatar. The goggles will scan for more details."

"What's my voice?"

He smiled. "A throaty girl from California."

She rolled her eyes. "Of course."

He pointed at the "x" on the right-hand controller. "Never press that button."

"Why not?"

Will cleared his throat. "Dad says there's a few bugs in the program. That button brings out ... uh, some crazy background noise."

She snickered. "Which to a mother's ears means you pressed it, and a bunch of throaty girls from California came running?"

"No, it taps into random thoughts, and screws up the experience."

"Okay, Dr. Frankenstein. Let's take this out for a spin."

CHAPTER FIVE

THE SUDDEN HIGH-PITCHED HUM made her think the headset malfunctioned or was attempting to download her brain. She concluded neither was the case when the irritating noise suddenly stopped. A full moon appeared at the horizon and rose slowly in the ink black sky. The orange orb appeared larger than any harvest moon on planet earth, and she felt like she could reach up and touch the lunar surface. The field of view was unlike anything she experienced with other VR headsets, and she lost the feeling of looking through goggles.

"Hey Mom, check this out!"

She looked down and to the right. Ten feet below she found William standing on the edge of a red-rock canyon bathed in moonlight. Her son's avatar appeared as an invigorated copy of himself, with every physical detail incorporated including the mole on his neck. A small backpack rested comfortably against his t-shirt and khaki pants.

Her picture-perfect son made her check herself out. She rubbed her virtual hands along brushed denim jeans before inspecting for the small round burn mark on her left forearm, an unplanned teenage tattoo she received when a fryer spit hot grease. "This is amazing!" she yelled.

Her son let out a whimper and put a finger to his lips. "Don't talk or you will blow-out my eardrums. Just think what you want to say."

Cassie heard a clear male voice say the words. Her mind became jumbled thinking how to reply. Her son noticed and smiled. "I did the same thing at first with Dad. Just slow down, and think of what you will say, like you would in conversation. Dad explained that most of the time we aren't focused on listening but forming our response."

"This feels super weird," she thought instead of saying.

He gave her a thumbs up. "There you go! Just take baby steps, and in no time, you'll be lecturing me nonstop like you do in the real world."

"But it sounds better in a sexy voice," she shot back and looked around some more. "This technology is mind blowing."

"You'll have to ask Dad about the special sensors and the crazy algorithms they developed because it's way over my head. He says they still have a few bugs that need to be fixed before launch." William held up his virtual hand and a menu appeared. "If you could be anywhere right now, where would it be?"

She scanned the red rock and would be content to stay here, but a tropical location beckoned. "St. Thomas," she said out loud, and her son winced. He clicked the controller. In the next instant, they were standing on a beach lined with palm trees, as gentle waves caressed the shore. She smelled coconut sun tan lotion and dug her toes into talcum powder sand as the warm trade winds caressed her skin.

The vibrant landscape brought back memories of their honeymoon at Sapphire Beach, and she fingered her wedding ring. The brushed finish was nearly gone now, and James urged her to bring it to a jeweler and have it reapplied. But she nixed the idea, because she viewed it as a testament of surviving every type of weather like the shingles on a Cape Cod house. Still, her heart quickened, remembering how James back then seemed mesmerized with her, and she sat at the top of the pyramid and everything else— job, interests, hobbies and friends fell in place below. Now the triangle sat inverted. She scanned the water and saw a man and woman bobbing about a hundred feet out. They looked an awful lot like her and James as newlyweds and her mind wandered to sand and sun and bare skin.

"Mom, knock it off! That's gross," she heard William suddenly bark.

She shook her head and glanced at her tanned and muscled son in orange swim trunks. "What do you mean?" she said again out loud.

William pointed at his head. "My ears are bleeding. You brag about graduating summa cum laude but can't follow simple rules. Were you absent the day in pre-school when they taught Simon Says?"

She smiled weakly.

"Well, Simon says no talking. Think what you want to say!" He glanced at the couple in the water and pointed down the beach and a series of circles appeared. "Let's teleport out of here."

A second later they were in a different location on the beach. Cassie looked back at the empty water. "Want to explain what happened back there?"

He picked up a mammoth conch shell and inspected its pearl finish. "Sometimes a strong memory interferes with the algorithm and inserts itself into the virtual world. Some present as the memory itself, while others grow into virtual nightmares. Dad says they have been working on understanding the parameters so they can disable it. Games are pretty safe because people concentrate on winning the contest, but tour a location and the risks increase. That you've been here before is a red flag."

"I don't know why you were grossed out back there. Your father and I were here for our honeymoon."

"Because you let your thoughts roam and I'll spend the rest of my life trying to forget what I heard. Once they work out this kink, it will be pretty cool because they will build apps to explore exotic destinations."

She looked at the water. "Can I stay here until spring?"

"You sound like an old fogie. I'd love to show you a zombie game, but you'd wet your pants."

"How considerate." She fingered the wedding ring again and frowned. James was an explorer in a new world and shared little of this adventure with her. When they were together, they discussed mundane things: finances, home improvement projects, what to have for dinner, watch on tv or what their son was up to. Conversations about their jobs were kept to a minimum, not that he wanted a brief on the mind-numbing project milestone meetings she ran, or conversely, how many software engineers could fit on the head of a pin. Years ago, they agreed this sort of minutiae sharing was exhausting, because it required explaining the background and context so the other spouse could understand. But this? Had she shut herself off so completely that he only shared this utterly fantastic world with others?

The wind picked up, and she looked down the beach and saw what looked like a motorized gurney slowly making its way along the shoreline. The heavy-set wheels were caked with wet sand.

William saw it too. "You must be thinking about your mom because she's on her way."

"My mom is always on my mind," she countered. William dealt with the tragedy for most of his life and probably viewed his grandmother like a great sandcastle that a rogue wave destroyed leaving only a small crater in the sand.

"We can wait for her, but it might be scary. Dad says some memories show up like a skeleton with only half the skin attached, and the algorithm fills in the missing pieces and it's not pretty."

"Sold. Can you bring up the list of destinations again?"

He touched the controller, and she read through a long list of cities and major tourist attractions around the world. At the bottom she noticed a few places in bold.

"What's with the nude beaches?"

"I saw that too. Dad said given the demographics—"

"I bet there were more than a few volunteers to work on that app. Hope you haven't been to any of these places?"

His cheeks turned red. "Want to play a game?"

She smiled seeing how the rules for embarrassment were the same in a virtual world. Guitar riffs suddenly filled her ears, and it sounded like they were emanating from the sand itself. Curiously, the song sounded like the hard rock her son listened to nonstop. William didn't acknowledge the music, and she chalked it up as part of the experience until she looked at the beach again. A familiar looking teenage girl ran past the approaching gurney. She had long blonde hair and wore dungaree shorts and a yellow tank top.

"Hey, isn't that Jill from next door? How did she get here?"

William's eyes got as big as the full moon and he fiddled with the controller as the music spiked.

A second later everything went black.

"What happened?" she asked.

William tugged at her headset. "The batteries ran down."

She looked around the family room and the real world looked awful dreary. "Let me guess. I mentioned the nude beaches and your imagination broke through?"

He ignored the question and placed his headset in its box.

"I won't embarrass you anymore than I already have." She rubbed his arm. "I appreciate you showing me around. If someone asked me what I just experienced, I would be at a loss for words. Let's do this again real soon. Next time we can play

VINCENT DONOVAN

some games— no zombies, but something that will give me a thrill. Okay?"

"Sure."

"Last question before I give back your phone. When you played with your dad, what memories of his broke through?"

Her son shrugged. "What happens in VR stays in VR."

CHAPTER SIX

"WHY DOES THE SHORTEST DAY of the year *feel like the longest?"* she thought. Three hours into the marathon project review meeting, her cell phone began buzzing. As she went to put it on silent mode, she noticed a text from Julie: *Mom's awake again and super alert. Get here quick!*

Everything that followed the starting gun became a blur. She spilled half a cup of coffee on the conference room table before excusing herself from the meeting, then got to her car only to find the keys were still back in her office. The frustration continued as she inched through two construction sites, three red lights before tailgating a vintage Oldsmobile that must have been restored with a lawnmower engine because it topped out at fifteen miles-per-hour.

When she finally pulled into the parking lot of the long-term care facility, she discovered her father's silver BMW SUV parked horizontally across two handicap parking spaces. Either his nerves were in overdrive too, or figured he was eligible for the reserved spaces based on his wife's condition and the checks he wrote every month. *Either way, why didn't he call me? Was he planning on keeping this a secret too?*

Naturally, the only parking space open in this comedy of errors was at the far end of the parking lot. When she finally shut the car off and reached for her purse, her hands were shaking. She sat still for a minute and concentrated on taking slow, deep breaths. An inner voice told her to check her makeup — because Mom had always been a stickler for looking her best in public. Stealing a glance in the vanity mirror, she saw how hope, fear, and dread were baked into her face. The flushed cheeks and glassy eyes reminded her of being in the Ladies Room after kissing her mother before they wheeled her into surgery. The recall made her stomach flip, and she sought refuge by scanning the landscape. Fifty feet ahead, a sizable field of pachysandra encircled an outcrop of granite. The unchanging rock was no surprise but her eyes locked onto the substantial ground cover which remained vibrant green despite the season. She stared at the stubborn plants that did not yell, "hey look at me!" in summer and did not wilt or brown when the rest of nature did. *I wish I could be as strong,* she thought. Love and fury welled up, and neither gained the upper hand nor called a truce. She hated how they had both taken up residence within her heart. Biting her lip, she could not say which would take the lead when she came face to face with Rose Owens. At work, she learned to project a calm demeanor no matter her feelings, but this was different.

She willed herself out of the car and practically sprinted to the building and reached the elevator before realizing she left work without a coat. After the elevator ignored multiple summons, she ran up two flights of stairs and reached ground zero panting. She paused in the hall, and wiped cold sweat from her brow and eyed the open door like a rock had been rolled away from the tomb.

Filling her lungs before diving in, Cassie entered the room and her peripheral vision took in her father sitting in a visitor chair in the corner. She did not stop but continued forward with a sensation of floating toward the center of the room. The head of the hospital bed was slightly elevated and her mother's head tilted to the left with her eyes open and fixated on the double window. The sun was streaming in. No doubt Julie's daily forecast had made an impression.

Cassie heard her father mumble something, but her racing heart drowned out the words. It took all her restraint from jumping into her mother's field of vision. Instead, she inched forward as if approaching an apparition. The light in the room took on a weird glow, and she felt the tightness in her chest relax as love overpowered resentment.

"Mom?" The greeting came out as a question, which surprised her, but then again, she wondered for a decade if any piece of the woman who gave her life remained. Did any spark of Rose persist through it all?

She watched for a reaction from the woman wearing a soft pink flannel nightgown basking in the light of a medium-sized star that most take for granted. The moment became a ripple expanding across still water. Her chest felt like it was about to explode before realizing she had been holding her breath. *What did I expect? Something out of the movies where my voice breaks the spell and Mom comes back to life?* She bit her lip as unbridled hope welled up with a reminder that sometimes she called William ten times before he answered. *Maybe it's the same now.*

She touched her mother's shoulder and gazed into blue marble eyes which looked bright and rested. "Mom, it's Cassie," she managed to get out. Hearing her own strained voice touched the little girl deep inside, producing hot tears that blurred her vision. *It would be heaven on earth of she could brush away my tears,* she thought.

Instead, she felt a large hand on her back. "I never thought I'd see those beautiful eyes again," her father whispered.

The tears continued falling, and all she could do was nod. Ten years ago, she would have turned around and buried her head in his chest, but held back, afraid this tender moment would be ruined if she smelled the other woman's perfume on his sweater.

"I dropped everything when they called," he continued.

You also dropped Mom years ago she wanted to add, but bit her lip instead.

"I didn't know what to expect when I got here." He leaned over his wife like he was inspecting a strange weed that suddenly appeared on his manicured lawn. "Her eyes are open, but is anyone home?" he asked evidently not concerned Rose might hear the comment. "Before you arrived, I stared at her for a good half hour. I've seen more life in a bucket of dead fish."

"You've always had a crass way about you," she spit back. "I look forward to the day Mom makes you suck on a bar of soap for that stupid comment." She shot him the same look she gave her husband whenever he ticked her off.

Her father responded by walking over to the window and blocking the sunlight Rose craved.

Cassie read her father's face and knew he got gruff when worried — a trait passed on to her as well. She took a few steps toward him. "I know you were hoping for more and feel let down but this is huge! Mom's always been the heart of our family and now she's awake. Embrace the miracle!"

Dad cleared his throat like she hit a nerve and continued looking out the window. *No wonder he looked troubled*, she thought. *What would happen to what's her name if his wife woke up?*

Nurse Julie breezed into the room carrying a blue patient binder and stopped in the middle of the room. "This is the family reunion I've been praying for."

Her father shot her a dirty look and returned his gaze outside.

The nurse came alongside the bed. "Good afternoon, Rose! So wonderful to see those beautiful eyes again."

Cassie watched her mother's eyes blink as if digesting the greeting. Then ever so slowly she turned her head toward the nurse.

"Dad!" Cassie called, and her father came rushing over.

Julie stroked Rose's hand. "Your husband and daughter are here. I wish you would say hello to them too."

The woman's eyes blinked a few times, and then pivoted to her daughter's face.

Cassie thought she saw recognition in those deep blue wells but feared it was just her imagination. She bent down and kissed her mother on the cheek. "I've been waiting forever for this day," she whispered. Memories of anger and frustration elbowed their way into her thoughts and she clenched her jaw. There was so much more she wanted to say, but given the audience refrained.

"Rosie, how about a look my way?" her father semi-barked ending the tender moment. The three of them waited, but his wife kept her gaze on her.

Her father grew impatient and checked his watch.

Julie felt the cold breeze. "This is a huge step," she added.

"What should we expect next?" Cassie asked.

"Why are you asking her? She's no doctor!" her father said sucking both the air and gladness out of the room.

"Dad! That's uncalled for!" she replied with twice the volume.

The nurse's face remained calm, and she opened the blue binder and studied the top sheet for a moment before smiling at her. "I'll update Doctor Thompson this afternoon."

"I think we're getting ahead of ourselves," Charles spit back not appeased. He pointed at his wife who was looking toward the window again. "Even plants know enough to face the sun." He walked away.

Cassie made two fists to prevent flipping him off.

Julie followed him. "Mr. Owens, I know mixing medicine and faith makes no sense to you, but I've seen enough to believe they aren't opposed to one another. They go hand in hand. I love that line from *Amazing Grace: I once was lost but now I'm found, was blind but now I see.* Rose waking up is a miracle, and this is the first glimpse of the sunrise. I believe with rehab and prayers; she will make a full recovery."

Her father spun around. "There you go again!" He pointed at the blue binder. "Let me guess there's a Bible hidden behind those pages so you can proselytize between emptying bed pans and giving sponge baths." He pointed at his wife. "You think her eyes popped open from all the ornaments you hang around her neck like she's a Christmas tree. The only miracle here is she hasn't hung herself."

Cassie put up her hand. "Dad, knock it off!"

The nurse smiled. "Your daughter told me your wife is a devout Catholic, and I asked her permission before adding St. Jude and the Miraculous Medal to her crucifix necklace. Saint Jude is the patron saint of impossible cases and something is happening here that fits that description. Regarding the Miraculous Medal—"

"Spare me!" he said cutting her off. "So, what should we do now? Hold hands and sing gospel songs?" He waved her off and looked at Cassie. "I'll call you later when we're not in La-la land."

She did not acknowledge the comment and waited until he left the room before turning to Julie. "Talk about impossible cases! I'm terribly sorry for his behavior."

"No apology needed. He's frustrated and—"

"Hey ladies!" a booming voice interrupted.

Cassie turned and greeted a young guy with shoulder-length brown hair. It would be hard to describe the rest of his features, as he had a camera up to his face and clicked away.

CHAPTER SEVEN

CASSIE DESPISED January's cold dark dance before it became synonymous with death, destruction and despair. She dreaded one day in particular, and today marked the tenth anniversary of unresolved misery. Over the years she learned there is a third option for the flight or fight response— hunker down and get as small as possible. This strategy ran the gamut from avoiding the limelight, shredding anything of importance that roving freelance reporters pawing through their trash might use, and having no social media presence. But even the best plans wilt under the needs of everyday life. *What choice do I have,* she asked herself, *but venture out since I have a husband that lives at the office and a teenage son constantly pillaging the refrigerator and complaining there's nothing in the house to eat?*

This January 6th began as a typical winter day with the sun tucked behind a thin blanket of clouds and radiating muted shades of pink and yellow on the horizon. The sky was pretty enough to sit on a park bench and admire if not for the biting wind that made her speed walk from the car to the supermarket while scanning the ground for black ice.

A train of carriages sat next to the courtesy booth, and she retrieved one and automatically stopped and sanitized the handle with a wipe, a hangover from the never ending COVID plague.

The trash barrel sat a few feet away, and as she disposed of the wipe, she scanned a wire rack holding copies of the *Eagle Tribune* and *Boston Globe* on the first two shelves. The headlines were a rerun of yesterday— *Continued Inflation, Washington Divided, Fighting Breaks Out in the Mideast.* She was already turning back toward the carriage when the bottom rack brought her to a full stop. The *Salem Insight,* a local rag with a rabid following that believed conspiracies were as common as orange pine needles in October, announced in bold type: *Salem Witch Wakes!* Picking up a copy, she noticed under the disgusting hook, a photo of her mother's room with her and Julie in the foreground looking ambushed. Behind them lay her mother, propped up watching the invasion.

Her stomach dropped into the heels of her boots, and she knelt down and put a few copies of the *Tribune* on top of the nightmarish slander. Before standing up again, she pulled her red wool hat down over her ears and scurried for refuge in the dairy aisle which felt colder than outside. The headlines were in the forefront of her eyes and blocked out everything else. Salem was a popular gateway from Massachusetts into New Hampshire; a shopper's delight with no sales tax and several tourist attractions. While many outside the area were only familiar with the Salem Massachusetts aura, this local publication tapped into the regional anger given the multiple fatalities and perceived lack of accountability.

She picked up a container of Greek yogurt and pretended to check the expiration date while wrestling what to do. She could abandon her cart and call James and ask him to stop on the way home and pick up what they needed. He would sigh and moan and revisit his tired arguments she was not the guilty party here. Cassie tried buying into that perspective for the first year after the tragedy, but clearly the friends who deserted her had a different outlook.

Another scan of the aisle confirmed there were few shoppers for a Saturday morning, but that would change shortly. For a second, she toyed with the thought of wearing sunglasses as she roamed the store, but concluded it would draw attention.

As the panic attack peaked, she clutched the handle of the carriage so tightly her fingers turned purple. She began a frenzied pace, tricking her mind into seeing the store as a giant Pac-Man maze and she a monstrous blob devouring the grocery items. Ordinarily, she would follow the grocery list which matched the flow of the aisles, but the list was in her pocket and her legs would not stop long enough to retrieve it. Not that she could decipher it since everything suddenly looked blurry. She grabbed whatever her eyes registered: milk, eggs, cream cheese, pickles, tuna, bread, chips, baked beans. All were thrown in the cart with no thought about what items would go together for a meal. At the end of one aisle, the deli came into view with the usual dozen people waiting their turn so they could order a quarter-pound of everything in the case sliced extra thin. "Cold cuts are so over-rated," she mumbled and moved on.

Nearly panting when she reached the produce section, she slammed on the brakes and wrestled opening a plastic bag to throw in a few green apples. Her ears were fine tuned to hear the beating wings of a fruit fly when she heard a carriage stop behind her.

"Is that you, Cassie?" a woman called out.

She dropped the plastic bag puzzle and found Kendra Jacobsen standing next to the blueberries. A blunt bob cut complimented Kendra's thick blonde hair while the running pants and form-fitted jacket advertised a level of fitness she could barely recall. They were good friends in high school and reconnected when their sons were on the same Little League team a few years back. Kendra never asked much about the troubles and while that may seem insensitive to some, Cassie took it as a mark of real friendship. When baseball ended, they drifted apart again. She thought of calling last year and checking in, but never made the effort.

She gave her friend a hug and smelled lemon citrus. "It's nice to see a friendly face in the fruit section," she whispered.

Her friend had the same easy laugh from their youth. "You always crack me up." Scanning the weird population of items in her cart she asked, "How have you been?"

Cassie wished she could tug on her hat; positive a few gray hairs were showing. She needed a cut and color badly but canceled the appointment to spend time with her mother. Not much had changed in the past couple weeks, except Rose's left hand began waking up with jerky movements.

"We're all doing fine," she replied lying through a fake smile she put on every morning with her makeup. How is Hunter?"

"Good. He's in a couple classes with Will this semester."

She nodded like she knew, which was another white lie and pointed at her friend's cart filled with cases of bottled water, fruits and vegetables. "What's your cholesterol? Negative ten?"

Kendra laughed again and glanced around to make sure they were relatively alone. "Look, I'm really sorry about what your family is going through." She held up her iPhone. "I've seen some ugly posts about your mother lately. Sometimes, I wonder if these devices are bringing the world together or tearing it apart."

She held up her flip phone. "To stay sane, I've kept things simple. If I had my way, I'd ban cell phones for a week. It would be good therapy if everyone had to talk instead of texting."

"Unfortunately, you can't put the genie back in the bottle. Imagine what our kids and grandchildren will see."

She nodded in reply thinking of the headsets and imagining the number of people that would ditch the real world for a virtual one.

"Look, I've been hoping to run into you," Kendra said haltingly like she was wrestling with herself before reaching into her purse and pulling out a business card. "I'm a reporter with the *Tribune* now." She handed her the card. "If you ever want to set the record straight on all the misconceptions out there, call me."

Cassie took a step back surprised by the ambush. The last she knew Kendra was teaching creative writing at Northern Essex Community College. *Everyone wants a scoop to make their career,* she thought. Her father might be a business leader in the community, but he did not flinch in telling anyone to go to hell if approached on the topic. The strategy worked as he courted a fair amount of the sympathy vote as the suffering husband of a brainless killer. Writing some big checks to sponsor community events also helped. The net effect was a portion of his guilt by association ended up being transferred to her and William. She looked at the carton of eggs in her cart, and calculated if she counted all the ones thrown at her house, she could make an omelet every morning for the next year.

"I hope I didn't offend you," Kendra offered.

She responded with a weary smile and looked at the green bananas across the aisle. Within a few days they would be brown and bruised. The reunion with her high school friend felt the same.

CHAPTER EIGHT

WHILE POURING a generous second glass of Cabernet, she heard Lucy from *Charlie Brown* setting up her infamous psychiatry booth in the kitchen's corner. Cassie did not need to wait for the "doctor is in" sign advertising help for five cents to know she could spend many rolls of nickels on a mental autopsy. *Heck, I could blow a paycheck just analyzing Mom and Dad's relationship*, she thought. Before she could raise her glass and toast the know-it-all cartoon character, the garage door made its trademark guttural moan. A glance at the clock on the wall confirmed the minute hand only tiptoed a few steps since she last checked.

Fleeing the needy wife routine, she quickly transported the wine back to the couch in the family room and found the leather seat still warm. She debated about turning on the television or picking up a magazine, but James would see through the staged event. No, sitting alone with her wine and her demons would be the norm.

The sound of heavy footsteps in the kitchen were followed by car keys skating across the granite counter. *Does he do that to piss me off or is he just an idiot?* she thought. The plastic key hooks were conveniently located by the back door, and she explained their function a hundred times.

"Hello?" her husband called out.

"Hell----o!" she replied and took a sip of wine hoping for an accelerated calming effect.

A minute later, James appeared with wine glass in hand. He paid no attention to the lonely environment, and instead of giving her a peck on the cheek, clinked his glass with hers.

James sat down next to her and stretched out his long legs on the wooden coffee table. "I'm beat," he moaned and closed his eyes.

She frowned at his feet on the table and bit her lip. The lack of a reply produced the intended effect within seconds, and James opened his eyes and held up his wine glass in the dim light. "I see you're drinking the cheap stuff tonight." He took a sip and grimaced. "How you can stomach this rotgut is beyond me. I told you there's a reason the Liquor Commission is practically giving this stuff away. Every bottle we've opened, tastes like gym socks. They should relabel it Brettanomyces Supreme." He let out a self-satisfying laugh and rocked side to side on the couch. "I wish I could hire a sommelier to describe the putrid barrels they use in bottling this crap. On second thought, why don't you send a few bottles over to your dad and what's her name?" He shot her a smirk.

Ordinarily, she enjoyed his wit, and if she played along, the stressed-out tech guy would relax after another glass or two. Then his cheeks would get flushed, and he would begin talking in shorthand about designing new modes of entertainment in the not-too-distant future or some silly video he watched. After another glass, she would see glimpses of how James once looked at her before the cataracts of other pursuits fogged his lenses. But no amount of liquor would fuel a couch date tonight.

"The only vintage I would gift Dad and that tramp is after it turns to vinegar." She held up her glass. "I would have asked William to help me polish off the bottle instead of waiting for you, but he's underage."

Her husband's expression froze for a moment before sitting back on the couch and resting his head against the pillow. "I apologize," he began like he expected the blowback and practiced his defense. "I planned on leaving by mid-afternoon. I thought with the time you've been spending with your mother you wouldn't miss me. But then one of the software guys found a huge glitch in the controller interface everyone overlooked." He shrugged. "I'll spare you the techno-geek explanation."

"How considerate, but you practically live there now. Maybe I should forward your mail there too?"

"That's not fair! I remember when you were leading big projects, and I had to hold down the fort. This won't last much longer."

"Hold down the fort? Like you should get a medal for taking care of our son when I had to travel?" She paused to calculate for a moment, and then looked at her data driven husband. "In five years, I traveled three weeks."

"I didn't mean it that way." He took another taste of the wine and screwed up his face. "Where is the boy wonder?"

"He went to see a movie with Cameron."

They sat in silence, and she felt too tired to press the matter. "Well, it's nearly eight o'clock and I'm starving. What do you want to order?"

James took a deep breath. "I'm afraid you're going to make me gargle with this bad wine or break the bottle on my head. I've already eaten, but I'd be happy to get you something. Just name it."

Cassie counted to five before replying so her husband could not accuse her of overreacting. "I don't understand. Your crack team lives on potato chips and Snickers. Junk food is not dinner in my book."

Her husband began pumping his right leg. "No, but hold your fire. It got to be late afternoon and everyone skipped lunch.

I felt guilty because I made the team work another weekend, so I took them to Tuscan."

A nice Italian dinner, while I munched on stale pretzels and drank spoiled wine? "I understand and if I'm upset, it's because you're shortsighted."

His head jerked back. "What do you mean?"

"Well, how about calling your wife so she knows what's up? You know how much this day haunts me, and I had a hell of a scare at the grocery store this morning." She glanced at her watch. "Ten years ago, we were out to dinner. Who knew it would be the last time we had any peace?"

"Why do you do this? I beg you to be done with it but here we go again. Most couples celebrate the anniversaries of good things in life; first date, wedding day, son's birthday. Not you! You're fixated on the darkest of all days."

"Your obsession with a make-believe world makes you blind to what's real. You never ask how my mother is doing."

He sighed. "How is she?"

She tightened her grip on the wine glass, combating the urge to throw its contents in his face. Instead, she leaned in to explain how his lack of concern hurt and caught a whiff of his cologne. It caught her off guard, and she sat back and studied him, aware that after years of marriage you have an image in your mind of your partner and sometime miss the little things. James wore the new jeans she got him for Christmas along with a light gray crewneck sweater.

"So, how many went to dinner?" she asked looking to outflank the geek's defense.

"Ah...." He hesitated and looked away. "Four or five of us."

"It's such a big number you have to estimate? Don't you know?"

He reached for the skunk wine and took another sip. "There were four of us at dinner. Sam came for a beer...but had to get home."

She met his team at a summer company cookout. There were about two dozen and most were in their late twenties and thirties. In particular, she remembered a woman named Halle with long dark hair and deep-set eyes. She seemed intent on winning her husband's attention and teased him about it on the ride home.

"Who went? Anyone I met at the cookout?" She did not want to come across as that type of wife.

"No, I don't think so," he said quickly.

She was still analyzing the squishy reply and debating whether to ask for names and rank of the attendees, when he grabbed her hand. "Look, I'm sorry about not calling. We're so close to launch, all my brain cells are maxed out thinking about one thing."

I'm wondering what that one thing is? she thought still smelling the cologne.

"After the launch, the investors will get off our backs and things will return to normal," he continued.

Normal had taken up residence on the dark side of the moon for the last decade. She looked at the band of gold on his finger, the precious metal signaling a life-long commitment. *He should have a ring of steel on his right hand too as a visible sign of his other marriage to work.* "You're being naïve. The launch is only the beginning."

"I'm sure there will be kinks after the rollout, which will require updates to the installed base, but—"

"I do this for a living remember?" she said interrupting. "The projects will grow faster than fat hen weeds, especially serving the consumer market."

"I hear you, but we will have the revenue to hire more people."

"Will took me on a VR trip, but I've been meaning to ask about the list of game rooms. What's with the nude beaches?"

James put up his hand. "Don't blame me. That was Marketing. Think about the demographics and what makes teenage boys tick."

She rolled her eyes. "All I'm saying is the pull from the market, never mind how the competition responds, will suck the life out of you for more content. Your weakness has always been looking at the potential without considering what a company will do to make a buck. That said, you don't have to think too hard to know what type of content oversexed teens and perverted men will want." She felt like she was taking an axe to her husband and saw him beginning to lean.

He rallied and sat up straight. "Don't go dark on me now by looking at all the risks. If we pull this off the rewards will be huge. Besides not worrying about how we will pay for our son's college, I will hire an army of engineers to manage the demand."

"That's true, but when Will took me through the application, I sensed massive potential your company is overlooking."

He put his hand to his forehead like he was exhausted from listening to another consultant. "Such as?"

"Think about the medical applications! How about those afflicted with terrible diseases like ALS? To communicate would be a real blessing for them and their family. Or how about all the bedridden folks in nursing homes staring at blank walls? Imagine if they could walk on a beach!"

He nodded. "Believe it or not, I'm not an ogre and understand how this technology could help many. Even school kids could use it for history lessons and virtual field trips. I'm sure we will tackle those opportunities down the line once this startup turns a profit and goes public. We also have some things to work out so it's safe."

"I found two instances where imagination takes on a life of its own."

"Yeah. I felt conflicted about letting Will try it out because of that." He touched her hand and laughed. "I got a sense of what's under his hood…. Typical teenager with raging hormones."

The dinner came back to mind, and she searched his eyes. "If we put on the headsets now, what would I find out about you?"

He hesitated for a second, but she read the fear. "I could say the same thing about you, but remember imagination like dreams are not real." He reached over and kissed her on the cheek. "But this is." He stood up and checked his watch. "Will won't be home for a while. Let me open a nice bottle of wine and we can enjoy it upstairs."

She remembered a time when they didn't need a buzz to fuel intimacy or moreover when sitting on the couch and cuddling was more than enough.

She stood up. "That would have been nice, but I haven't had dinner.

CHAPTER NINE

WHEN THE DOORBELL RANG at eleven-thirty, her heart sank. Her son did not push the boundaries on curfew but eleven o'clock came and went. Text messages went unanswered. Cameron's mother drove them to the movie theater and also offered to pick them up, and she kicked herself for not getting her cell number. Her teenage years were more adventurous than William's so far. She used to tell her parents she was going to the movies or the mall, as cover for attending an underage beer blast.

Opening the front door, she expected a policeman. Instead, it was Cameron's mom, Beth. In the few times they were together, she came across as someone constantly sparring with chaos which made her resting face look like sandwich wrap stretched too tight. She knew it was sick, but she took a liking to Beth, probably because it made her look calm in comparison. Now Beth was standing in the doorway bug-eyed and looking like she threw on a pair of baggy jeans and a gray hoodie for the chauffer duties. Before she could inquire about anything, her son came up the walk with Cameron in tow. William held an ice pack against his mouth, and there were multiple drops of blood on the front of his white ski coat.

"What happened?" She rushed out and embraced her son as a cold gust suddenly kicked up. When he did not reply, she hurried everyone into the house.

"I wanted to bring Will to the hospital and get him checked out, but he would have none of it," Beth said once the front door shut. "Then I headed for the police station, but Will said he wanted to come home."

Cassie thought Beth sounded like a woodpecker hammering a tree searching for bugs, and could never be a journalist, because she sucked at summarizing the facts. *Why isn't she telling me what happened?*

Beth was still rambling on as she put her arm around her son. He flexed his shoulders a bit, like he did not want any sign of motherly care.

Pulling the ice pack away, she discovered an ugly two-inch gash on his lower lip. "Did you get in a fight?"

He shrugged and pulled away and put the ice back in place.

"See! He wouldn't tell me anything either," Beth continued.

William might have a future with the CIA or be comfortable in the witness protection program, but his buddy had loose lips like his mother. She put her hands on her hips and gave Cameron a hard look that even made James wilt. "Your turn, buddy! What happened?"

The teenager looked up at the ceiling like he was trapped under the ice with no way to escape. William would have to fend for himself.

Beth got in her son's face. "Start talking!"

The teenager took a deep breath. "Well, the movie ended .... we were waiting in the parking lot," he stuttered, and then stopped as if tasting the rest of the confession, "Then some guys … uh, they came over and started picking on Will."

"Do you know them?"

Cameron gave his buddy a side glance, hoping William would intervene and when he did not, simply shrugged and looked at the floor, willing to suffer parental retribution rather than break the code of silence.

An uneasy stillness followed until Beth cleared her throat. "All I know is when I got there, they were in the lobby. Someone from the snack bar gave him ice for his lip."

Cassie looked at Beth wanting to ask why she didn't call her from the theater? *Cell phones are such amazing devices that allow for instant communication! My son could have given you the number!* she imagined herself yelling, but held her tongue and looked toward the kitchen where Lucy held out her hand for another nickel and whispered, "*What good would that have been? After three glasses of wine and no dinner, you could not drive, especially on this cursed day!*" James was no good either. After their tiff, he sulked for a bit and then went to bed. Attempting to wake the dead at Pine Grove Cemetery would be easier.

Her head ached, and she wanted to talk with her son alone. She gave Beth a quick hug. "Thanks for everything."

Beth's face remained stiff but her shoulders drooped, disappointed the whodunit had no resolution. She pointed at her son. "Be sure and see your dentist and make sure nothing is loose or cracked. My cousin got whacked by a two by four, and he lost three teeth from the injury."

Beth was half way down the sidewalk and still rattling off a list of complications like a pharma commercial, when Cassie closed the door.

William began slithering down the hall when she stopped him. "We need to talk. Let's go in the family room."

Her son headed for the stairs. "Really? I just want to go to bed."

She ignored the protest. "I'm not arguing with you. I'll get you some ibuprofen and a gel pack for your lip on the way."

He turned around looking like he took another punch.

"You can't play *Rocky*, cuddling a pink bag of ice," she said with a forced smile.

When they reached the family room, William collapsed in a recliner, and she sat on the floor in front of him.

"Enough with the silence. Tell me what happened."

Will put his head back and closed his eyes.

She dug her nails into the short nap carpeting as the silence lengthened. "Look. Your father won't be this patient when he asks you in the morning. He's overworked, overtired and will ground you for a month with no hope of parole." She hated using James as an excuse. The "wait until your father comes home" was a cop out, not to mention James was rarely home and when he was, dead asleep or tinkering with prototypes.

"I'll take my chances with Dad. He's a guy and will understand."

The words were like a rusty box cutter that made a ragged slice across her heart. She loved her son deeply and though she appreciated how close he was to James, she wondered why they could not develop something special too. James wanted another baby but after the tragic affair with her mother the desire disappeared along with the opportunities. Deep down she knew that after pushing him away so often, he classified her as ninety-percent untouchable.

"I might be a woman, but I could probably take your father, so give me a break about not understanding."

William half laughed, and she waited through another period of silence and measured time by listening to the furnace kick on. She almost called it a day when he sat up in the recliner.

"You'll get mad, and I know how difficult this day is for you."

She gripped the carpet harder. William was too young to remember his grandmother. As much as she tried counterbalancing what he heard and read by sharing stories about her mother's goodness, the void seemed too big to fill. She was not surprised when he refused visiting her. The curious thing was she never mentioned the anniversary to her son, yet somehow, he knew. Maybe James told him. Her son's sensitivity surprised her from time to time.

"I love you for your concern, but I'm all right. I promise not to flip out regarding what happened," she replied.

He touched his swollen bottom lip still not convinced.

"I mean it, honey. Just tell me what happened."

William shifted in the chair. "Well, it was that article in the *Insight* that caused this," he said pointing at his lip with his free hand."

She curled her toes and swallowed hard as the image of the newspaper flashed in her mind. "What article?" she asked hating herself.

"The one that called your mom the Witch of Salem. It had a picture of her in bed, and you looking pretty angry."

She nodded. "I'll be honest. I saw it when I went to the store today."

"Did you read it?"

She shook her head. "Why would I? It's the same garbage."

"Well, three jerks from school held me down in the parking lot so they could read it word for word to me. It went on and on about what she did to all those people, how she mowed them down and wouldn't stop like some evil witch. The paper claims it has a source at the nursing home that says she's awake and improving. The goons beat it into me that she belongs in a prison hospital."

She wondered who spilled the beans. It wasn't Julie but everyone else was suspect.

"So why did they take it out on you?"

Her son shot her a look with one eye, and if looks could kill, she would clutch her chest instead of the carpet. "I shouldn't have said that. I get it."

"The guy who punched me in the face a couple times is the cousin of the woman that had her leg amputated."

Cassie ran through the victims in her head. She had them all memorized by name and injury. Tanya Lagasse lost her leg, and her cousin was one of the five that died. She looked away, too numb and dehydrated for another glass of wine.

"Why are we still here? She's caused so much heartache and it continues!" William's voice was on the cusp of breaking. "If we moved a few towns away, it wouldn't be in our face every day."

She and James talked about it over the first year, but hated cowering to the mob. After all, they were innocent, which James wore like a coat of armor every time it came up. They thought with time the memory would fade. Plus, their son had a different last name, but with social media, no infamous connection is ever missed or forgotten. In a couple years, William would be college bound. Would the stigma follow him there too?

"What can I do?" she asked softly blinking to keep the tears at bay.

He leaned toward her. "Help your mom really wake up so she can face the music, instead of everyone taking it out on us. I'm tired of the rumors on why she hit all those people. It alternates between saying she was depressed, mad at grampa, angry at the world, or too drunk to care. It's been ten years and still wherever I go, someone points their finger at me and tells me they haven't forgotten what she's done." He stared at the ice pack. "I know how this is killing you. If I were her, I don't know if I would want to wake up either. It's a no-win situation— remain asleep tucked in a nice bed, or wake up and be the target of a prison knifing."

"You're not saying anything I haven't thought. I have a lot of mixed feelings and wish she could explain what happened. This tragedy has been a millstone around our family's neck for years."

He got up and began walking toward the hall. "This sucks! I wish we could read her mind." He glanced back at her. "I'm going to bed."

She listened to his heavy footsteps navigate the hall and then up the stairs. Her son's words reverberated in her head and they would for the rest of the night. *"I wish we could read her mind."*

She looked across the room at the custom built-in shelves which featured hundreds of video games. When she complained about the cost, or dusting them, James said it was his research archive. She had fantasized using the virtual reality headsets with her mother, but filed it away as a daydream. But the more she thought about it, the only risk was it would not work.

"What do I have to lose that I haven't already?" she whispered.

CHAPTER TEN

THE FOGGY MORNING made her question where the monochrome land ended and the sky began. On the short drive to the nursing home, she imagined limbo looking like this— a misty, formless world which led to her mother.

She entered the building still grappling how to pull this off and tamping down the strong urge to abort this nutty mission. Seeking guidance from Julie would help but also brought mixed feelings. Not that the nurse would nix the idea, but if she probed what she hoped to accomplish, Cassie would be at a loss explaining. Consequently, she hurried through the halls, afraid someone might inquire what was in the rectangular white box. *If I said it was a time machine, would I be lying?* she thought.

She found her mother sitting upright in bed and intently twisting her wedding band.

"Good morning!" she chirped loudly, aware how uncharacteristic it sounded.

Rose immediately looked up. Before giving her a kiss on the cheek, she studied her mother's lips. Over the last few days, she thought she could detect the beginning of a smile at the corners of her mouth, but Julie chalked it up to hope's reflection. Still, she thought the same a few weeks earlier about the ever-slight hand movements, and time had proven her right. Her mother's fingers were still somewhat gnarled, as if frozen in a weird ritual, but the pretzel-like knots were softening from the special exercises. The doctors and physical therapists were astonished by the progress, but sadly not her husband. Whenever she called her father to report the latest milestone, he would listen, and if he commented at all, it was the same retort: "Don't get your hopes up."

Cassie put the box containing the headsets on the bed and took her mother's hand. "I'm sure you remember my husband James," she began slowly and with a wide smile that had become a recluse. "I can't explain how, but the company he works for came up with a marvelous invention that allows you to enjoy different locations and communicate without talking. Someday, we will have a conversation why the target of this unbelievable innovation is to play games, instead of something more worthy." She bit her lip realizing this must sound like gobbledygook to a woman still grappling with reality, so she pointed at her mouth as the empty eyes followed. "Let's just say it's a magic carpet that takes us somewhere special," she said slowly and deliberatively.

Her mother's eyes followed as she unpacked the box. After laying the headsets on the bed, she crossed the room and quickly closed the door. What would follow would be hard explaining to any of the residents roaming the halls and occasionally wandering into the room, hungry for conversation. She also feared another ambush from the media, even though her father and the administrator lodged complaints against the *Insight* and Security was on the lookout for trespassers.

Rose did not move when she slipped the headset over her eyes and adjusted the strap. As she did, her fingers trembled and she concentrated on her mother's luxurious strawberry-blonde hair. She remembered being eight years old and putting dozens of ribbons and Bobby pins in the human-sized Barbie. The more ridiculous the better, and her father laughed and took pictures.

Cassie glanced toward the closed door and listened intently. Hearing nothing, she looked back at her invalid mother wearing a ridiculous looking headpiece which brought a new wave of doubt. Before it could take hold, she put on her headset and began working the controller. She quizzed William at breakfast about the basics until he was ready to scream, telling him she wanted to surprise Dad and fly solo. That was no white lie.

Her heart beat louder than the introductory music as the presets she selected at home floated before her eyes. A couple of clicks and the blackness transformed itself into a lush forest with the sun high in the bluest sky this side of Eden. She urgently scanned the surroundings looking for her mother among the giant pines, maples, and white birch but remained alone. Just as she was about to rip her headset off and see if the other unit malfunctioned, she heard a woman giggle.

Selecting a packed dirt path that ventured to the left, she followed the growing laughter. After making her way down a short embankment, she discovered her mother ankle deep in a fast-moving stream, her toned arms outstretched and looking up through the canopy at the sky. Cassie hid behind the trunk of a massive birch, mesmerized by the apparition of her radiant mother. Rose wore a loose white blouse and khaki shorts highlighting shapely legs securely anchored on a boulder in the middle of the rushing water. But it was the expression on Mom's face that took her breath away. The feeding tube and blank look were replaced by an expression of sheer child-like joy.

She moved ever so slowly from her hiding place, and all the plans she made about how to proceed were lost in the euphoria. The only thing she remembered was her son's repeated instruction not to talk out loud. She battled all the emotions welling up and concentrated on thinking one word, "Mom!"

The ecstasy that kept Rose's eyes heavenward were immediately severed, and she fell backwards into the water. The strong current began carrying her downstream. Cassie rushed into the ice water and after struggling a bit, helped Rose to the shore and onto a thick carpet of grass.

Her mother began shivering but did not seem to mind her clothes being soaked through. "What a lovely dream," she heard her mother think.

Cassie held her breath and felt all the pain, frustration and anger disappear. She reached for her mother's soft hand and let the tears come, wondering if she took her headset off, would her eyes be wet in reality too?

"Mom, this isn't a dream," she continued and thrilled she did not have to explain the rules about not talking because Mom was still incapable. "This is what I was telling you about going someplace special. All you have to do is think what you want to say and this machine picks it up and amplifies it."

Her mother did not acknowledge the explanation but pulled her in for a tight embrace. "I love you … love you … love you," she repeated like a litany finally falling free.

Cassie basked in the words and thought it miraculous how she heard her mother's Boston accent, not some surrogate. Strangely, she also had use of her hands without a controller, and chalked it up to an unknown option in the settings. However, she did question if she understood what this was all about. "This place is make-believe, Mom. We're just wearing headsets. This is a game of sorts."

The words— or rather thoughts, were like a cattle prod, and Rose jumped up. "I've prayed night and day not to be led into temptation. Be gone evil one, and damn you for taking the form of my daughter!"

Before she could offer words of assurance, Rose ran toward the woods. She ran after her mother, but her sneakers were not motivated like the woman being pursued. The deeper they ran into the woods, the darker and more ominous they became. In short order, the sun disappeared, dusk set in and the spectacular trees gave way to picker bushes and treacherous bogs. The air itself changed from smelling of pine to a deep putrid decay. Cassie could hear her mother yelling up ahead and for an instant thought she detected a hulking figure darting between the scrub pines.

A feeling of impending doom gripped her, and she stopped running. Working the controller, she noticed the Chapel of the Holy Cross in Sedona as an alternate location. In the blink of an eye, they were transported to the architectural marvel built into the red rock. She found her mother standing next to her and now wearing a light sweater and jeans. Rose took in the new environment for a moment and then made her way to a kneeler and knelt in front of a ninety-foot metal cross. The crucified Jesus, eyes wide open looked down at them in pain and resignation.

Cassie watched her mother's lips move in silence and strangely did not hear what prayers she recited. When her mother finally stood, she took her hand and led her outside to a small garden. The contrasting blue sky and red rock were mesmerizing.

Rose sat down on a bench and admired a small ceramic angel kneeling in prayer. "If you were an evil spirit, this is the last place you would bring me. Tell me, how long have I been gone?"

She looked around. "I know time in make-believe feels different, but we just got here a couple minutes ago."

"No, I mean since ..." She buried her face in her hands.

The realization her mother was present took her by surprise. "Ten years," she replied, though it sounded cruel being so direct.

Her mother looked up. "That's all? Then I have a new sense of what forever feels like." "Can you describe it?"

Rose took a deep breath and closed her eyes for a long moment like she was reliving it. "It was like flicking a light switch on and off — present one moment and then swallowed up by the blackness. But slowly I was more aware than not. Then there were the dreams, some vivid, others disturbing, sometimes both, but few happy. I began counting days by how much light I sensed against my weighted eyelids. Then one morning, the stones crumbled. When I saw my room and looked out the window, I questioned if this was just another dream."

She knelt down and gave her mom a tight hug. The lyrics from *Awake* from Josh Groban came to mind: *So, keep me awake to memorize you. Give me more time to feel this way.*

"My hearing came back some time ago." her mother continued, "I welcomed it, but there's nothing worse than being buried alive in your body. I know what a piece of furniture feels like because that's how I felt— except for Julie's love. She combed my hair, rubbed my back, sang me songs and prayed I would wake up."

Cassie looked away, as her cheeks grew hot. Being her father's daughter, she felt the shield go up as the internal demons rallied. "Forgive me for not being present more, but it goes to the heart of what put you in a coma."

"What do you mean?" her mother asked.

"You don't remember?"

"I've had an eternity to think over everything in my life. Days and weeks and months to examine every joy, every mistake, every missed opportunity." She caressed her cheek. "I held on to tender memories of you." She looked away. "Other recollections only brought nightmares."

The sky suddenly turned overcast and the wind picked up. Cassie stood up, and her eyes followed the long driveway down the hill. About a half mile away standing against the red rock, she could make out two men in the approaching dusk. The taller of the two pointed up at them.

"Do you remember being in the car with Dad the night of the accident?" she asked watching the figures.

Rose got up from the bench and looked down at the men. Her face became tense like she knew who they were.

"Mom?" she asked, hoping for a reply and wondering if she remembered any of the carnage.

Rose glanced back at the chapel like it might be a refuge and flexed her right hand. "I have a few flashes … winter …. speeding … trying to open the car door." She studied the shadows again. "Then not being able to breathe and drowning in the blackness." Fingering her wedding ring, she sat down again on the bench. "I'm exhausted."

Cassie nodded. "So am I," she replied but ecstatic by the magic carpet ride.

CHAPTER ELEVEN

THE HONDA CIVIC DROVE ITSELF home as she replayed the last hour in her mind. When she took the headset off her mother, she half expected their conversation would continue. Instead, Rose remained wrapped in a cocoon and gazed at the ceiling. It made her wonder if the entire session really happened.

Pulling into the driveway, she discovered a blue Mazda MX-5 Miata parked in front of the garage. She did not recognize the vehicle and noticed it had temporary plates, indicating it had just been purchased. Before she could look for additional clues, she saw William come bounding out of the front door and as usual, without a coat.

He sprinted toward her car. The last time she saw him this flushed was after Malcolm Butler's interception at the goal line in the 2015 Super Bowl. He took after his father and usually ran pretty low key. It made her question if some of it rubbed off on her, since she should be jumping up and down after talking with Mom. She was half way out of the car when she caught sight of her father emerge from the house and saunter down the front stairs in his standard gray pea coat.

"Hey Mom!" her son sang coming to a stop in front of her.

It felt like she was looking up higher every week to address him. "What's up, buddy? You look like you won the lottery which is too bad because your underage so the millions are mine."

Her dry humor usually irritated him, but he just laughed and waited for his grandfather to catch up.

Her father wore that knowing smile of his which made her moan, but this time she just held her breath.

King Charles put his arm around William. "Thought I would stop by and visit with my grandson since I haven't seen him in six months."

She nodded in acknowledgement of William being his grandson but rejected the premise of the visit. Every year she invited him to Thanksgiving and Christmas dinner and like a scene out of *Groundhog Day*, he repeatedly refused because it would be uncomfortable for *her*. She laid awake many a night wondering what unearthly powers Rachael possessed to make a tough guy cower like that. Normally, the holiday skirmish would trigger a series of Scud missile voicemails. By Christmas Eve a different type of silent night would settle in until negotiations commenced in January. This year however, the missiles were few and radio silence averted given the many updates on Mom's progress.

"You are always welcome here," she replied with special emphasis on the first word. "The holidays were pretty quiet this year with James working so much."

"I thought he played games for a living. Did he switch careers?"

She glanced at her fidgeting son instead of taking the bait. Her father never understood the value of anything not made from wood, steel or concrete.

"No, he's crushing it. I just wish he didn't work so much." She flashed a smile hoping to change topics. "I just visited with Mom."

Her father rolled his eyes. "You've been making a lot of deposits into that guilt account of yours." He glanced at his grandson. "I make memories with the living." He put his hand up to his mouth to shield William from reading his lips, "and someone not under indictment."

Cassie sucked in her breath, and the shadow figures pursuing her mother in Sedona flashed through her mind. *Her father must have been one of them. Who was the other guy?*

William began pulling her toward the Mazda. "Isn't this a cool car?" he said gushing.

She admired the vehicle's streamed lines. Not that she considered herself a car buff, but thought the Miata shared some DNA lines with a Corvette, while the deep blue color really popped against the snowy landscape.

William pointed at the roof. "Notice the retractable hardtop?"

"Oh?"

Her son laughed. "That means it's a convertible, Mom."

"Perfect for a January thaw, if it ever shows up." She shot her father a puzzled look. "I thought you only drove trucks and SUV's? You haven't owned a car since—" Her mouth froze as her heartstrings became knotted again.

Her father flashed a smug smile. "You know me well, daughter." He winked at his grandson. "I think we've toyed with her enough, my boy. Tell her about your super-duper surprise."

William reached in the pocket of his jeans and extracted a key and held it high above his head. "Gramps bought the Mazda for me!"

Her eyes locked on the dancing key. "What!"

William gave his grandfather a hug. "He knows I'll have my license this summer and wanted to buy my first car."

Cassie tried mimicking her poor mother by keeping her expression frozen. "You bought him a new car before he even knows how to drive?"

"No, it's a few years old, but in mint condition."

Her first car was a minivan that her father used to transport his band of hourly workers from site to site. It had a couple hundred thousand miles on it and smelled of sweat, tobacco, sawdust and skunked beer.

"Remember my first set of wheels, Dad?"

He laughed. "Sure, but you had a dozen boys willing to drive you around town. This will give William an aura of coolness."

"The only aura I see is an ambulance with flashing lights after this two-seater becomes a pancake when he gets t-boned."

"You're being a killjoy, Mom!" William protested.

Her father waved her off. "Stop being so dramatic. Look at it this way. He can only have a wingman so he won't be hauling a car full of his friends around. It's also too small to go parking in."

Did he really just say that? What is he? Sixty-five going on seventeen? she thought.

Her father read her thoughts and after clearing his throat pointed at William. "Just remember it's rear wheel drive and very light, so keep it in the garage when it snows."

That's great! I lose the garage too? A sudden gust underscored the point, and she saw the opportunity for a sidebar with her father. "William, you're going to catch pneumonia out here. Go in and get your coat."

"I don't need one!" he protested.

Her father's eyes narrowed like he was itching for a cage fight too. "Listen to your mother, son. Go in and grab your coat and then you can show her the interior of your pocket rocket."

As William galloped toward the house, she wasted no time in moving toward the center of the imaginary ring.

She knew she would only get one shot, and immediately went for the TKO. "How dare you! What are you going to do next? Set him up with a supermodel for his junior prom?"

"C'mon Cassie. William's a nice kid but he's no genius or super athlete and takes after your husband and has zero chutzpah. A nice car can be a alter ego and level the playing field a bit. Why make things so hard for him?"

"Because there's no shortcut in building character and that doesn't happen being a helicopter parent or buying unearned popularity. We told William he could drive my Honda, and if he wanted his own wheels, he would have to get a part-time job and start saving toward it. If he kept his grades up, we would kick in a few bucks and help him find something reliable." She pointed at the blue beauty glimmering in the dying daylight. "Now you've ruined a valuable lesson on how your grandson should approach anything he wants to achieve in life." She took a deep breath. "William will be devastated when James makes you take it back."

Her father shortened the gap between them as if preparing to unleash a body blow. "Make me take it back? You can tell your hubby that will not happen. Maybe he acts all macho at home, but he has no balls when it comes to me."

"Do you talk like that to all the women in your company?" she asked. "Where I work, HR and Legal would be all over you, regardless of title."

He waved her off and walked to the edge of the driveway and kicked at the frozen snowbank with the toe of his expensive Italian leather shoe. "Tell me," he said without turning around, "why are you visiting her so often? Nothing has really changed."

Cassie wondered if she had time to tackle the insensitive jerk before her son returned. "Her?" she repeated. "I only use that pronoun when referring to your blonde squeeze."

He spun around and punched the air. "Knock it off! This act of yours about Rachael expired years ago so put it to rest." He rushed toward her. "Stop hoping your mother ever leaves the vegetable garden she's inhabiting. That stuff only happens in the movies, and I don't care how many novenas that holy roller nurse says, it is what it is. Like Ben Franklin said, *the only things certain in life are death and taxes.* In your mother's case it's coma or jail. I think fate chose the less painful option."

Before she could scream, the front door slammed shut, and William rocketed across the front yard and did not stop until reaching the car.

"Mom! Slide in the passenger seat and check it out!" he said.

It took every ounce of self-control not to walk into the house and lock the door behind her. Instead, she swung herself low into the leather bucket seat and immediately noticed the car had a six-speed manual transmission.

"My old man is delusional!" she whispered under her breath.

William threw himself into the driver's seat and rattled off a long list of the vehicle's features. She said, "Wow!" and "Cool!" a half dozen times for show, but felt like she was back in the virtual world and having an out-of-body experience.

After several painful minutes, William began repeating himself, and she decided on making a graceful exit. She put her right hand on the door handle and froze.

"Do you remember being in the car with Dad?" she asked in their VR session.

Her mother flexed her right hand. "I have a few flashes ... winter .... speeding... trying to open the door.

She looked over at her son's left hand, the one he would open the driver's door with and her jaw fell open.

CHAPTER TWELVE

CASSIE ARRIVED at Dunkin Donuts ten minutes early and ordered a decaf coffee because she already felt jittery. The coffee shop was the most convenient location to meet her high school flame and probably the safest. Other locations on Route 28 would trigger too many memories and be a distraction.

She chose a table by the window and watched the mid-day traffic. Most of the cars, trucks, and SUV's no matter their age looked dingy given this week's trifecta of slush, salt and sand. All needed a good scrubbing before rust and rot took over. "Rust and rot, what a perfect pairing," she mumbled into the black ink coffee.

Looking out the window again, she watched a silver sedan pull into the parking lot much too fast. She knew the unmarked car belonged to Sean. He was born with a heavy foot which in high school proved to be a nice annuity for the town given his many speeding tickets. *How ironic the perpetual teenage offender went into law enforcement and recently made detective,* she thought.

As Sean got out of the car, she surveyed his tailored gray suit and blue tie, and wondered if he specifically chose it for this reunion. She would be lying to herself not to admit the extra time she spent this morning brandishing a curling iron and mascara brush.

Cassie stood up as he entered the lobby and hurried over, flashing the same smile that first got her attention in biology class.

She pointed out the window. "Son, my radar gun says you were doing twenty miles an hour over the speed limit," she said in a low voice mimicking one of the cops that pulled them over.

"Sorry Officer, my girlfriend is starving for a Big Mac and they close in ten minutes," he replied right on cue. "If I remember correctly, I got off with a warning and you got your sandwich, so we both won."

"Close, but it wasn't a Big Mac— just a cheeseburger with extra pickles."

They both laughed, and she gave him a hug. *Ah, to be seventeen and out cruising with someone that wants to impress me. It's true what Shaw said, youth is wasted on the young.* She pointed at the table by the window and her lonely cup. "Can I get you a coffee?"

He glanced at the table and then back at her. His eyes shifted ever so slightly, like he was trying to size her up. "No thanks. My New Year's resolution is cutting back on java."

"How's that working for you?"

"Not good. Drained half a pot this morning and the day is still young."

She shrugged. "There are worse vices. How about a donut?"

Sean smirked. "What are you doing? Typecasting me?"

She led him to the table, and they sat down. His athletic six-foot frame straddled the chair, and he moved it back in order to get comfortable. She used the opportunity to study his blond hair. It looked a few shades darker now and he wore it very short— no doubt to control those locks that were a barometer and curled at the first hint of humidity.

"I can't remember, the last time we saw each other," she began.

He shot her a quick look before his hazel eyes stared at the Formica table top. "That's because we haven't spoken since graduation. When I got your voicemail yesterday, I played it a few times to make sure I wasn't hearing things." He looked outside for second like he wanted to make sure no one was egging his cruiser, or having difficulty finding the right words. "It's been a lifetime," he said gazing into her eyes. "You look great."

"You're too kind," she replied knowing everyone longs to hear that compliment. She likened herself to the Titanic where all the damage was below the water line. Sean was too sentimental to see she was listing. *Few others see it either*, she thought, *and maybe instead of the ship, I'm more like its stoic band that played on despite the rising waters.*

She took in Sean's fuller face and could still recognize the boy she made out with. "You've changed some, but still as handsome. I read about your promotion. Congrats!"

He nodded, and she pointed at his bare ring finger. It was the first thing she surveyed when he walked in the coffee shop. She lost any special privileges long ago, but pressed anyway. "Single? What gives?"

He held up his left hand. "There's the girl I remember who never let me get away with anything. I was married for ten years, but this line of work takes a toll on relationships. We have a beautiful daughter named Nora, who's eight years old and in second grade." He leaned in. "You would know all this if you came to any of our class reunions. Actually, a few of us have an ongoing bet on whether you'll ever show up."

"Well, I hope you didn't bet I would." She did not need to mingle with old chums to be remembered. The *Salem Insight* kept her in everyone's memory.

Sean stroked his chin. "As a detective, I should know all about you, but your social media presence is zero. But I stay in touch with the old gang and know some of your profile: married, one teenage son, house on Main Street."

She nodded and took a sip of her coffee. It would be fun reminiscing, but that was not the purpose of this meeting.

"Your police powers are impressive. That's why I wanted to meet."

His face shifted quickly into a professional mug featuring a deep frown that would bring wrinkles as he aged. "Why didn't you want to meet at the station?"

"Have you seen the paper lately about my mother?" she asked and looked around the lobby. A few patrons waited in line, but all the tables remained empty.

He nodded. "Yeah, but slinging mud is their shtick. I wouldn't be too worried. Did you see what the *Insight* wrote about the police union last week?"

That was Sean, always supportive. James used to be like that too, before the Ice Age set in.

The detective glanced at his watch. "So, what's this all about?"

"Most days I refer to it as my mother's terrible accident or the family affliction, but some days the reality of it gets to me. Then I repeat all the charges she's facing out loud. I always choke when it comes to aggravated manslaughter."

He reached for her right hand wrapped around the Styrofoam cup and cradled it for a long moment. Electricity shot up her arm. "I was devastated for you and your family after it happened," he said softly. "I feel terrible for all the victims and that includes you."

"Thank-you. We might not have spoken, but I always knew you were in my corner and that's why I called. I have some questions about what happened that night. When it all went down, I was in a state of shock, and my father handled everything. Besides having some questions, I'm ashamed that I filtered everything about the tragedy on how it impacted my life instead of my mother's."

The detective cocked his head. "Don't be so hard on yourself. There is no playbook for what you went through, and with the media frenzy any mother would round the wagons to protect their family. I'm sure you have many unanswered questions, and all the vigilantes on social media do too. Look, the only thing that would put an end to it is for your mom to wake up."

"She has."

"So, the rumor is true?"

"Yes, though there's a lot of fake news blended in. Mom is alert and making progress but it's a long road. The doctors told me not to get my hopes up that she makes a full recovery given the head trauma sustained in the accident. But they also thought she wouldn't survive the night when she first arrived at the hospital."

He looked into her eyes and nodded. "That's the best news I've heard in a long time. Maybe someday, she can clear up everything, even if it comes with consequences. Your dad must be over the moon."

Cassie rolled her eyes. "More like Jupiter. Isn't that the planet that has a lot of gas and the big eye storm?"

He jerked his head in surprise. "Maybe he's afraid of getting his hopes up? That's understandable given the number of years she's been in a coma. From what I've seen, it looks like he threw himself into work given all the construction projects he's managed."

She took a sip of coffee. "Given the blowback, he skated with bankruptcy for some time. Many of his friends deserted him and he worked nonstop to hold on."

"Have you discussed any of this with him?"

"I would need more that a diamond drill bit to get inside his head." She locked eyes with Sean like she used to do when she wanted her way. "Would I be able to see the case files?"

"Sure," he said quickly agreeing like he did at seventeen, "but why not ask your dad's attorney instead? I'm sure with all the lawsuits, he has multiple copies."

"His lawyer is a good friend of his and I don't want it getting back." She touched his arm hoping to close the sale. "Look, my father and I can't talk about it without things getting …. shall we say, more difficult than they are already."

"Okay, I understand. Well, you can certainly make a simple request. You don't need me to pull any strings."

"True, but I need someone to review it with me. I'm afraid I'll miss something. Will you help me?"

He sat back in the chair and smiled. "What's that line from *Jerry Maguire?* You had me at hello."

CHAPTER THIRTEEN

JAMES SAT on the edge of a wooden stool, meticulously soldering a component on a circuit board. A half dozen headsets in various stages of disassembly cluttered the workbench.

Cassie watched from the doorway and studied a level of concentration she could not match. Whether working, watching a movie, or reading a book, lightning could strike the room and her husband would continue unperturbed. It was the same when he slept— the moment his head hit the pillow his spirit entered the valley of the dead until dawn. She lived in a parallel universe where a grasshopper crossing its legs would distract her. Likewise, sleep came in small increments, like the space between raindrops.

She met James junior year in college, when they were both competing for a summer internship in marketing, which turned out to be code for tele-sales. Quite by surprise, the manager hired both of them, probably because he needed two hundred calls a day to make a run at the ridiculous sales target. Summer was nearly over when he finally got up the courage and asked her out. He was such a gentleman, or too much of one, that she initiated their first kiss. Like most things, timing is everything and the new love of her life had just finished an onion bagel when she grabbed him by the collar and they locked lips. The face she made when she pulled away remained a source of laughter ever since. If she were to bookend the romances in her life, it would begin with Sean and end with James and the people in-between merely short stories. She thought over the years how they were such opposites: Sean possessed a certain swagger and competed for recognition, whereas James slouched and when accolades came his way attributed success to the team.

Her husband sat up and arched his stiff back, and she took the cue.

"Hey hon," she said meandering over to the workbench.

He glanced her way, gifting half a smile before looking down again at the circuit board. In the first few years of their marriage, they greeted one another with a kiss. Few were passionate but they underpinned a connection no matter what the day brought. Somewhere along the way, the ritual stopped and made her ponder bigger questions which had no easy answers. More than once, she used it to fuel a dumpster fire when a petty argument outgrew its parameters. The memory of Sean touching her hand verified she might be numb but still very much alive.

He inspected a stamp sized board under the intense light of an overhead lamp. "I didn't hear you come in. Long day at work?"

She took a deep breath because she called out again, but did not think the news would go over well. "I'm about to start dinner. How much longer will you be?"

He pushed the rolling chair back from the bench. "Man, I need a break. If this project doesn't kill me, nothing will."

The disassembled headsets caught her attention and made her realize the plans for a second virtual meeting with her mother were now in jeopardy. She pointed at one flayed unit with tentacles of red, white and black wires sticking out. "Our son will be devastated."

"Why?" He shot her a confused look.

"You rock his world whenever you bring prototypes home, but this VR technology … well, I even enjoyed it. I planned on taking another trip into that wacky world but I see you're autopsying the headsets."

James smiled. "Then we must really be onto something. You've never been impressed with any of the other devices."

She touched his hand, wanting electricity from him and not an old flame from high school. He looked surprised and nodded at the workbench. "None of these are the units you played with. I'm taking them apart so I can determine a certain failure mode that's driving the team nuts. You and William can experiment with the beta headsets for a while longer. Competition is cut-throat and senior management wants to lock everything down soon. I can smell the paranoia in the air."

"What does it smell like?" she asked, while thinking she needed to move fast and have another session with her mother.

He laughed. "Like that stinky fruit.

"Durian? They say it smells like rotting flesh."

"Yeah, that about sums it up, and I think it's from the team pulling eighty-hour weeks." He looked at her like he was inspecting a component before giving her a kiss on the cheek. "You still surprise me from time to time," he said shaking his head, "but not our son. He gave me a lot of lip about the Mazda when I got home. He went on and on."

"What did you tell him?"

"That his grandfather could not have purchased a worse car for his age and driving ability — not to mention he will look like a spoiled, entitled kid. It wouldn't surprise me if someone punctured the tires or keyed the car to make the point." He glanced down at a notepad. "Your dad is a real piece of work," he muttered.

She could give a dissertation on that comment but focused instead on William. "I'm sure that went over big."

"Yeah, he will probably give me the silent treatment for the next month, or needs twenty bucks to go out with his friends." He chuckled. "I'm forty-three and have never driven a car like that!"

Suddenly an idea welled up within her. "Maybe there's a middle ground here."

He looked up from his notes. "How so?"

"Well, we could tell him if he keeps his grades up, he can have the car after graduation. In the meantime, he can only drive it when you're in the passenger seat. You two can be like Batman and Robin until he heads off to college. Think about it! You would also get some quality time with William in this world instead of a virtual one."

James puckered his lips like he did when he was emotionally against an idea but his intellect recognized the logic. "Let me give it some thought."

"We can also add the caveat he needs to get a part-time job and pay for the insurance and gas too," she added quickly to put more pros on the scale.

James did not acknowledge the suggestion and made his way over to his desk in the corner and opened up his laptop. Cassie followed planning on cementing the idea further when she noticed his screensaver: James and a half dozen of his team sitting around a conference room table littered with dozens of headsets, pizza boxes, long neck bottles of beer and an empty handle of tequila. The smiles on everyone's faces were brighter than their neon green t-shirts. Even from ten feet away her eyes locked on the woman with her hands wrapped comfortably around her husband's shoulders. She glared at Halle.

"That's quite the team pic," she said pointing.

James looked up from the keyboard and smiled. "Yeah, they're phenomenal and work hard," he replied with a chuckle.

"They play the same way too. I sometimes wonder which gives the greatest hangover."

She looked at Halle's seductive face and the silly smile her husband wore. *I'm too tired to go there tonight,* she thought and began moving away.

"So, long day at work?" James repeated.

She turned around. "Why do you keep asking?"

He looked her up and down. "Because I called your office and Joan picked up. She said you called out today." He started pecking on the keyboard. "I felt like a fool."

"Sorry about that. You left early this morning and I decided on taking a personal day."

He thought for a moment then frowned. "What are you talking about? We had coffee together!"

Cassie laughed. "Was that today?"

James shot her a hard look. *This must be how he looks at his staff when they disappoint him,* she thought. "I spent some time with my mom." She bit her lip wishing she did not have to keep their session secret because he would flip his lid.

Her husband sat back in his chair and looked at the ceiling like he was begging heaven for patience. "It's not like your mother is sick or migrating south for the winter! I don't get this daily obsession of yours since she opened her eyes. Any progress will be painfully slow. Why are you risking the career you worked so hard for?"

She pointed at the workbench. "You pride yourself on taking things apart and finding the root cause of a problem. But your logic puts a blindfold over your heart. You more than anyone else should understand what this miracle means to me."

James shook his head and started typing.

"When you're finished with your report, can you pen a note to my manager requesting a parent conference?"

The dig went unanswered.

Leaving the room, she decided against telling James about reviewing the police report because he would say it was a big waste of time. She doubted he would care she met with Sean either and that bothered her as much as flirtatious Halle.

CHAPTER FOURTEEN

A SHORT STOCKY WOMAN wearing a loose-fitting housecoat featuring monster-sized butterflies and dandelions blocked her mother's door. Cassie tightened her grip on the box containing the headsets as she approached.

"Good morning," she offered with a forced smile realizing the nondescript greeting hardly defined the day so far. If it did, she would be shouting about the frustration she felt waiting for her husband to leave so she could retrieve the headsets and make sure they were fully charged.

The odd-looking woman with an elongated head like a summer squash did not reply and kept her feet planted. Even without the benefit of a neck, she still gave her a full body scan.

"Are you the daughter?" a raspy voice inquired.

She felt her smile drooping and looked beyond the human boulder. Her mother waved at her from the bed. "Yes, I'm Cassie."

The woman slapped her on the arm. "Nice to meet you! I'm Madelyn." She let out a deep cough, the calling card of someone that smoked unfiltered cigarettes by the gross. One pale green eye winked at her. "But my friends call me Mad."

Cassie nodded in reply, thinking maybe she stumbled on the set of a new comedy show.

The woman watched for a reaction and a few seconds later, expelled a congested laugh which smelled like mice had crawled up her nostrils and died in her sinuses. "It's always fun watching people's expression when I tell them that!" she replied and moved aside to let her pass.

Cassie was still processing the combo of butterflies, dandelions, summer squash and rotting mice when she felt someone tugging on the box under her arm. She turned around.

"What's in the package?" Madelyn asked. "Hope they're tangerines because the fruit in here sucks."

She shook her head. *Little wonder a nut is categorized as a fruit. I don't have time for this today,* she thought. "This is something for my mom."

The woman let out a protracted sigh. "I wish I knew where my mother lived so I could visit, but she ran away with some hairy creep from the circus. I haven't heard from her in years—except for an occasional postcard telling me she works for peanuts." She let out another laugh and shuffled over to a chair by the window.

It took a moment for the shock to wear off. "What floor is you room on, Madelyn?" she inquired gently, willing to escort her back. If needed, she would tie her up in the shower curtain in order to postpone her from wandering back for the next hour.

Madelyn responded by smiling and pointing at the door.

As if on cue, a young orderly rolled a bed overflowing with clothes and other personal effects into the room.

"What's going on here?" Cassie asked the young guy in blue scrubs as he positioned the bed ten feet away from her mother.

Julie came rushing into the room and looked at both of them. "I wanted to make the introductions but see you've beaten me to it."

"I don't understand this," she said.

The nurse ignored the comment and glanced at Madelyn seated by the window and smiled before moving to check Rose.

The orderly smiled and sensing the tension, quickly left.

"Rose, did you meet Madelyn?" Julie asked.

Rose smiled and nodded.

"It will be fun having a roommate," Julie continued. "It will feel like a sorority."

"What?" Cassie asked much too loudly.

The nurse nodded at her. "Why don't we take a walk and give Madelyn a chance to settle in?"

She marched out of the room with the box instead of leaving it to prying fingers. They barely made it to the nurse's station before she unloaded on Julie. "What's going on? My mother has a private room." It took quite a test of willpower not to add a colorful adjective or two.

The friendly nurse shrugged. "You should ask your father. From what I understand, he made the change."

The oxygen in the room suddenly vanished and she started hyperventilating. "What?"

"Yeah, it surprised me too, but given the cost of long-term care and your mom's medical needs—"

"Which he can more than afford!" she said interrupting while thinking of their strained conversations. *Why is he punishing her like this?* She envisioned what's her name looking over the bank statements and spouting off about the money they could spend on tropical vacations if Mom got a roomie.

Julie watched the anguish on her face with sympathetic eyes. "Look, if it's any consolation, Madelyn won't be here long. She just needs to regain her strength before going home."

Cassie clutched the box. "Define long. A week?"

The nurse shrugged. "More like a month."

"After I get through with my father, I'll need a bed in here to regain my strength too. She swallowed hard. "On the bright side, if anyone can motivate Mom to get better quick so she can go home, it's probably that wacky woman."

The nurse held back a laugh. "Once you get to know Madelyn, you'll see she's a spitfire, but a sweet woman. Hey, what's in the box?"

She looked at the package to conceal her eyes. "Just some stuff from home I want to show Mom, but I don't want Miss Mad eavesdropping. Could you get her out of the room for an hour?"

Julie glanced at the box and nodded. She was too much of a professional to ask more.

When they got back to the room, Madelyn was showing Rose a shoebox collection of garish fingernail polish.

She looked at the nurse and if her eyes could scream, they would blow out all the windows in the facility.

"Madelyn, why don't I show you where you can store that tremendous collection?" Julie suggested. "It would be a shame if a bottle broke." A few seconds later they were headed down the hall.

Cassie watched them until they disappeared around a corner. Closing the door, she wondered if she just met a walking representation of a monster from virtual reality.

CHAPTER FIFTEEN

THOUGH WINTER WAS HER LEAST FAVORITE season, Cassie knew her mother loved it, so after firing up the headsets, she chose a vintage New England farm blanketed with a fresh foot of snow. The mid-afternoon sky had a purple tint making the landscape look like a paint by number scene.

With the parameters set, she walked around the Hallmark like setting and found her mother standing in front of a weathered barn, dressed in a red snowsuit and matching knit hat. Rose smiled as she approached and picked up a handful of snow and put it to her mouth.

"Be careful," she warned. "You don't know where that comes from!"

Her mother bit into the virtual snow and lapped her lips. "After having a tube down my throat for so long, I'd eat yellow snow just for the moisture. You have no idea how much I longed for this," she said between bites. "I felt like the rich man in the parable begging Abraham to send Lazarus to cool his tongue with a drop of water."

Her mind flashed to pictures of herself standing in her mother's room during the obligatory visits, thinking the woman in the bed was dead to the world. To learn she could hear everything and desperate for a drink of water was too much to bear. "That's terrible," she replied more as a comment on her own behavior than the coma hell her mother endured. It was also curious that Rose wanted nothing stronger than H2O.

Rose ignored the comment and picked up another handful of snow.

"With the progress you're making, the doctor says you can try some soft foods soon," she continued. Following her mother's lead, she took a bite of the snow and it tasted like she remembered.

Rose watched and smiled. "When you were in preschool, you sampled some after each storm thinking there might be different flavors."

"Well, Dad made me think that after introducing me to snow cones."

Her mother followed up by biting an ice crystal off her pink knitted glove. "Don't get me started about the dreams I've had about food! Not gourmet food mind you, but simple things like biting into an overly ripe peach and letting the juice slide past your lips to your chin. Ah, the things we take for granted! Now, I would eat shoe leather and relish the taste." She screwed up her face. "Whenever the feeding tube backed up, I would taste chalk for days."

She made a mental note to look for a virtual reality destination with an all-you-can-eat buffet for their next trip. How this technology could tap the memory centers for taste were beyond comprehension.

"Regarding strange tastes, I'm sorry about your new roommate," she said switching topics.

Rose looked beyond her at a snow-covered stone wall separating a large pasture from the woods. "Makes me wish things were vice versa, and this was the real world." She nodded to herself. "If that were the case, I wouldn't visit a hospital bed for a million bucks." She looked at Cassie with suddenly shiny eyes. "Be gentle on Madelyn, honey. She has nowhere else to heal, and it's nice having someone dote on me. For months at a time, I had no visitors."

Cassie heard a distant rumble of thunder, and her mother cocked her head and listened. "I appreciate how silence is a rare gift," she continued. "There is always some sort of background noise marking the passage of time: water gurgling through baseboard radiators, a window shade beating against the sill, the hum of fluorescent lights, cascading chatter between nurses. When I opened my eyes there were few surprises because I took in everything with my ears." She shook her head. "Why they call it a rest home, I'll never understand because there's little of that. One of my biggest motivations for getting well is giving a piece of my mind to the halfwit that decided the tv could be my companion. Purgatory can be defined as listening to the entire catalogue of Sesame Street and Barney songs. Those tunes droned on day after day until I thought they were in my feeding tube and coating my insides. Sometimes, it made me pray for the nothingness to return."

A yellow light began blinking in the upper right section of Cassie's eyepiece, indicating the battery was running low. *How is this possible? I charged them before I left!*

Her mother suddenly let a laugh erupt and threw herself down and began making a snow angel. "Then one day the clouds lifted when I heard Julie's angelic voice praying over me." Her mother stood up an examined the snow sculpture. "Why, she even had Father McGowan come and bless me. I was surprised when I opened my eyes and she didn't have a halo over her head."

Cassie sought refuge from the pins and needles crisscrossing her chest by studying the snowy field. Soon spring would come, and the owner would plant corn and pumpkins and maybe some sunflowers— all annuals in contrast with the perennials Mother Nature tended to beyond the stone wall. She could make out a trio of cardinals as they flirted from one thicket to another, their red snowsuits lighting up the snow lined branches. "Nature versus nurture," she whispered to herself. Before her mother was wheeled into the OR, she called a priest and he provided the anointing of the sick. But as the days multiplied into months and years, she left her to wither both emotionally and spiritually in a sanitized bed. No wonder her mother was thirsty.

The lump in her throat came back, and she felt the snowpack underneath them sink a bit.

"I'm sorry Mom. I should have visited a lot more and been as thoughtful as Julie. I'm not making excuses, but—"

"Don't beat yourself up, my child," she said interrupting and closed her eyes for a long moment. *We even boast of our afflictions, knowing that affliction produces endurance, and endurance, proven character, and proven character, hope, and hope does not disappoint, because the love of God has been poured into our hearts through the Holy Spirit that has been given to us,*" she said slowly. When she finished, she opened her eyes and gave her a kiss on the forehead. "You will see how the kiln has changed me." She fished in her shirt and pulled out a small silver medal on a delicate necklace. "It took me some time to discern the meaning of that verse until Julie gave me this Miraculous Medal and explained how the Blessed Virgin promised all who wear it will receive special graces. I feel its power."

Cassie nodded but her mother read her face. "I see the doubt, but here I stand playing in the snow and talking to my sweet daughter. You don't call this a miracle?"

She wished she had half her mother's faith, but that was missing in the virtual world too. *That said, if the situation were reversed, would I have survived all those years in solitary confinement without faith?* The pit in the bottom of her stomach provided the answer. She would have withered away.

The trees were listening and responded by shaking off some of the snow clinging to their branches. The muffled beats made the ground shake.

Cassie felt a warm breeze kiss her face. The sudden melt combined with the low battery warning light, not to mention Madelyn pacing somewhere nearby, told her time was short.

"Mom, last time we were together we talked about the accident."

Her mother ignored the comment and kissed the Miraculous Medal before putting it back under her shirt.

She reached for her mother's hand. "Remember how you said you tried opening the door before the crash?"

Rose thought for a moment and then shrugged. "Isn't it strange what we remember and what we forget? For the longest time, I thought we recorded every second of our lives, and in the end the Good Lord wouldn't have to pass judgement because we could take in the totality of our lives and know the verdict. Now, I'm not so sure."

"Don't be too hard on yourself. I know you remember the million and one details that defined you and also made us a family— penuche fudge, the *Beatles,* walks on the beach, silly laughs watching reruns of *Seinfeld.*" She stopped to check-in.

"Of course, but I came across many gaps, and no matter how hard I searched pieces of me were lost." She took a deep breath. "That's because what started out as a friend to numb the hurt and loneliness and boredom… well, it became my jailer. I put messages in all those bottles of booze waiting to be rescued. What I failed to grasp is everyone is treading water too." She touched her heart. "Despite the drinking, I always had good intentions, but that's not enough. It's only action that counts, and I'm determined to make amends for the rest of my life."

"Mom, you're shredding my heart. I knew about your struggles with alcohol and understand why. But you shouldn't be confessing to me. I stayed away from visiting you because I was both angry and ashamed."

Her mother face fell and her eyes became little slits. "Why?" she gasped.

The melting accelerated. Cassie could hear a loud torrent as if some great glacier had been microwaved and expected a tsunami of ice water any moment. There was no time or battery left to change locations.

How can I put words to the tragedy? Her mind blanked until she recalled the *Insight* slander and the terrible ditty. "Your name around town is the Salem Witch because you killed five people and injured seven others in a drunken hit and run before plowing into a utility pole."

Rose collapsed into the snow angel which was rapidly turning to slush. "I don't understand," she said with pleading eyes. "Didn't your father tell them what happened?"

"No! Tell me!"

She looked away.

The background faded with the dying battery. "Yes or no, were you driving?"

Gingerly feeling the slush with her glove, she shook her head once.

Suddenly, a terrific noise filled the air. Turning, they saw a landslide of biblical proportions rushing toward them, rocks and trees and huge chunks of ice devouring everything in its path.

She wanted to rip the headset off, but had trouble feeling her real hands as the virtual pair were lifting her mother up from the slush puddle.

Seconds before the landslide arrived, she finally located her fingers and wondered what happened if you died in this make-believe world. She had no desire to find out.

CHAPTER SIXTEEN

DEFINING THE OVERSIZED CLOSET containing a small wooden table and two metal chairs as a conference room certainly stretched the definition. The new police chief made a lot of headlines by promising more feet on the street versus additional infrastructure spending, but this setup also underscored his disdain for meetings.

Cassie took off her coat and wrapped it around the back of the gray metal chair. Taking a seat, she felt the cold radiate up her back as Sean shuffled into the room balancing two cups of coffee on a laptop.

She pointed at the cups. "I thought you were cutting back?"

"Mine is decaf," he replied.

"If you say so." She reached over and touched the dingy looking tan wall. "I see you still have a thing for meeting in small cages. I'll never forget that cozy bar up the street that had tree trunks as tables. I can't believe they served us since the fake IDs looked like something out of a kindergarten project."

The detective sat down across from her and put his finger to his lips. "Remember anything you say in here can be used against you. I also recall your drink tasted like a Shirley Temple, so maybe they were on to us." He slid a Styrofoam cup toward her. "Hey, I offered to do this over lunch, but you were all business."

"Well, I didn't want you trucking in all the case files never mind watching you devour raw hamburger."

"Says the girl that once had a monthly subscription for beef jerky."

They looked at each other for a moment, before she cracked first and laughed. "So, where's all the files?"

He responded with a smirk. "Something tells me you watch a lot of those police and lawyer tv series?"

She let the question hang in the air and took a sip of coffee. "In most shows, the characters complain about the coffee at the station. This isn't bad."

He gritted his teeth. "Then you should try the decaf." He straightened his blue striped tie that complimented the crisp white shirt. "You won't find any donuts around the station either."

"You're killing all the stereotypes."

The detective opened the laptop. "Then I'll really rock your world. All the original files are in storage," he said pointing at the laptop, "but there are these remarkable devices called computers that allows one to access scanned copies."

She rolled her eyes. "I asked for that."

He smiled and continued typing. "To get started, I pulled up the report when your mother hit the utility pole." He stood up and came on her side of the table and sat back down. "Take a look."

Her eyes scanned the block style lettering logged by Officer Brian Dowd.

At 1:30 a.m. on Sunday, January 6th 2013, I was dispatched to Nettle Avenue. Upon arrival, I found a 2012 black Mercedes sedan which sustained heavy front-end damage after colliding with a utility pole. The passenger side of the vehicle took the brunt of the impact. Approaching the scene, I found Mr. Charles Owens alive and unconscious in the back seat of the vehicle with multiple facial abrasions. The driver, Mrs. Rosemary Owens was also alive but had serious head trauma. I called for an ambulance and secured the scene.

Before the ambulance arrived, Mr. Owens became conscious and I advised he not move and wait for medical personnel. Mr. Owens disregarded the request and exited the vehicle. He was quite unsteady on his feet and slurring his words. He stated his wife hit several people on Lawrence Road minutes before and left the scene of the accident. He explained further how he and his wife had been at a company celebration. After consuming several alcoholic drinks, he let his wife drive home while he slept in the backseat. Soon afterwards, he woke up when his wife's driving became quite erratic. After hitting several pedestrians, Mr. Owens stated his wife became quite agitated and sped away from the scene despite his pleas to stop. Mr. Owens also disclosed his wife had a long-standing problem with alcohol. Upon inspection of Mrs. Owens purse, I discovered three unopened nips of whiskey.

After husband and wife were transported to the hospital, I noted missing trim from the right fender of the vehicle which later matched material left behind at the accident scene on Lawrence Road.

Cassie closed her eyes. The report backed up what her father told her that night and highlighted incessantly in the papers and on tv.

The detective exhaled. "I know reviewing this is tough no matter how long it's been. You said you have questions. What are you hoping to find?"

How can I tell him, my mom says she wasn't driving? "I … don't know … yet," she stammered. "These are just painful words on a page. Does anything look out of place to you?"

He shook his head. "I read the report ten years ago and again this morning. It seems so unlike the woman I remember. She made a very poor decision getting behind the wheel after drinking. Even so, I have a hard time believing she would leave the scene after hitting all those people. I remember how kind and caring she was."

Cassie stared at the computer screen. "Everyone says the same thing, it's totally out of character." Occasionally, she would see the short-tempered side of her mother when drinking, but even then, she never drove. When Mom asked her to run errands, it was code for being impaired.

Sean looked up from the laptop and glanced at the closed door. "Look. I hate stating the obvious here, but your father doesn't come off looking like a model husband in the report. First, there's no mention whether he asked about the condition of your mother, although Officer Dowd might not have included it in the report. Second, instead of keeping his mouth shut like someone of your father's stature would know, he blabbed on and on about what happened. For a drunk man, he seems pretty motivated on making sure his version of what transpired was captured." He shrugged. "Maybe that's just my jaded view after seeing too much of the seedy side of things."

"The other thing that always bothered me were the nips found in her purse. My mom hated hard liquor."

"Did you ask your dad about it?"

"Sure. He said when things were bad, she would drain a bottle of vanilla extract. Can you pull up the other ... report?" *Even to this day, I can't say hit and run accident— that type of cowardice is the antithesis of Mom.*

A few more clicks and the other report popped up. This one was filed by Officer Steven Riley. She scanned the screen instead of reading word for word ....

12:45 a.m. Sunday, January 6th ... Arrived at scene. Hit and run accident with multiple fatalities and injuries.

Interviewed Nancy Meese, owner of Sunrise Tours. She stated their chartered van was returning from a Boston concert when it broke down with a flat tire on Lawrence Road. Passengers from the broken-down van were being transferred to another vehicle when a black sedan approached from the south at a high rate of speed. The vehicle struck people in the roadway resulting in multiple fatalities and injuries. There are unconfirmed reports of people in the river… Divers called.

Sudden nausea made her push her chair back. "Maybe you're right. Some things will remain unanswered unless my mother recovers."

The detective swiveled the computer his way and began toggling between screens.

"What is it?"

"Maybe nothing, but I'm always in the weeds over the details. The hit and run happened at 12:45 and we received a call at 12:52 when a neighbor heard the Mercedes kiss the pole."

"So?"

"Well, Officer Dowd would have been on the scene within minutes, especially since all units in the area were looking for the car."

She looked over his shoulder at the screen. "But the report says he arrived at 1:15."

Sean sat back and pulled on his lip. "Maybe he meant 1:05? Working the third shift can make you forget your name never mind making a typo."

"Are there any pictures of the passenger side of the car?" she asked.

He looked through the files. "Hmm, I'm sure there are, but am having trouble finding most of the pictures. Maybe they're in another database."

"Didn't you say something about computers being marvelous devices?"

He shot her a gimme a break look. "Before I go hunting for them, what are you looking for?"

"I'm not sure. Did Dowd say where he found the purse in the car?"

"After the car hit the pole, anything not belted down went airborne. What are you insinuating?"

She didn't answer and thought about her mother's head injury. "Any pictures of the windshield?"

He looked for a moment and pulled up the image. The tempered glass looked like a picture frame stomped on by an elephant.

"Did anyone compare my mother's head wound to the windshield? Maybe see where her blood was located?"

The detective closed the computer. "When you're holding a winning lottery ticket, do you think about the other twenty losing ones you purchased? Dowd had your mom unconscious in the driver's seat and your father's statement. Why look further?"

"Because she's facing aggravated DUI, leaving the scene of an accident, multiple counts of manslaughter and a rash of other charges. Plus, you said a minute ago, my dad went to great lengths to get his story down at the scene."

"So, you'd rather trade one parent for another? There are no winners here, Cassie."

"I know that. I just want the truth. What about this Officer Dowd? Where is he now? Is he your boss?"

"No, and that's why I wondered why you weren't asking your father. Dowd works for him."

CHAPTER SEVENTEEN

ON THE ELEVATOR RIDE UP to the third floor, Cassie recalled a recent trek to the C-suite for a strategic project review meeting. After two hours in the rarified environment replete with fine china and linen napkins, the resulting fatigue, lower back pain, and ringing in her ears made her wonder if she had a case of the bends.

This building made her feel no different, even though her father owned it. Over the past ten years, she could count on one hand the number of times her shadow darkened this crystal palace. This time she made sure King Charles was not present.

When the elevator door slid open, she came face to face with Catherine, the gatekeeper and executive assistant occupying a desk large enough to fill two conference rooms at the police station. The attractive middle-aged blonde welcomed her with a pleasant smile but as usual revealed no teeth. Her theory was she either reserved them for family or had none left after grinding them away from spending fifty hours a week in a deep pool of testosterone.

"How nice to see you, Cassie," Catherine said before turning the fake smile upside down. "I'm afraid your father is at the worksite today. Shall I call him for you?"

Be direct and don't raise any flags. "Actually, I'm here to see Brian. Is he in?"

Catherine cocked her head like she didn't hear correctly. "You mean Mr. Dowd?"

She wanted to reply and say Officer Dowd, but glanced at her watch to make it appear she was in a hurry. "Yes, please."

An uncomfortable silence descended, and she held her breath hoping the request would be viewed strange but trivial enough not to probe further.

Catherine stood and instead of escorting her to his office, pointed at the guest chairs in the corner. "Take a seat and I'll see if he's available."

She flashed a grin. "I don't mind waiting if he's on a call or in a meeting." *I have all day free since I called out of work again,* she thought.

The admin shot her another curious look before sauntering down a long corridor in three-inch heels. Cassie looked down at her flat shoes. *No wonder Catherine has a joyless smile.*

A stark stillness kept her company and she pondered why this quiet felt different. The best she could come up with was intent. Silence in a library represents standing in supplication at the well of knowledge, in a church it stands for transcendental reverence, and at a veteran's grave honor and sacrifice. The quiet in executive corridors emanate innovation, strategy and ego. As the minutes passed, she expected Catherine to make the catwalk back and say Dowd slipped out, after repelling down the side of the building.

Instead, she heard footsteps from an adjacent hallway and stood up straight and put her shoulders back like her mother taught.

Catherine appeared with a short, husky man in tow and they parted ways at the reception desk.

For the first time on the fifth floor of this building, she witnessed a broad smile and pearly caps. An extended hand sprang toward her. "Brian Dowd."

She scanned her opponent's face as they shook hands. Late thirties, large nose dominating a full face, close-set brown eyes, receding hairline. She took a step back and noticed he dressed the part; dark suit with a crisp blue striped button-down shirt, expensive dress shoes and no wedding ring. A musky cologne permeated the air.

"So nice meeting you! How can I be of assistance?" he asked.

Cassie felt the x-ray while her peripheral vision took in Catherine. The admin's chair moved ever so slightly, while her long white neck leaned toward them to catch the reason for the unannounced visit.

"I thought I knew everyone in my father's boys club. Would you have a few minutes to talk?"

Dowd kept his smile, but dialed back the intensity. As they made their way down the hall to his office, she sensed Dowd was dragging his feet like he was being led to the electric chair. *Maybe he thinks my father is bringing me on in some capacity*, she thought.

His office was a replica of her father's except in square feet and minus any family photos. She took in the large mahogany desk, oversized leather chair, colossal bookcase framing ceiling to floor windows. It made her want to gift him a copy of *Little Men*.

She chose one of the chocolate-brown leather chairs in front of the desk. It felt a tad low which made her look up at the executive. She almost laughed.

He scanned the bare desktop like he was waiting for some work to come his way. When he looked up, the way he stared at her bust gave her a creepy feeling like his stubby fingers were unbuttoning her shirt. Back in grade school, her mother taught her where to kick if a boy offended her. The school principal was not amused shortly afterwards when two of her classmates feared they might sing soprano for the rest of their sorry lives given her pinpoint accuracy. Her mother wore a red blazer when she went into battle that day, and after an hour with Principal

Cohen, he asked if she wanted to be a kicker for the junior high football team.

"So how long have you worked for my dad?" she asked to break the perverted stare.

It was a simple question to ease into the specifics, but Dowd responded by looking at the white tiled ceiling. "Hmmm, it's going on … I don't know … eight, nine years?"

She laughed. "You sound like a lot of husbands when asked how long they've been married. Mine just says forever and leaves it at that."

Dowd turned the oral dimmer switch clockwise and the teeth lit up again. "Hope you don't mind if I borrow that one!"

"Were you always in construction?" she asked.

"Yes and no. I spent summers roofing houses back in college, but started out in another field. I looked for a career change and interviewed with your father. He offered to take me on, but I had to pay my dues by being chief, cook and bottle washer." He leaned forward and pointed at her. "I know more about how your father takes his coffee and what type of soap he likes than you do." He sat back and let the high-back leather chair frame his inflated head. "But I rolled up my sleeves and learned as much as I could and worked my way up to Chief Procurement Officer. It's been quite a ride from coffee runs to negotiating million-dollar contracts." He hesitated a moment feeling smug, and Cassie knew this was a man that saw no imperfections when he looked in the mirror.

Dowd ended his rags to riches biography with a snap of his fingers. "I might have the title, but believe me your father jumps in whenever he thinks we're paying two cents over the norm for anything." He leaned forward. "The man is an animal."

"You think you have it tough?" she replied. "Try negotiating a weekly allowance from him when your nine-years old."

He let out a laugh that sounded like a pig doing the jig in fly infested mud. "Maybe you can tell my daughter what it's like having to save up for things. She's eleven and I spoil her rotten."

Cassie smiled. "Better address it now before she's a teenager."

"I don't know. Your dad tells me about the soft spot he has for his grandson." His eyes began wandering over the front of her shirt again, and she started rocking her right foot. "He told me about the little convertible."

"Yeah, that little car is a big problem."

Dowd opened a side drawer and pulled out an iPhone and showed her the screensaver — a cute eleven-year-old girl in pig tails and braces. The little sweetie had her head back enjoying a good belly laugh. "This is the one person I will never negotiate with. We almost lost Savannah twice."

Cassie sunk deeper into the chair. "Oh?"

He took a deep breath like he did not have the strength and explain. "Yeah, two bone marrow transplants. The first one didn't take and ..." He looked away.

"How old was she when she went through hell?"

"Five the first time and then repeated the process three years later."

She nodded. The piss and vinegar she stormed into the building with was dissolving like she downed an entire bottle of antacids. "Is she okay now?"

He nodded and pointed at the picture on his phone. "Look at her! Isn't she the picture of health?"

Cassie let him linger on the center of his life while she fought with herself. If William were in a similar predicament, she would have committed any crime short of murder to get the needed resources. Her mom's face flashed in her thoughts and she watched her bite into a handful of snow. *I have a noble motive for this sword fight too,* she thought.

"So, what field where you in before my dad intervened?" she asked putting the picture of Savannah out of her mind.

The Chief Procurement Officer moved the phone to the corner of his desk. "Law enforcement," he replied quickly.

He will not make this easy, she thought. "Whereabouts?"

Owens drilled his eyes into hers minus the lust. "I was an auxiliary officer here and there. It's been really nice meeting you Cassie, but your father runs a tight ship. I have a ton of things to accomplish this afternoon or I'll be back making his coffee full-time. Is there something I can help you with?"

Her mom taught her never to cower, and always look the slug in the eyes before kicking him where it counts. She stood up and looked down at him. "I can ask my father to include janitorial duties in your career development plan, or you can answer a few questions about the accident report you filed."

White could be defined as the latest shade of guilt after the color drained from the ex-cop's face. He shook his head. "Are you joking? That's why you're here?" He stood up and leaned across the desk. "My report covered everything, and I have no further comment. I live my life looking forward. Your father operates like that too."

She pointed at his phone. "I do too. But some things, like your daughter's illness, cannot be forgotten."

"How dare you bring Savannah into this!"

"Then humor me. How long after the accident did my father offer you a job?"

He pointed at the door. "This meeting is over."

"So is this coverup. Regardless of when you started, I know for a fact your interview was early in the morning of January 6th."

CHAPTER EIGHTEEN

GAZING AT THE WESTERN SKY ablaze with streaks of pink and orange made her want to sit on the trunk of the car and admire the sunset. That was the thing about winter, the short days and stark conditions sharpened the senses. Spring and summer brought a constant smorgasbord of colors and textures overwhelming the senses, whereas winter felt like living within the confines of an old television set with nuance found in the multiple shades of black and white.

Her eyes left God's celestial masterpiece and she scanned the white colonial, still decorated with Christmas greenery, but a few sprigs were now tinted orange. "Boring and a pain in the butt to put up and take down," William would dismiss. He had a point, but this house could be decorated in plastic flowers and she would still not condemn the extended member of the family that lived here.

Half-way up the sidewalk, the garage door opened, revealing her father's best friend and former partner boxing up spotlights.

"Hey, Uncle Phil!" she called out. "I hear Logan airport is building a new runway and short on materials. Maybe you can make a deal."

The thin man turned around and pointed at his Patriot's sweatshirt. "I'd rather trade my strategic reserve of lights for some tickets." He thought about it for a second and then shook his head. "But the cold bothers me now so it would have to be an early season game."

Cassie pointed at the shrinking snow. "Unless, it's a day like today."

He followed her gaze and sighed. "Today was tolerable. I love January thaws, but it feels like the eye of a hurricane. You get a breather for a couple days before getting walloped in the second half of winter. That's why I'm out here today, because it will be March before I get another chance to dismantle any of this. Want to bet we get a blizzard next week?"

"I would, but dad told me you were a lousy loser after betting your paycheck at Rockingham Park."

He waved her off. "Yeah, I would paint houses in the summer for tuition but every so often would swing for the fences. If there were a Hall of Fame for most strikeouts in betting on the ponies, I would make it on the first ballot. Forgive and forget will never be written on my tombstone." He looked down for a moment and contemplated the comment. "Given everything I put my poor wife through, maybe I should add that line to hers."

Cassie had not seen Phil since the funeral six months ago. His face looked a lot thinner than she remembered. Usually dressed to the nines and clean cut, today he wore baggy pants and his white hair looked like a wrung-out mop.

He glanced at her like he read her thoughts. "My sister got me a cappuccino maker last year and I've never used it. Want to come in and we can give it a whirl?"

It was a struggle not to glance at her watch, suddenly aware the answers she sought would not come in concise bullet format, like the project updates at work. If they came at all it would require some cajoling. *Why rush home anyways?* William would turn his nose up at anything she cooked, and it would be hours yet before James made a pit stop home and fall asleep on the couch.

"If it's any good, I'll leave a tip so you can play the horses again."

Phil's face lit up like the Christmas lights he was taking down. "No, I retired once Rockingham closed. The only horses that interest me now are at Canobie Lake Park. My niece loves the Merry-Go-Round."

She followed him into the well-appointed kitchen and quickly discovered Phil did not know how to operate the new contraption. After ten minutes and producing nothing but a puddle of frothy milk on the marble countertop, they teamed up and made tea.

Taking a seat at the kitchen table, she eyed a box of corn flakes and a fat jar of peanut butter on the counter. *Some diet!* she thought. "How's your sister these days?"

He sat down across from her and looked in his mug. "Laura is doing fine. Her and Bruce decided they've had their fill of snow and moved to Scottsdale. It really doesn't matter where their located since Bruce travels so much for work. She complains he's on call 24/7."

"Sounds like my husband's company."

"Or the business your father and I built."

Proceed carefully, she thought. "Have you seen him lately?"

"Not since Christmas Eve, when he delivered a horrible fruitcake like he always does. We have a good laugh as he watched me put it in the closet on top of the other dozen. He's such a tease! I bet he puts in his will something about funding perpetual fruitcakes for my grave every Christmas. I think to spite him, I'll have my ashes spread."

She laughed. "Yeah, he told me about that time in college when you got drunk on spiked eggnog, and after eating moldy fruitcake got sick all over your girlfriend."

"That was not my finest moment and the end of Debbie. Thankfully, Ellie overlooked all my stupidity from the day we met. She hated drama and would nip it in the bud." He looked away. "She even made peace with the damn cancer … had it for so many years she said it felt like an ugly sister."

Cassie did not know what to say. Drama was her family's adopted surname.

Phil let out an unexpected snicker. "This year your father brought Rachael to witness my fruitcake humiliation."

"Who?" she asked out of habit.

The widower's eyes narrowed. "Rachael. Your dad's—"

She flashed a stop sign. "Yes, I know who," she interrupted and felt her mouth go bone dry. "Like I told you at the funeral, I'm here for you."

"I know you are, my dear."

"Well, we need to put some fat on your bones. Let me talk with James, and we will have you over for a nice dinner soon." She pointed at the counter. "You can even bring your cappuccino maker along and we can have a team event figuring it out."

"That would be fun."

"*Stop delaying and get on with it!*" an internal voice yelled. "*I would rather face a dozen gawking Brian Dowd's than do this,*" she spit back.

She watched Phil take another sip of tea and waited for him to swallow. "Did you hear Mom is awake?"

Completely out of character, Phil did not look up from the tea. "Yeah, that's incredible," he whispered. He must have thought how it looked because he quickly strapped on a smile that did not match the worry lines on his forehead. "I'm so happy for you!" he added and took another sip.

"For me?" she repeated and it came out rather curt and moved immediately to soften it. "It's like a January thaw in my life."

He finally looked up, and his eyes were moist. "That's a lovely thought."

"But there's a big storm coming if she gets well. There's no statute of limitations on what transpired."

"I agree, though I can't imagine much can be done unless she really comes around."

They both retreated into their mugs. Cassie thought the house echoed with the silence of his wife's absence. She tried thinking back and could not remember a similar gnawing echo at her parent's home. Every time she stopped by the house to comfort Dad, he would rail how his life was ruined because of the colossal crime. *He never uttered one word about the dead and the maimed. It was all about him.*

"I've been thinking a lot about that night," she began softly and minus the various foul prefixes she normally added.

"I'm sure it's never been far from your thoughts."

Though she knew Uncle Phil would never blush like a nun, it was time to gauge his reaction. She glanced at the sliding door leading out to an expansive deck and in the failing light noticed the thin blanket of ice on top of the broad railing. Beyond that, dark trees stood like sentries watching and waiting.

"With Mom waking up, I decided to go back over the details."

Phil nodded and slid his cup away. "Gee, that was good tea."

She found the comment odd, but no doubt a sign he wanted to move on. "I reviewed the police reports," she continued.

The host squirmed a bit in the wooden chair. "Why would you put yourself through that? It's like me wanting to review all the notes from Ellie's oncologist. It doesn't change a damn thing."

"Certainly not the outcome, but having a sense of what led up to the hit and run is crucial if it ever goes to court. I'm sure you and Ellie questioned where the cancer came from? Was it hereditary or environmental?" She watched Phil take a deep breath and nod. *This is going as well as Dowd talking about the bone marrow transplant for his daughter.*

"Uncle Phil, I'm sorry but have to ask you about that night."

He looked her in the eye and folded his hands.

She started with an easy question to put him at ease. "Why did you have the party here?"

He shrugged. "That's what partners do. Your father landed a big contract that would put us on the map and we wanted to celebrate. I looked into chartering a bus and going into Boston and making a splash in the North End. But your dad wanted something more intimate. So, when Ellie had a break from chemo and went to visit her sister in Maine, I hosted the party here. Your father was very appreciative because he feared with a few drinks the roughneck crew would end up in a Boston jail." He smirked. "We laughed thinking about having hangovers and spending the next day bailing everyone out. Plus, your dad asked and that's what you do for your best friend since first grade."

She heard all of this before. "How many came?"

"It feels like ancient history now. My guess about two dozen people."

She looked toward the dining room recreating the scene.

"There was so much food left over, I could have fed the entire neighborhood." He sighed. "After what went down that night, I threw it all away."

"Even the liquor?"

"No, I used it as Novocain for many months."

"Anything stand out about that night?"

"No, we simply had a blast," he replied and stood up. "It was a typical party. Food, booze and schmooze."

She stood up too. "Did you see my mother drinking? You know she had a big problem."

"Like I told your father and the cops a hundred times, no I didn't." He picked up their mugs and transported them to the sink. "What are you insinuating?" he asked with his back to her. "That I lied?"

"No. I'm just reviewing everything. How did the party end?"

He turned around. "How do all parties end? Everyone goes home."

Force field deployed, she thought. "It drives me nuts, when James' family has a party and there's a mass exodus. Did everyone leave at once?"

"Your parents left last, but you already know that."

"Humor me and walk me through it."

Phil shook his head and walked over to the glass slider. It was dark enough that his sad reflection showed. "There's not much to say. Charles celebrated a bit too much and Rose offered to drive home."

"Why did you put him in the back, instead of the passenger seat?"

"Because his legs were like spaghetti, and after picking him up a few times my back was killing me. I also didn't want him bothering your mother on the way home."

"If he was such a handful, why didn't you just let him sleep on the couch?"

He folded his arms and hung his head. "You don't think I've thought that? If I could go back and change things, I would, but I can't!"

She rushed forward and grabbed both his hands. "Believe me, I've thought every day what could I have done to change the outcome too. You claim you would do anything for your best friend since first grade. I'm asking you to honor his wife and daughter. Did my father drive home that night?"

He let go of her hands and backed up. "Of course not! Your mother did." His eyes filled with tears, and his hands were trembling.

"If Ellie was standing here, what would she say?"

"She would comfort you by saying it is what it is, and then offer you something to eat."

She eyed him. *More like it is what it isn't.*

CHAPTER NINETEEN

ON THE WAY TO THE NURSING HOME, her father called five times, but she let it ring. On the sixth attempt, he left a curt two-word message. "Call me!" he barked and hung up. If she had to guess, Dowd got to him before Uncle Phil.

Still weighing how long to delay the verbal flogging, she reached her mother's room and could not believe her eyes.

Madelyn was sitting on her mother's bed spoon feeding her.

"What are you doing?" she yelled.

The odd-looking woman turned and shot her a puzzled look. "What does it look like I'm doing? I'm feeding my roommate vanilla yogurt."

She grabbed a napkin off the nearby tray and wiped a glob of the fermented milk from her mother's chin. "You can't be doing this! What if she chokes?"

The woman ignored the warning and refilled her spoon. "I think she will starve first." She pointed toward the hall. "The nurses are short-staffed this week. Heaven knows when they will get around to feeding her and it's getting late."

She grabbed the spoon out of her hand. "My mother had a feeding tube for ten years so we have to take it slow. We started feeding her a few ice chips, then some gelatin—" She stopped and sighed. "I don't owe you an explanation."

"Madelyn jumped off the bed and pointed a crooked finger at her. "Get off your high-horse and stop barking orders." She showed her the half empty yogurt container. "What you don't understand is I'm here with her all day, every day, and look after her too."

Cassie looked at the container and then at her smiling mother and felt her jaw bounce off the floor. "Wow! You fed her all that?"

Madelyn snorted like a frustrated horse. "Julie is wonderful but the poor thing is racing between rooms taking care of three dozen residents. In my experience, if you're trying to be everywhere, you're nowhere. From what I've observed, the nurse you drool over has gotten your mom to sample a few things, but most of it ends up on her chin." She smiled at Rose who was watching her intently. "I feed her like a momma bluebird tending to her babies," she sang before breaking out in laughter. "Scratch that comparison because I hate yogurt and would never put that paste in my mouth first to feed her." Madelyn smiled at Rose. "I tell her funny stories and before she laughs, I pop in the spoon."

Her mother nodded in agreement, and Cassie patted the good Samaritan on the back. "I apologize. I'm just concerned if we don't follow doctor orders."

"That explains things. You're a rule follower."

"After losing my mother for ten years, you bet."

Madelyn waved her away. "I've learned the hard way that when you let others make the rules, your window of potential shrinks." She looked at the yogurt container. "In my case, I was fed a story and agreed to the rules before I checked the expiration date. Now I find the whole thing is rancid."

"I know what you mean," she replied thinking how she relied on her father's version of events while James urged her to move on.

"Do you want to see the other magic we made today?"

"Magic?"

"I think the term fits, but you have to trust me first."

She gave a slight nod because trust encompasses reliability, and she was not prepared to go that far with this character.

Madelyn stuck out her hand. "Give me back the spoon."

Cassie reluctantly obeyed.

She dug out a small spoonful of the yogurt and held it in front of Rose's face. Cassie watched her mom's eyes lock onto the spoon. The smell of vanilla wafted through the air and reminded her she had not eaten today.

"Rose, say my name and I'll give you a treat!" Madelyn commanded.

This is too much! She's not a puppy! She reached for the spoon to end the charade but the feisty woman used her other arm and blocked her.

"C'mon Rose! Show Cassie we make a great team! Say my name."

Rose's eyes got big and her mouth moved. "Mmmaaaadddd!" she called out.

CHAPTER TWENTY

AFTER A DAY OF SPARRING with Dowd, Phil and Madelyn, the last thing she needed was another brawl. But when she finally made it home and dragged herself into the kitchen, she found a sink full of dishes and a pot on the stove containing the encrusted remains of macaroni and cheese. She called the cheap dish "yellow death in a box" because some health nut claimed each serving reduced your life by ten minutes. By that calculation, James should have died as a junior in college.

Her elevated blood pressure did not improve after wandering down the hall and finding James in his office working on his laptop. He was wearing headphones which he did when catching up on emails. The smell of the orange processed cheese emanated from a green plastic bowl sitting in his lap. As she approached from behind, James did not stir which was surprising since he bragged about the eyes in the back of his head.

But this day of surprises continued, as she glanced at the computer to see what captured her husband's undivided attention.

There on the screen, she watched Halle jogging down the middle of a tree-lined suburban street wearing light blue gym shorts and a matching t-shirt leaving little to the imagination. Her long dark hair was pulled back in a tight pony tail and somehow despite the sprint, she broke no sweat to disturb the fake eyelashes and red lip gloss. The camera panned every few seconds from different angles all of which were complimentary. Cassie quickly took a side step and watched her mesmerized husband's lips curl into a devilish smile. It made her forget the dirty pot on the stove and recall the big stainless steel one she boiled lobsters in. It might take a concerted effort but she felt confident she could cram him in face first before putting the burner on high so he could scream like a crustacean.

James reached for the plastic bowl of yellow death on his lap, and she waited until he shoveled in a big mouthful before tapping him hard on the shoulder.

The ambush proved successful as James jumped up and the toxic macaroni spilled all over the hardwood floor. Unfortunately, perky Halle kept right on jogging, as the camera panned.

James whipped off his headphones. "What the hell are you doing?"

She pointed at the monitor. "Yes, what the hell are you doing?"

He looked confused and glanced at the screen. "Huh? That's Halle—"

"That's Halle!" she said imitating him. "And here I thought you only ogled her at the office." She pointed at the mess on the floor. "Now you bring her home for what? Dinner and a show?"

Her husband waved her off. "You're just like your father! No filter and shoots before getting the facts. The truth is, we found a few hiccups with the avatars. Certain mechanics like running look gimpy, and we're making some final adjustments in the software based on human models. It's critical we fine tune things before the release."

"Let me guess, the class pet volunteered."

James gave a slight you caught me grin, but shrugged. "It was her or Wally, and given his beer belly ... well, that would have created a whole set of ancillary issues we don't need right

now. Besides, he wouldn't be able to jog for over ten seconds."
He glanced at Halle still running and stopped the video. "She's
been a good sport."

"I bet."

James nodded. "She's good looking too. Okay, I said it."

"Attractive and cunning, what a combo." She looked at the
monitor then back at him. "With the large team you manage,
why didn't you delegate this? A junior member of your team—
maybe someone closer to Halle's age, could fix the problem if
not drooling over the eye candy."

Her husband's head recoiled. "Okay, that's enough."

"Is there something more you want to tell me?"

"Yeah. You used to run circles around a girl like Halle," he
said looking her up and down. "You probably could still take
her in a 5K." He pointed at his temple. "But your head has been
screwed on backwards since the night your mother played
pinball with all those poor people." He glanced at the mess on
the floor. "You might as well have been run over that night too."

Her legs felt like they might buckle. "Shame on you for
denigrating my mother and playing the victim again." She
pointed at his computer. "But I guess it lets you rationalize a lot
of things. Like her."

"Her? I thought you reserved that tag for the woman living
with my father-in-law. I'll tell you one thing. Halle doesn't
belong in the miserable piss pot you created for things you can't
face. She's a bright young woman that wants to get ahead."

"We both know how she plans on accomplishing that."

"I'm through arguing about this." He knelt down and started
cleaning up the macaroni mess. Their marriage survived because
they opened the pressure relief valve every once in a while, even
if it never addressed the root cause. Maybe it was time.

"I want you to support my mother's recovery."

He stood up and snickered. "Why? So, the town will follow
suit and give her a second chance because her brain rebooted?

Give me a break, Cassie. I find it surprising how you're overlooking the horror she committed."

"That's not true."

"Isn't it? After crying yourself asleep for years, and sampling every anti-depressant on the market, you're at her side like she's going to jump out of bed and wave a magic wand and make everything right. Unless she can turn the clock back and raise the dead that's not happening. The only thing I see here is another high tide that will pull you under." He held up the yellow encrusted mac and cheese bowl. "I'm eating in here instead of our new kitchen to stay away from the windows and prying eyes from the news truck parked out front. Plus, the crank calls have started up again. Seems everyone wants the overdue bill paid." He took a deep breath. "That includes me."

I can't tell him what I know because he wouldn't understand, she thought. "Did you ever think maybe we have it all wrong?"

He let out a sarcastic laugh. "Now you're the one living in make believe."

CHAPTER TWENTY-ONE

SHE KNEW MEETING SEAN for a drink was a colossal mistake and more than once slowed down to turn the car around and head home, but the image of Halle running across the computer screen and into her husband's imagination nixed the impulse.

Walking into the Mexican restaurant, she found the detective sitting at a booth near the bar and felt her pulse quicken. She called Sean after the fight with James reached the stony silence stage. He invited her out for a drink to discuss the case, though down deep she wanted someone to look at her the way James ogled Halle. Childish maybe, but after everything the day threw at her, the distraction felt timely.

Sean watched her approach which heightened the feeling this was a mistake. When he finally stood, he hugged her a little too long and then pointed at the glass of white wine waiting on the small table. The empty glasses in the corner indicated he was enjoying his third draft beer.

"Thirsty?" she asked.

He nodded as they sat down. Instead of addressing the empty glasses, he kept his hazel eyes fixed on her. She watched them change from a greenish tint to light brown, like he was trying to deepen the hue to match hers. As her cheeks burned, he smirked and checked his watch. "You said let's meet in ten minutes. That was almost an hour ago."

She shook her head. "You're mistaken. I said let's meet at ten to eight."

"Most people I know, mark time by the quarter hour. You've always been weird that way." He laughed. "Actually, it worked out because I hadn't eaten today and inhaled some nachos and salsa. Are you hungry?"

"Not at all." She took a small sip of the light chardonnay.

Sean glanced around the bar. "I've never been here before. It's quaint and makes me feel like we're having a secret rendezvous."

Though the meeting was innocent, she did not need one of her neighbors spotting her at a more popular hangout. "Well, I didn't want to hog the front page of the *Insight* again this week."

"Good point, though you can never be infamous enough. They probably have spotters all around town, you know."

"If not, I'm sure there's an app for that." She took another generous sample of the vino. "What made you order me wine?"

"Because you got so sick on rum back in the day, I figured you'd steer clear of hard liquor for the rest of this life."

She pointed at his beer. "I wish you didn't remember that tidbit of ancient history, but given the mess you had to clean up in your car, I can see why you refrain from the hard stuff too." She shook her head. "Believe me, I wasn't much fun when James and I toured the Bacardi factory on vacation."

Sean glanced at her wedding ring and took a hit of his beer. "So, how is hubby? It's Jimmy, right?"

She chuckled. "James hates that nickname because a bully in grade school threatened to grind him into jimmies for the class ice cream party." She never could get out of him whether he stuck up for himself— probably because she told him if she had been there, one of her infamous kicks in the bully's privates would have ended it. That said, tonight she sided with the bully and might even call him Jimmy when she got home.

"That's hilarious!" he commented.

"Well, Vice President Jimmy MacLean loves his career, maybe too much," she added and glanced toward the door expecting Halle to run by any moment.

"That's the reason Tina and I split up. I was married to the job instead of her. The hours were brutal." His voice trailed off and he took another hit of the beer. "We all know how that story ends." He sat back in the booth, and his eyes locked onto her lips. "Jimmy should appreciate what he has... because if I had you to come home to..." He let the comment hang in the air for a moment before clearing his throat, like he came to his senses. "I wouldn't be sitting in a bar guzzling beer and eating chips and salsa for dinner."

Nice recovery, she thought and retreated into the wine glass. She hoped to recall this not-so-subtle exchange tomorrow as harmless flirting. *Is there a full moon tonight?* Sean was suave over coffee in their first meeting and extremely professional at the station. How should she read this alter ego?

"So is your daughter living with you?" she asked hoping for firmer ground.

"Every other weekend, but I talk with her every day." He dug an iPhone out of his jacket and laid it on the table. "I spoke with her an hour ago about a science project coming up. How old is your son?"

"Fifteen. We have a good relationship when he lets me in." She frowned thinking since getting a fat lip, Will went underground and provided one-word answers for most questions.

Sean shrugged. "I'm sure our folks wrung their hands when we were his age and wandered around the Methuen Mall, Canobie Lake Park, and cruised up and down Route 28." He stared at her, and a sly smile slowly appeared. "Hey, what do you say after we have a couple drinks, we take a ride through some of our old haunts for a laugh?"

The invitation ended with hungry eyes which eerily reminded her of Dowd's this morning. Back in high school, she admired Sean's confidence and went along with his spontaneous road trips which were innocent adventures until they weren't. Twenty-five years later, he was evidently still using the same playbook. She remembered Mom lecturing her on rip currents and how to escape them by swimming parallel to the shore.

"Did you think of anything else from looking at the accident reports?" she countered.

He blinked hard which she read as aggravation when she didn't jump at the memory lane tour.

"I looked through the files again."

"Find anything?"

"Nothing other than what we've already discussed."

The case is the last thing on his mind right now, she thought, *or rather how he can use it to his advantage*. "C'mon detective, impress your prom date with your police skills. Did you find the missing pictures of the car?"

He looked in his nearly empty glass. "Senior prom! Man, that was some night." He twirled the mug in his big hands for a long moment but when he looked up, he was a detective again. "A rash of muggings and domestic disturbances have kept me pretty busy, so I haven't had time to check the lost and found bin."

She took a mouthful of wine that pushed most of the smart reply down her throat. "Because you think I'm on a fishing expedition?"

He raised his hand. "Whoa! Those are your words, not mine. If you recall, all you asked was for an extra set of eyes. I'm happy to provide that, but that also means being honest. I see nothing that would take your mother out of the driver's seat."

"Fair enough."

He reached across the table and put his hand over hers. It felt big and warm and once upon a time she thought they would hold hands forever. It suddenly occurred to her that in the last ten years, she truly embraced no one — not James, William or her father. Her arms were either locked by her side or wrapped around her head as the community tried stoning her. The revelation sucked the wind out of her lungs.

"Look, it's still early," Sean continued as his face softened. "Let's take that ride and we can get another drink somewhere else if the spirit moves us. Don't worry. I promise you'll make it home before Jimmy worries too much."

She looked at his hand still over hers and wished Halle would run by the booth so she could make introductions.

He read the hesitation and removed his hand. "If you'll excuse me, I have to use the Men's room before we hit the road. Enjoy the rest of your wine."

As he hurried away, she put on her coat, wishing she had not come. She was thinking how best to excuse herself when his iPhone lit up. Picking up the device, she read someone named Dedra was calling. Against her better judgement, she answered it.

"Where are you?" a woman yelled.

She hung up — and leaving a ten-dollar bill under the phone, hurried for the door.

CHAPTER TWENTY-TWO

MADELYN CAME RUNNING down the hall so fast, Cassie thought one of her ex-beaus might be in pursuit. Give her five minutes and she would boast how she took them all for a ride when the relationship soured.

As the wild woman sprinted past in white furry slippers, she slowed down and pointed a stubby finger in her direction. "I don't cuss often, but your old man is one mean bastard!"

Before she could ask what happened, the woman's short legs were on the move again, pushing rapidly against a restrictive house coat. Cassie watched her disappear down the corridor before repositioning the small box in her hands. It would not be the first time her father had that effect on someone. If there were a silver lining in the upset, at least she did not have to come up with some cockamamie excuse to get rid of her for an hour.

Entering her mother's room, she almost smiled thinking about another virtual meeting. Unfortunately, the good feeling evaporated when she found Dad hovering over her mother. For half a second, she considered joining Madelyn and they could become the town criers about horrible Charles Owens.

King Charles must have read her thoughts because he shot her a dirty glance before carefully placing a spoonful of applesauce in his bride's mouth. But unlike a baby bird waiting to be fed under Madelyn's care, Rose did not smile and watched the spoon like an outfielder following a fly ball. Once she secured the prize, her eyes shifted immediately back to her husband's face as the lines across her forehead deepened.

She placed the headsets on the visitor chair and quickly covered it with her coat. Her father paid no attention as he reached for a napkin.

When the spoon made its way back to the dish again, she had enough. "Are you giving me the silent treatment, or did you use up all your charm on Mom's roommate?"

Her father did not acknowledge the comment but put the utensil down and rolled the napkin into a little ball and threw it at her. The missile hit her in the chest where James once frequented, but now only attracted the roving eyes of men like Dowd and Sean.

"My throat hurts from yelling at that lady. Madelyn needs her mouth cemented shut because she can't mind her own business," her father replied in a hot whisper.

"She means well. What happened?"

He shook his head. "I'm not going there."

"Well, you were the one that got rid of Mom's private room, which I can't understand. It's not like you can't afford it."

"How would you know? Like I say every time we talk— it's none of your business." He continued glaring at her. "How dare you come into my office and harass one of my employees! Who do you think you are?"

The intensity on his face when angry, always made her tremble inside, and she looked down on the floor and studied the weaponized napkin. She considered throwing it back at his inflated head, but one of them had to be an adult. When she looked up, she found his attention had returned to the small glass dish of applesauce and thought it interesting he did not mention her visit with Uncle Phil.

She watched her mom take another spoonful before realizing she had not said hello. She leaned over and gave her a kiss on the head and received a wonderful smile in return.

Disappointment did not cover how she felt, since she planned on asking many questions in today's VR session. Her father really mucked up her plans. Now she would have to return at another time and deal with all the logistical challenges.

"What are you doing?" she asked.

"Are you talking to me?" he replied.

"Well, I know why Mom's here, but your presence not so much."

He smirked and spun the spoon in the glass. "What does it look like I'm doing? I'm feeding your mother."

"Who is also your wife," she added. "You don't visit often, and now you're feeding her? What's up with that?" *Maybe my meetings with Dowd and Phil rattled him, and he's checking things out,* she thought.

He put the spoon and applesauce down on the tray and came around to her side of the bed and did not stop until he got within two inches of her face. "From now on, if you have nothing nice to say, keep your mouth shut. While I think of it, when your father calls you, pick up the damn phone! I deserve some respect and won't be treated liked some telemarketer you ignore."

The woody floral cologne he showered in overwhelmed her. "Why do you get so upset when I don't answer? Because you jump whenever you get a call or text from what's her name?" She looked in his black eyes and wished she could screw a VR headset on his sorry head.

He took in a great gulp of air, and she braced for a slap across the face when a terrible moan suddenly came from the bed.

They both froze and watched Rose flexing her mouth in multiple directions like an angel was applying WD-40 to get the rusted muscles moving again.

"Stooooooooop!" Rose yelled in a harsh voice.

Cassie glanced at her father who suddenly took on the appearance of a deflated balloon. He pointed at his wife.

"She's talking?" he said to himself.

Cassie grabbed her mother's hand and looked at her father. "Like I keep telling you, but you never listen, Mom talks whenever she gets aggravated or excited." She looked at her mother and the deep lines on her forehead. "I'm sorry we got you upset. We were wrong to argue in front of you, but this is huge! I think we should ask the doctor about speech therapy."

When her father did not add a comment, she turned around and caught him inching toward the door, like he was afraid to turn his back.

"Where are you going?"

He motioned toward the hall. "Take a walk with me."

She nodded and waited until he left before she looked back at her mother. "I brought the headsets with me so we can talk some more, but with Dad here we will try another time." She rolled her eyes at the smiling woman. "You know how Dad is, always in a tizzy about something. I'll be back in a couple minutes after I calm him down."

She found her father pacing in the hall, and he led her to a small room used for board games.

"We can't argue in front of Mom like that," she began.

Her father folded his arms and smirked. "Argue? Is that what you call it? Because it feels more like insolence. I cannot believe you had the gall to ask Brian about that night. Why on earth would you do such a thing?"

Defending her motivation without revealing the implausible virtual reality trip would be a stretch. *Just speak about what you know,* she reasoned. "Well, I was going through the police reports and—"

"What police reports?" he said interrupting her.

She shook her head. "Don't play stupid with me. The only ones that ever mattered in our lives."

He took a deep breath and exhaled. "I should have named you Difficult."

She understood again why Cassandra meant the descendant of the curly haired, but unheeded prophetess. Her mother used to laugh and pointing at her curls ask for the winning lottery numbers whenever the jackpot soared. She drilled her eyes into her father's chest where his heart beat for another woman. "Sometimes the truth is difficult, Dad. Mom doesn't have a choice what you're shoveling in her mouth, but I do."

"Stop with the nonsensical riddle. What are you saying?"

"Let's start with Officer Dowd. You never told me he works for you."

Her father cocked his head. "Dowd is a common name so how did you know Brian was the same cop? There's no way you figured that out by yourself," he replied as his voice ramped. "I give enough to the police benefactor's association to find out who helped you."

She waved her arms. "Quiet down or a news crew will be here in minutes."

Her father took a deep breath and exhaled through his nose. "His employment is just a coincidence, so you can drop the conspiracy theory. Brian and I never talk about it."

She nodded. "I'm sure you don't. You won't even talk about it with me."

"Good grief daughter, it's a wonder you haven't lost James given your obsession with this sad saga. How can he love you when you have a dragon as an emotional support animal? My grandson tells me he's tired of tripping over that monster, setting a place for it every mealtime, bunking with it on vacations. The net effect is your family is marinating in bitterness because the wife and mother is MIA." He licked his lips like he tasted the acidity. "William says it's only grown worse since your mother's eyes popped open. I agree."

The air between them was thick with flak but she kept her sights on her mother's recovery. "Eyes popped open? Are you kidding me? You heard her talk minutes ago."

"You're the one kidding yourself hoping for more. The doctor says it's unusual for someone to wake up after all this time and yes, it's fortunate she can mumble a few words, but we shouldn't get our hopes up. This may be as good as it gets."

"My, aren't you the optimistic one!"

"No matter what you think of me, I'm a realist, honey. You live with the hand you're dealt."

She thought of the tears in Uncle Phil's eyes. "Unless you have an ace up your sleeve."

He frowned. "Now you're acting like Madelyn, but listen up. I won't put up with any more blowback from you. I'm taking control of this situation for the good of our family."

Cassie felt a wind wanting to blow her against the wall. It had been so many years since they fell under the definition of family, that it sounded ludicrous. "What do you mean?"

"It's time for some major changes. That's why I was calling you yesterday. I've made arrangements."

"Arrangements?"

"Your mother deserves some peace away from the prying eyes of the mad roommate, and the praying nurse. The recent stunt from the *Insight* also confirms the paparazzi will get more aggressive when they find out she's talking. Your mother needs additional tests to determine if any of these improvements are real. If they are— though I doubt it, she will need rehab. More likely, she will plateau and need continued long-term care. I pulled some strings and found a nice facility near Mount Washington. I'm having her transferred up there."

"Are you kidding me? With work, I'll only be able to see her on weekends."

"Which will give you more time to focus on your husband and son. It will take a few days to get the move north scheduled. In the meantime, I will be here and help take care of my wife."

"I bet you will."

CHAPTER TWENTY-THREE

SHE LEFT THE HOUSE early for the meeting, thinking how her father accused her of being neurotic because she prided herself on being punctual and built-in extra travel time in case of a delay. She never understood how a successful businessman like Charles Owens could disdain clocks. "My dear, someday you'll realize the world doesn't revolve around you!" was her mother's standard line whenever they ran late, which meant always. It got so bad her mother once set all the clocks in the house fifteen minutes ahead, thinking the crutch would help the affliction, but Dad ignored any device except his Tag Heuer watch. The silver lining was it honed her subtraction skills.

So, it came as a surprise when she pulled into the lower parking lot of Salem High School ten minutes early for the eleven o'clock meeting, and found Kendra kneeling by the front wheel of a silver SUV.

Cassie pulled alongside and rolled down the window. "Car troubles?"

Kendra stood up and shrugged. "The low tire pressure light keeps coming on but Carl tells me to ignore it."

"Sounds like something my husband would say."

"In the fall when we get our first cold night, sometimes the warning light comes on and I reset it." She laughed. "I could have been a star witness for the Patriot's in the Deflate-gate fiasco."

"I still have stains on my carpet from James and William throwing things at the tv."

Kendra frowned at the tire. "But it never happens this time of year. All I know is if it were his car—"

"He'd have you make an appointment and get it checked," she said completing the indictment.

"Touché."

Cassie got out of the car and hugged her high-school chum. "Thanks for meeting me."

"No problem." Kendra sniffed the air. "When the wind dies down and you feel the warmth of the sun on your face, you can almost imagine spring."

Cassie thought of her mother advancing the clocks. "As long as you ignore the groundhog that saw his shadow last week," she said in a serious tone.

Her friend rolled her eyes. "Do you ever wonder what that inner circle is smoking since they are supposedly speaking to the same groundhog from 1837?" She pointed at her black leather boots. "Call me conflicted— my spirit is embracing an early spring, but I'm still dressed for winter."

"Then I'm in total denial." Cassie glanced at her flat shoes before looking at the high school that recently underwent a seventy-five-million-dollar upgrade. It felt like her four years there could be measured in dog years so much happened.

"So many changes with the expansion," she said pointing, "but I'm glad you can still see the original bones."

Kendra nodded and pointed. "Hey, the sidewalk looks clear all the way to Kelley Library. It's a nice day. Why don't we walk and talk?"

She remembered Kendra's running outfit from the grocery store. "Can I translate the plan?" she asked. "You overslept and had to blow off the gym."

"Something like that, but if you remember, I can't sit still."

She nodded while studying the rivulets of melting snow running the length of the parking lot and knew the sidewalk would feature the same challenge. She wished she wore better shoes, but would go barefoot if necessary for this conversation.

They locked their cars and started the quarter-mile jaunt. Neither spoke for a minute as if both were plotting their strategies.

"What made you change your mind about meeting with me?" Kendra finally asked.

The image of their chance meeting at the supermarket flashed in her mind. It was the same morning she saw the terrible article in the *Insight* about her mother being the Witch of Salem. The paper continued lamenting every week since then how Rose enjoyed a country club existence in the nursing home. *Talk about a sick exaggeration,* she thought.

"Unlike everyone else barking at me, you wanted my perspective," she replied slowing the pace, "and I thought maybe it would counter the fake news being spread around by the frontier justice gang."

Kendra touched her arm. "True journalism prides itself on reporting the facts and letting people decide for themselves. But certain stories touch a nerve and trigger a media feeding frenzy. Objectivity is quickly sacrificed to make a buck. Unfortunately, your mom's story is like throwing chum in the water and it attracted a lot of sharks and other bottom feeders. There's no denying what happened on that bridge was beyond tragic but the whole concept of innocent until proven guilty can be a slippery slope. In your mother's case, the public is tired of holding its breath."

"Tell me about it. On the first anniversary of the tragedy, some sicko from out of town arrived at the nursing home with an eighteen-inch machete and asked what floor Mom was on."

"I remember reading about that. I was teaching at the time and had a class discussion about vigilante justice. Honestly, I'm surprised there haven't been other attempts. That's why I think a story from your perspective would be a powerful antidote in describing who Rose Owens is and how what happened impacted your family and friends."

"Friends? I found out I never invested in the pressure treated variety." A few of her supposed close friends spoke up at first but it was like pretending a nor'easter is nothing but a summer shower with an attitude. It wasn't long before they were lost in the snowdrifts and no one stood by her side shouting, "*let he who is without sin cast the first stone.*"

She pointed across the street at the town hall. "Back in the seventies' crushed cars were displayed in front of town hall to underscore the danger of drunk driving. I'll be honest, when I think of the death, pain, and suffering my mother caused …. well, I hated her many days too."

Kendra stopped. "That's past tense. Do you still?"

Cassie took a deep breath. *Keep the lid screwed on tight*, she thought. "It's complicated, but no, I don't."

They resumed walking, and Cassie honed in on a blue jay squawking in the distance. The air smelled of wet snow and reminded her of a musty cellar.

"Let's talk about setting the record straight," Kendra said re-engaging, "and pour some water on fire-starters like the *Insight*."

"And risk having the nursing home invaded by the crazies?"

"The risk is already there from all the vulgar posts I've seen on social media. For example, this morning—"

"Spare me the details!" she said interrupting. "I don't look at any of it, though it hasn't stopped William from getting beat up."

"Yeah, I heard about that from my son."

She stopped and looked the reporter in the eye. "I know it's next to impossible changing people's opinion on my mother. If that was the objective, we wouldn't be having this walk and risk ruining my good leather shoes."

"Shoe damage aside, then why?" Kendra asked.

"I have little to go on, but believe there's more to the story."

"Such as?"

She faced the same issue confronting her father. *I can only talk about concrete things and not miraculous apparitions in virtual reality.* "I'm going back through all the reports and finding some things that were glossed over. For instance, when my mother slammed into the pole, the first officer on the scene ended up working for my father."

She watched the reporter's eyes narrow. "That's interesting."

"More than interesting, I call it suspicious. I just discovered that nugget and had a chat with ex-Officer Dowd. It didn't go well."

"I don't see how it could have. What did your father say?"

She grabbed her friend's arm and they started walking again. "You know him. How do you think?"

"I always liked your mom, but your father … reminded me of a caged tiger that hadn't eaten in a month. What else?" Kendra asked.

"Sean's going through the files with me. I'm waiting for more pictures of the car."

It was Kendra's turn to stop. "Not *the* Sean?"

She gave a slight nod and felt herself blush. He called a few times since she left him at the bar, but like her father's calls they went unanswered.

Kendra pointed back at the high school. "Seems we should walk that way if we're taking a trip down memory lane. You two were such a cute couple. My eighteen-year-old naïve self, thought it would last forever."

"Me too," she replied as the latest fight with James came to mind. "I've talked to my father's partner that threw the party that night. He still says he deposited my father in the back seat."

They began walking again and reached the parking lot for the library. Across the street, a FedEx truck pulled in to make a delivery to the Boys Club.

"Well, this is a surprise," the reporter remarked. "I thought we were discussing a feature story about your mother and the impact on your family, but what I'm hearing is a possible investigative piece. Enlighten me."

"I want to establish beyond a shadow of doubt who was behind the wheel that night."

"Well, the only other person in the car was your father."

She nodded.

"What does Sean think?"

"That I'm on a crazy fishing expedition." She shrugged. "He's probably right but I'm determined to reel in whatever happened."

"But you have little bait."

She pictured her mother eating snow again. "But my fish finder says there's something lurking right below the surface. Perception doesn't equal reality in this case. If I confessed my suspicion to anyone else, they would have the same look on their face as you do now, but wouldn't be as polite. All I'm asking is for you to look into the details. If you find nothing, I'll still give you the interview about our sad family saga."

Kendra looked at her and shook her head. "Unfortunately, if you're right, the family saga will only get sadder.

She looked down at the white salt frosting the edges of her leather shoes and nodded.

CHAPTER TWENTY-FOUR

USUALLY, THE SWEET AND SPICY SALMON rice bowl at Pressed Café was her favorite lunch. But today she picked out the chopped grilled salmon and abandoned the supporting cast of baby spinach, broccoli, carrots, zucchini, summer squash, red and green peppers, onions, charred pineapple and avocado.

Her manager pointed at his empty bowl, and the way he eyed hers, she thought he might steal it any second. "Normally, you devour that combo like you're in a hot dog eating contest. What's wrong?"

Cassie gifted Ray with a weak smile. "It must have been the appetizer."

The sixty-year-old man's eyebrows spiked northward. "Huh? Did you have something when I stepped outside for my call?"

"No. I'm still digesting what you said about my performance and feeling disappointed."

"Disappointed I get, but is it surprising?"

The last ten years taught her the best defense sometimes meant leading with a blank face.

Ray pushed his plate away and took a quick sip of iced tea. "C'mon Cassie, let's be honest with each other. Anyone else on my team that called out as often as you have the last couple months, would be looking for another job instead of eating lunch with me. Look, I respect your accomplishments and the potential is there for continued career growth, but it means bringing your 'A' game every day." He sat up straight and looked her in the eye. "I strive to be fair so expect the next warning won't include lunch."

She felt her façade crumbling and took a long drink of seltzer water. It stung her throat, but she used the pain as mortar to dam the tears. "I'm not looking for special treatment and pride myself on being judged on my performance. I also appreciate all of your support in providing opportunities for advancement," she said and then hesitated for a second. "I didn't say it before, but I've been a bit consumed with my mother lately." Glancing at the next table, she watched a young boy play with his sandwich. She could not stand the pity look that came whenever she bridged this topic.

Ray bit his lip for a long second. "You should have told me. I hope you don't think I'm some type of cold-blooded lizard. My folks are getting older and facing some challenges that have kept me up nights. Look, the company has benefits that allow — "

She held up her hand. "I've been dealing with this longer than you've known me. I don't want it coloring how I'm treated."

"I understand and that's commendable," he replied with a wince. "I'd be lying if I said I didn't know about your mother coming out of the coma."

There it is, she thought. The *Insight* article might as well have been posted on the company bulletin board. If she could check the search history on everyone's laptop, it would be there too. "Thanks for being honest."

His face brightened. "You must be very excited on her improvement."

She nodded and left it at that.

The seasoned manager must have felt the chill and checked his watch. "Okay, I have to run and make a few calls before the two o'clock project meeting. See you there."

She said goodbye and lingered behind to finish her drink. By the time she got to her car Ray was long gone. A quarter-mile later, she noticed blue lights in the rear-view mirror. Pulling over, she expected the cruiser to whip on by, but it stopped behind her.

"You have to be kidding me!" she mumbled and glanced at the state inspection sticker thinking it must be expired, but it was current.

The side mirror revealed a beefy looking, middle-aged officer slowly strutting toward her.

Her fingers trembled a bit on the controls as the window opened.

"Good afternoon, Officer?" she said with an inquisitive face.

"License and registration," the policeman barked.

She noticed the cop wore no coat in the frigid winter air and hoped it signaled a short stop. "Sure, but why did you pull me over?"

He backed up a step and she read his badge. Clive Trulie. *Seriously?*

"Did you hear me? License and registration."

"Okay, but I just—"

Trulie folded his arms, and she decided not to press the matter. Leaning over, she retrieved the car registration from the glove compartment and license from her wallet.

The Officer took them and sauntered back to the cruiser.

Minutes passed and Officer Trulie did not return. Looking at her watch, she groaned. The project meeting was scheduled to start in fifteen minutes. Even if she left now, she would be late. *How will I explain this?*

Time stood still. Whenever she looked in the side mirror, she noticed the cop was just staring straight ahead, like he decided she should serve some time in solitary confinement for whatever offense she committed. Car after car went by, and a good number of drivers slowed down to get a look at the woman who broke the law. After another glance at her watch, she imagined Ray sitting in the conference room shaking his head thinking she flipped him the bird for the gentle warning about her performance. At this rate she wouldn't have a job by tomorrow. She picked up her iPhone to call him, which ended up being the key that unlocked the cruiser's door.

"Put the phone down and step out of the car!" Trulie yelled.

She put her head out the window and noticed the cop standing at the rear of the car. "I'm just telling my boss I will be late."

"I said get out of the car now!" he repeated.

She opened the door and stepped out.

"Walk to the front of the car so we don't get hit," he ordered.

She quickly marched to the front of the Honda and turned around. "I don't understand any of this! I have a right to know why you stopped me."

"You were weaving approaching the rotary. Either you were on your cell phone which is not permissible or were drinking. Which is it?"

"Neither! I just met my manager for lunch and was on the way back to the office."

"Where did you eat?"

She pointed at the one-story brick building in the distance. "Pressed Café."

He cocked his head and looked at her. "So, you were drinking."

"Yeah, seltzer water," she replied rapidly.

"Mixed with what?"

"Limes!"

"Then you won't mind performing a field sobriety test?"

She put her hands on her hips. "Are you kidding me?"

"No, and you have the option of refusing. If so, I'll arrest you for suspicion of operating under the influence. With a good lawyer and ten grand you should have your license back in six months."

The words were like frozen clumps of earth which plows drive into the snowbanks lining the roads; things that get stuck together, but do not belong. "I wasn't drinking and will take a breathalyzer."

He stepped closer. "Close your eyes and touch your nose."

She did it quickly with her right hand and to prove the point repeated it with her left. He followed up by making her walk a straight line along the edge of the snowbank risking another pair of leather shoes.

She turned around to repeat the performance, when an unmarked car pulled in behind the cruiser. Sean jumped out of the car also wearing no coat.

"What's going on here?" Sean barked.

The cop smiled. "Possible DUI."

"I only drank seltzer water!" she yelled.

Sean called Trulie over and the two law men walked away and left her standing there. Car after car slowed down as they passed, as if some major crime lord or drug dealer had been captured to garner this much police attention. Any moment now, she expected the media would arrive. The *Insight* would have a field day.

Trulie finally trudged back, but this time with a broad smile. "Your detective friend vouched for you." He handed back her license and registration. "That's what friends do for one another, right? In my case, Officer Dowd and I went through the academy together. I would do anything for him." He pointed a long finger at her. "Think about that on your way back to the office. I suggest you keep your eyes on the road and not in the rearview mirror if you know what's good for you."

Sean waited until the cruiser left before joining her. "I was on the other side of town when I heard him call in the stop. What's this all about?"

She studied the snowbank that ruled the roads in February and all the things hidden underneath.

CHAPTER TWENTY-FIVE

ENTERING THE ROOM, she found Madelyn hovering over her mother's bed. In the dim light, she could not tell what the batty woman was up to this time so she stopped mid-step. She watched Madelyn study the sleeping woman for a long moment and then adjust her pillow. The gentleness and concern were touching.

Cassie backed up a few steps before announcing her presence so not to startle the nutty but good-hearted woman. "Good afternoon," she announced.

"Hey there," came a curt reply punctuated by the pack-a-day-cough.

After depositing the box containing the headsets in the visitor chair, she opened the shades on the double window. Outside a light rain continued its assault on the snow and made her think Kendra's hopes of an early spring might come true after all.

"Why are you messing with the shades? I don't like the rain because it's depressing," her mom's roommate barked and came toward her fast like she might wrestle over the shade controls.

"Nights are long this time of year," she countered. "We have to cherish the light. I also like watching the snow lose its grip."

Madelyn gave her underarm a good scratch. "Winter dries me out terribly."

She ignored the display. "You can't apply enough moisturizer this time of year."

"Well, I'm peeling like a snake from my belly to my knees." She reached for the zipper of the floral housecoat. "Let me show you."

"Please don't!" she replied much too loud. "Why don't you ask Julie if she has any ointment?"

The woman responded by puckering her lips like she just kissed a lemon. "I'll ask for something topical but hate the 'O' word."

"Huh?"

"Ointment. The word gives me the creeps." She pointed at the chair. "You bring that box almost every time you come. What's in it? A hamster or baby sugar glider?"

She sought refuge by looking outside. "Funny," she said slowly, at a loss what she could make up that would make the nosey lady would yawn. "Just some personal stuff."

Madelyn put her hand up like a stop sign. "You mean like pictures and other mementoes to help your mom remember?"

"Yeah, something like that." *If she asks to see any, I'll tell her they're all smeared with ointment,* she mused.

Madelyn eyed the box. "Our bingo game is canceled today, and there's nothing on tv so can I stay? This morning I had her laughing."

She pasted on a fake smile. "That's very kind of you, but I use it as a special bonding time with Mom, after the years we lost."

Madelyn sighed in disappointment. "That's pretty much what your dad said at lunch. I think it's a riot that Rose never smiles at him."

Her stomach sank with the sudden air turbulence. "My father was here again today?"

Madelyn gifted her with a knowing grin. "Yeah, he's been coming most days around lunchtime. Spends an hour or so and feeds her some applesauce. I asked him today why he doesn't provide a little variety? I told him I love milk chocolate but if I had it every day, I'd get bored with it."

"What did he say?"

"Told me to mind my own business in that quiet voice that rumbles like it's going to backfire any second."

The warning bells continued ringing in her ears. "Thanks for sharing that tidbit with me." *Get back on task and get rid of her,* the internal voice commanded. "On a different topic, I know how much you like coffee."

"Yes, and I haven't had a decent cup since I arrived at this outpost. All they serve here is piss-poor water that's never kissed a real bean."

"Well, as a special treat for looking after my mom, I'll buy you a coffee or cappuccino from Dunkin or Starbucks later." She glanced at her watch. "In the meantime, go relax in one of those big comfy chairs in the lobby while I spend a special hour with Mom." She winked at her. "I'll get a cream filled donut to go with your coffee too. I suggest you savor it in peace downstairs because if you bring it up here, everyone will want a bite."

"Bless you my dear!" The words had not reached her ears before Madelyn came running across the room and embraced her. She quickly discovered the flabby rolls were rock hard flesh.

The moment the pesky roommate left for the lobby, Cassie shut the door and quickly retrieved the headsets. Approaching the bed, she gently shook the sleeping woman. "Wake up, Mom!" she repeated several times, but the best she could get were thin eye slivers like a cat mid nap.

She hesitated moving forward but concluded why not try? After all, the system worked when her mother was barely out of the coma, why not when sleeping? James and William never mentioned it, but she saw the headsets as Bluetooth for the brain.

After gently slipping the headset on her mother, she put on her own and fired up the unit. This time she noticed Marco Island as a preset destination and did not hesitate selecting it.

Seconds later, she found herself at low tide on Tigertail Beach, and she could practically taste the smell of sea salt. The early morning sky was filled with a purplish hue which gave the blue-green water lapping the shore an eerie look. Letting her eyes wander, she noticed an irregular dark line running the length of the beach that marked high tide. It was also where the sea deposited spectacular treasures making Marco Island one of the best locations in the world for shelling. She hurried on the white powder sand to the first clump and fell to her knees. Her fingers ran through a myriad of whelk, scallop and banded tulip shells of various colors, shapes and sizes. A raking noise made her look up and she surveyed a dozen people of different ages a hundred feet away pawing through the rich collection. They reminded her of angels sent to gather extraordinary souls which would prove to be an impossible task, since each piece possessed extraordinary color, shape and texture. Even the broken shells could be admired for their beauty, despite the chaos they faced underneath the waves. Her pious mother had a fervent belief that in the end, there was enough good in everyone that all would be saved. From what she experienced in life, that was a minority opinion.

Out of the corner of her eye, she saw something moving along the sand; a fiddler crab sneaking back to the water before sun or seagull intervened. She picked it up and transported it back to the water so it could rejoin the living. *Isn't that what I'm trying to do with Mom?* she thought.

Turning around, she looked back at the wet sand and discovered hundreds of other displaced crabs chasing the retreating waves. *Too many to save.*

A cool breeze hugged her tight, and she reasoned it was winter. If so, she thought Punxsutawney Phil should stop whispering to those strange men and move south and free up his February calendar. Her eyes drifted over the sand again and then back toward the line of high-rise hotels and condos for the one percenter's. In between sand and cement, she located a blue canopy and a woman lounging on a beach chair. Even from a distance, she knew the long-legged lady was Rose.

Drawing near, she found her mother still asleep and thought it strange how the real and virtual worlds were in sync. James teased she looked angry when sleeping, but Mom looked like a poster child for serenity.

The sand felt surprisingly warm without the sun, but the growing breeze was brisk and she welcomed the shelter.

"Mom?" she called shaking her gently.

Her eyes popped open for a second before closing again. "Hello dear," she barely whispered.

She shook her harder. "C'mon, you've been sleeping for ten years! Don't you think you've had enough?"

Her mother licked her lips. "For sure, but today I feel like a bag of dusty bones."

"Maybe if you move around a bit it will help." She grabbed her hand. "Stand up."

The effort required to get Mom out of the lounge chair sucked the life out of her too. After catching her breath, she thought her life force must have been transferred to her mother as Rose was suddenly awake and looking at the tall buildings behind them. Tears began streaming down her face.

"What's the matter?" she asked.

"I recognize this place! It's Marco Island." she replied wiping her cheek. "Your father took me here when we were first married. We had little money and stayed at a motel a few miles inland. We would park our car at the Marriott and enjoy this beach for hours." She blinked hard and graced her with a sad smile. "Such simple but happy days."

Cassie wished they could linger in this memorable spot, but worried Madelyn's obsession with coffee and donuts would mirror Einstein's definition of time as flexible.

She rubbed Mom's shoulder. "Seeing you this happy, breaks my heart and we'll talk more about this place. But right now, we need to focus on that terrible accident. You were severely injured, but do you remember anything after hitting the pole?"

"Why are we talking about this again, when there's so much here to enjoy?"

She grabbed her hand, and it felt warm and soft. "I know Mom, but it's really important. Anything?"

"Everything was a blur. My head hurt and I felt encased in ice. Then I saw a tunnel of light above me."

"Dad thought you were dead."

Rose closed her eyes and frowned. "I started drifting upwards into the light. When I glanced down at the wreck, I saw the ugly gash on my forehead and all the blood. Charles was near the front of the car crying, which I thought strange because I never saw him weep before…. even when his parents passed.

"Anything else?"

There was a long delay. "Voices."

"Of who?"

She opened her eyes. "Everything is jumbled. A motherly voice is telling me it's not my time, that I have to leave the warm embracing light and go back to the cold and pain. In the background, I hear Charles crying, and Phil is trying to calm him down."

Sounds like a textbook near death experience but not helping her cause. "Are you sure you heard Phil? I thought he put Dad in the back seat of the car after the party was over?"

"Party?"

"Yes, the one for the company. Dad had too much to drink and you drove home."

"I could drink that man under the table," she replied. "He would be half lit after a couple beers, which I considered pre-gaming." She shook her head. "But I never drove even if a little buzzed. When my hearing started coming back, I heard whispers about some caged monster and realized they were talking about me." New tears spilled on her cheeks. "There's no corner of hell more painful than being punished for a sin I cannot remember."

Her mother turned and walked away and she followed. The sun looked untroubled in the east, but in the western sky, white funnel clouds were marching toward the shore as the wind began picking up.

She took her mother's hand. "I'm sorry for being obsessed with the details about that night. Please understand, I'm trying to find the weak spot in a dam that's held back the truth for ten years."

Rose shot her a knowing look. "The truth is I believe in my heart of hearts I didn't drive that night. But my memory is like this beach, the tide comes in and leaves all these memories to pick through. Before I can finish, sleep carries me away. When I wake up, some memories remain but others are underwater again."

Cassie gave her a tight hug. "We all try and make sense of our yesterday's, and in the process find out we are nothing but sand sculptures at the mercy of the wind and the rain." She felt tears well up. "The sun sure can be a fickle friend."

Rose pulled away and felt for her miraculous medal. "But if you use river sand, the walls will hold." She thought for another minute. "I remember little, but have a gut feel of being upset with your father."

She was angry with her father too, but knew why. The growing waves and distant rumble of thunder made her scan the horizon. Hoping to extend the session, she searched for a setting on the controller that might change the landscape parameters or provide shelter from the coming storm. She came across the "x" button which William vaguely warned her about. Without thinking it through, she pressed the button.

Day immediately turned to night, and a million stars lit the warm sand. Suddenly, Halle came out of nowhere and ran past her, smelling like lavender and taking small sips of air as she sprinted toward a tall dark figure standing at the water's edge.

Cassie started toward the couple, but the soft sand no longer supported her weight and she fell three times. Still short of the goal, she watched Halle reach up and pull James in for a long kiss.

She tried to scream but her tongue would not move.

Ripping off the headset, she wondered if that kiss was her imagination or a recorded session.

CHAPTER TWENTY-SIX

A BLINDING LIGHT made her think the upsetting visual of James and Halle triggered an ocular migraine when a deep voice began singing: "five gone and dead, four broken arms, three fractured legs, two lost limbs, and a killer in a coma free."

She swung a fist in the direction of the light source and smacked something hard and sharp.

"What are you doing? Channeling your mother's mayhem?" the male voice yelled.

Her eyes adjusted, and she took in a tall skinny twenty-something wearing blue hospital scrubs with an ancient video camera propped on his right shoulder. Some sort of headlight was attached to the contraption and looked tilted. Given the pain in her knuckles, she assumed that's what she punched.

"Get out of here!" she yelled.

"Wow! She's a feisty one!" another high-pitched voice from behind said.

Spinning around she found another man, this one dressed the same but a half foot shorter and given the peach fuzz on his chin, younger.

"Welcome back!" Junior said with a laugh. "Did they beam you and mommy up to the mother ship?"

She glanced at the bed and her mother remained dead to the world, but looked ridiculous wearing the headset. Mister Peach-Fuzz-Punk pointed his iPhone at the bed and clicked away.

"I'm going to sue the *Insight* into bankruptcy!" she yelled.

The two men looked at each other and shrugged. "Go ahead. We're not with them."

"Then tell me who you work for?"

"No one. We're just a couple of freelancers trying to make a few bucks in this crazy world," the tall one replied and shifted the camera on his shoulder. "Given the freak show you and Mommy provided, the *Insight* won't be able to afford us." He smirked at his sidekick. "I see tropical beaches and top shelf liquor by the weekend."

Cassie looked around for a weapon intent on maiming. A curling iron on Madelyn's nightstand caught her attention, and in a scene reminiscent of a *Matrix* movie, she hurled herself sideways while her enemies reacted in slow motion. In an instant, she had the weapon in her hand and swung it at Junior's iPhone. She missed the device, but not his stomach. If it had been a sword, she would have cut him in half.

The punk's eyes got big, and he doubled over for a moment before pushing her hard. She fell backwards on Madelyn's bed.

They ran for the door, and she chased the duo down the hall while screaming for Julie at the top of her lungs.

The good nurse came flying out of a resident room just as the pair found the stairs. Between heavy breaths, she told Julie what transpired in short spurts. The way Julie looked her up and down it seemed like she was more concerned with her condition than the ambush. As the residents started gathering in the hall, they had similar expressions. She looked down and realized she was still brandishing a curling iron with a bloody hand.

Julie yelled to another nurse to call Security and then led her to the nurse's station for first aid.

Security called before her hand was bandaged and reported the two got away. They said they would pull the recording from the cameras and call the police.

Cassie considered calling Sean to see if he could help, when a somber looking gent in a starched white shirt rolled his walker into the small cubicle.

"I have a complaint," he announced flatly.

Julie backed away from the supply cabinet. "What's the problem, Carl?"

"Well, I read the calendar of events every morning and it says nothing about a masquerade party."

"What are you talking about?"

"Madelyn and the sleeping lady have funny masks on and everyone is fighting to take a turn. They won't let me get in line."

Cassie's feet didn't touch the floor on the way to her mother's room. When she finally braked, she saw a twig of a woman with blue hair inspecting her mother's headset. Glancing to the right, she caught Madelyn sitting on her bed with the headset on and playing with the controller. Three men and two women mulled about the room.

"Can I try it?" one bald guy barked at Madelyn. "I'm pretty good with technology and logged into a Zoom meeting last week."

Cassie made a beeline for Madelyn and touched her shoulder. "Hold still, while I take this off," she said sharply.

"What's this contraption?" Madelyn asked rubbing her eyes. "I pushed all the buttons and kept getting different screens but nothing happens."

She ignored the question and gently stepped in front of the blue-haired lady shadowing her mother. Before she could slip the headset off, Julie appeared on the other side of the bed.

"What on earth are you doing?" she asked. "You're worrying me!"

She shot her a desperate look. "I'll explain later."

The nurse frowned, clearly not satisfied with the answer and turned her attention to the uninvited guests. "Okay, show's over. Let's give Rose some quiet time so she can rest."

"Quiet time?" the bald man asked with a snicker. "She's been sleeping for years!"

Everyone followed Julie out of the room except Madelyn, and Cassie wondered why until she remembered this was her room too. She quickly boxed up the headsets and had her coat on before the silence became noticeable. Looking back, she found Madelyn standing like a statue at the foot of her mother's bed.

"A penny for your thoughts," she asked.

"Rose hasn't been much company lately. I enjoy having someone listen to my stories and smile instead of shaking their head." She shot her a sideways look. "I see how people size me up, like I'm an old chubby fool with nothing but expired air between my ears. I wish everyone could see how the boys fought over me back in high school and later, when I managed a clothing store, how my team respected me." She let out a deep sigh. "Given the reasons I'm stuck in here, I'd be happy to trade places with Rose most days." She walked to the side of the bed and stroked her mother's hair. "Rose gets a real kick out of me, which makes me laugh."

Cassie studied Madelyn. *Where did I learn to be so judgmental?* she thought.

"But now she just sleeps most of the day," her roommate continued.

She thought how tired her mother looked even in the VR session. "It takes a lot of energy to rejoin the world."

Madelyn rubbed her double chin. "I thought that too, but it's strange how she's so alert in the morning. Then after your father leaves, she's asleep and dead to the world until the next day."

"My father can be exhausting."

"I get that, but whenever I come back for a nap or to get something, he's feeding her applesauce. A few days ago, I asked if he was feeding Snow White another poison apple to put her back to sleep. He nearly took my head off."

Cassie felt her bandaged hand. She was prepared to fight above her weight.

CHAPTER TWENTY-SEVEN

CASSIE KNEW she should stop and pick up something simple for dinner, but her stomach felt like one of those retro larva lamps twisting and tumbling into different shapes. Even a pizza joint felt too daunting considering what she might reply when the waitress asked, "Can I help you?" Making Mom whole again was her top priority, but all the arguments made her see how the cumulative stress of the past decade were like termites attacking her marriage and family. Acknowledging that, meant repairing the rot and she did not have the emotional fortitude for the required demolition. Realizing that again, her stomach suddenly gnawed as a reminder she had eaten nothing today. Since her mother's eyes popped open on Thanksgiving, her appetite went into its own coma and meals were limited to a few nibbles. Even James, who noticed little outside the borders of a computer screen, commented on her protruding ribs. *Maybe that's why Sean acted like he did after a few beers,* she thought. In high school, she was little more than a curvy string bean. Maybe he wanted a trip down memory lane with the girl he remembered.

When she finally pulled into the driveway, the house sat in darkness. Hurrying to the front door, she planned on popping a couple ibuprofen and pouring a glass of Cabernet to mull over the crazy afternoon, before William and James blew in clamoring for dinner. If some newspaper printed pictures of her and Mom wearing the headsets along with a nasty writeup, it would cause problems on many levels. Those belonging to the holier-than-thou club would conclude if her mother was well enough to play video games, she could also stand trial. Worse, James would be out of his head worried about the exposure given the upcoming product launch. And then there was the matter of her father. He would probably roll the newspaper into a club after Julie informed him, he could no longer feed his wife suspicious applesauce. Maybe he could shovel the remaining inventory into the woman he lived with who had eyes bigger than her stomach.

She fumbled unlocking the door and after succeeding, soft jazz greeted her ears. *Maybe I've stumbled upon a thief with good taste*, she thought.

"Hello?" she called out and readied her phone to dial 911.

"I'm In the kitchen," her husband answered.

Cassie looked out the window wondering how she missed seeing his Jeep in the driveway, but it was not there.

Normally, she would stop at the hall closet and hang up her coat, but she smelled roast beef and headed straight for the kitchen and found James at the sink scrubbing a pan.

"What's all this?" she asked.

He stopped and pushed up the sleeves of his cotton sweater. "Just my luck! The one night you come home early," he said and let out a sigh. "I planned on meeting you at the door with flowers."

She looked at the assembly line on the counter: mixer, milk, butter, sour cream, and salt and pepper shakers. "I'm sorry, I must have the wrong house."

Her husband nodded and continued working on the pan. "Hopefully, you will say that after dinner." He pointed at the pots on the stove. "I covered all the bases: roast beef, mashed potatoes, ginger carrots, nice bakery rolls. For dessert, we have cannoli's from Piros Bakery." He began rinsing the pan. "I bought some nice wine too."

"Who are you? Buying wine by the bottle instead of the box?"

He dried his hands on a paper towel. "Easy now."

Cassie questioned if maybe she was still in the virtual world and slipped off her coat and hung it on the kitchen chair. "Everything sounds delicious. Can we make William give us a ten-minute head start so we can enjoy a few mouthfuls before he pillages everything but the wine?"

"Normally, we'd be in trouble with the human vacuum cleaner, but not tonight," he replied walking toward her. "Our son won't be home until ten."

She felt his hands around her waist. He kissed her more intently than he had in quite some time. The ice around her heart softened.

"You know our anniversary is next month, right?"

He squinted at her. "Not funny, and before you ask, I also know Valentine's Day is a week away too." He gave her a peck on the cheek. "Things have been crazy since I started the new job and thought it would be nice to have a romantic dinner and catch up on us." He reached for her hand and stopped.

"What happened?" he asked examining the bandage.

She held up the hand like it belonged to someone else. "It's just a small cut with one of those annoying bleeds." She heard a gushing noise and noticed a pot on the stove beginning to boil over and a perfect way to change the subject. "Your Irish heritage is calling."

He ran over and turned the heat down on the potatoes. "Go relax in the family room so I don't screw this up."

"How about I help and set the table?"

"No. I've got it all covered."

She headed upstairs for the ibuprofen and noticed James left his shaving kit on the bathroom counter. *"Have to admit, I'm impressed by the effort,"* she whispered and remembered James doing little things; like bringing home flowers or giving her a spontaneous hug in their first years of marriage which kept the passion burning. Now, his definition of getting lucky was hoping the drive-thru window in their bedroom stayed open past eleven when he finally dragged himself to bed. She shared the blame too as she hugged bottles of wine and antidepressants instead of him. Too often, she pretended to be asleep when he reached for her. She felt the needle on the resentment meter fall and felt her legs. Fortunately, they felt smooth.

The king-sized bed looked inviting, and she laid down and shut her eyes hoping the meds would quiet the tension headache. In short order, she drifted away and pawed through the shells on Tigertail Beach again. Suddenly, her iPhone beeped, and the text message announced, "Dinner is served."

After washing her face, she re-applied some makeup and went downstairs. James stood in the doorway of the dining room and had changed into a blue striped dress shirt and khaki pants. Beyond him, she could make out the place settings and lit candles.

He flashed a proud smile and escorted her into the room and held out her chair. The fairy tale would have been perfect except for one uninvited guest; his iPhone which occupied the empty real estate on the table between them.

She sat down and giggled like a nervous teen. "Maybe you should pull the shades down."

He screwed up his face. "Why, what are you proposing?"

"Nothing. If nosey Betty looks out her window and sees you doing all this for me, Tim will sleep in the shed."

They shared a good laugh and dug into the meal. The roast beef was tender, the gravy perfectly seasoned, the potatoes fluffy. Cassie looked at James as if he were a shapeshifter. "When we got married, you couldn't peel a potato and only worked your skills up to making grilled ham and pineapple sandwiches after William turned six. So, what gives? How did you learn to cook like this and why have you been hiding it? I don't know whether to kiss or punch you."

"Believe me, this skill is younger than the ice cream we have in the freezer. The short answer is I try to keep morale up as everyone is working their butts off. In the spring and summer, we play wiffle ball at lunch. When the weather turns cold, we make lunch on Friday's."

Suddenly, she imagined Halle running into the room and stopping to grab a ginger carrot off her plate, before continuing down the hall.

James poured the rest of the bottle of Cabernet into his glass. "Gee, bottles don't go far when you have a glass or two cooking dinner."

She eyed his glass. "Hence your love for the big bottles or the box with the built-in spigot."

"Are you mocking me?"

"Just reporting the facts, Chef."

"Well, lucky for us I hid another bottle downstairs." He wiped his mouth on the cloth napkin and made a beeline for the hall. She looked down and studied her plate. She had cut the beef into pieces small enough for a two-year old. Sadly, neither flavor nor presentation aroused her appetite.

The iPhone on the table pinged, and she could see James had a text message from Halle. She glanced toward the hall, and though she prided herself on not being that type of wife, she reached for the phone. After rapidly keying in her son's birthday as the password, she read the text. *Make sure you let the roast rest for twenty minutes before serving.*

She quickly scrolled up and noticed a lengthy thread about how to select the best beef and the optimal cooking times. Before she could go further back, she heard footsteps and put the phone face down on the table.

James came into the room with a serious look on his face and silently topped off her glass.

Did he see me reading his messages? she thought. "It's nice you're learning to cook, but I don't get it," she said quickly. "All you have in the break room is a fridge, microwave and a sink." She pointed at her plate. "C'mon. What gives?"

Quite out of character, he picked up the wine glass, spun the contents and took a careful sip. "We had a few culinary team building events offsite." he said flatly. "I didn't say anything, so I could surprise you."

How can I bring up Halle now? It might be harmless but their closeness is troubling, she thought. She sought refuge in the wine glass.

James pushed his plate away, and watching his eyes narrow, she recognized the brewing storm.

"Everything okay?" she asked pointing at his plate. "Usually, by now you're asking if I'm going to finish my meal so you can swoop in like a seagull."

He ignored the wisecrack and pulled on his lower lip like he was weighing something. "I've really tried to make tonight special."

"You have!" she replied bracing for the *but.*

"The big launch is next week, and Brad gave me an earful when I told him I was taking the afternoon off. I flew to the grocery store, the bakery, and the florist before hiding the Jeep down the street in order to surprise you and −" He hesitated and took a deep breath. "A fight is not on the menu, but I'm really sick to my stomach right now."

It was unlike her husband to be so melodramatic. "Just spit it out. What's wrong?"

"When I went to get the wine, I saw the box in the hall with two headsets and controllers. I brought everything back from the workshop to the office last week. Please tell me you found them under William's bed and boxed them up for me."

The reel of the wild afternoon played behind her eyes. *A blinding light ... punching the camera .... wisecracks from the two punks about selling the pictures ... beating the younger guy with a curling iron ... chasing them down the hall ... Julie bandaging her hand … Madelyn clicking through the menus … the blue-haired lady stalking Mom.*

She worked hard on controlling her face, but lost the battle and tears filled her eyes.

James listened intently, and his eyes got big like he refused to abandon hope. "I assured Brad everything was back in the lab and locked down for the launch." His shoulders slumped from exhaustion. "Please honey, tell me I'm just a worry-wart and everything's okay?"

His plea outflanked the fine food, good wine and the brand name ibuprofen. A painful pulsating pain ripped across her forehead. Instead of replying she bit her lip.

Her husband jumped up. "Are you kidding me? Who did you show it too? Someone at the office?" He pulled on his chin. "Please tell me it wasn't Carol. The town doesn't need a newspaper with that loudmouth."

She watched her husband from an out-of-body perspective. His anger, anxiety, and fear looked familiar since it was what she saw every time she looked in the mirror. It represented something beyond her control.

"Sit down James," she said and heard her voice harden like it always did to cope.

Her husband flung himself in the chair.

"I planned on telling you later, but when you surprised me, I figured it could wait until morning."

"Okay, now you're scaring me."

"I can't apologize enough," she began. Reaching for his hand, she had a flashback of Sean doing the same when they talked about the case. Except this time instead of feeling electricity, both their hands felt clammy.

"Take a shot of your own medicine, and stop beating around the bush and level with me," James said.

She nodded. "Remember that night we had a fight about the new VR technology?"

"Sure, because that's every night!" he replied sarcastically.

She ignored the comment. "I mean the night we talked about how this innovation could help outside of gaming, like from a medical perspective. It got me thinking about the possibilities after William gave me a tour." She hesitated and took a deep breath because she needed every molecule of oxygen available to explain the breakthrough. "I brought the headsets to the nursing home and tried it out with Mom."

"What! Why would you do that?" he yelled jumping up.

She stood up too. "Because the technology works! I've talked with Mom a couple times and it's a miracle. I found out—"

"Couple times?" He said interrupting and gave her the stink eye. "Why didn't you tell me?"

"You have every right to be furious. My only defense is I knew you would react like this." Cassie grabbed his arm. "This innovation is life changing. Mom told me she wasn't driving that night. It made me go back and study the police reports and I think—"

"Just stop!" James marched to the end of the table before turning around. "We are not getting back on that never ending rollercoaster so we can climb mountain after mountain trying to dissect that night." He ran his hand through his hair. "Because afterwards, we plunge into the abyss where the only sound you make for days on end is crying into your pillow. I vowed for better or worse, but it's not a one-way street. If you hadn't gone on an antidepressant, I don't know if Will and I could have hung on much longer. They say there's five stages of grief: denial, anger, bargaining, depression, and acceptance. But you're so wrapped up in the first three, our son nicknamed you D.A.D for a while and called me Pops."

"Wow, how long have you been waiting to launch that torpedo?" she replied and collapsed in the chair. "You should put that sound bite up in the cloud so you can retrieve it whenever you're playing the martyr." She scanned his face. "But sadly, you have to live in the real world to get any pity."

Her husband gulped the rest of the wine and walked over to the liquor cabinet in the room's corner and poured tequila in the wine glass.

"We have a bigger problem than beating each other up," she said addressing his back.

He spun around. "We?"

"A couple of freelancers got video and pictures of Mom and I wearing the headsets this afternoon. I didn't hear them come in."

Her husband's hand began shaking, and he put the glass down on the table next to the dish of glazed carrots that might be the featured vegetable of their last supper.

"How can I get in touch with them?" he whispered. "If they publish anything, I'm more well done than the roast."

She shrugged and held up her bandaged hand. "I don't know because I chased them out."

He hung his head and the silence lengthened. Suddenly, his phone began pinging on the table.

"If that's your girlfriend Halle, tell her we don't do doggie bags."

He grabbed the phone and headed out of the room.

CHAPTER TWENTY-EIGHT

THE WHITE RANCH with the black shutters sat at the end of a generous cul-de-sac and a good hundred feet back from the road. To the right of the house, a tight line of pine trees ran along the lot line and blocked a full view of the utility pole which nearly killed her mother and made her father someone she barely recognized.

She parked in front of the wooden pole which represented the family dividing line. Over the years, no matter the season, she came and sat here for a few minutes or hours depending on how much she missed Mom. Nothing against the indicted woman down the street fighting to make a comeback, but this location felt like a cemetery plot where the memory of her real mother passed away. Sometimes, she sat still and listened to the wind, or watched falling leaves or flurries dance around the pole, but more often than not, she just closed her eyes and let her mind run free and reminisce about the smallest details.... *holding her mother's hand crossing the street .... painting their nails bright pink .... making super hero costumes out of cardboard ... searching for salamanders in the brook behind the house ... laughing as they picked out prom dresses and a wedding gown.* The memories were ingrained like the rings of a tree, and for many years the growth lines remained healthy despite the clang of empty wine bottles being thrown in the barrel or the whispered yelling between her parents. The megadrought of the past ten years made her wonder if the withered tree had died. Invariably, waves of regret would rise from the floorboard of the car for the many "lasts" she could no longer recall — the last shared meal, hug, saying "I love you." Feeling emotionally spent, she would head home hoping to make lasting memories with her husband and son, but would find hope is not a strategy. The feedback from James and William if they looked up at all from their scrolling and texting, terminated her feeble efforts.

Sitting here today, she mouthed a spontaneous and quite unexpected, "Help me dear God," and imagined a tenacious blade of grass struggling for survival in the crack of a busy city sidewalk during the dog days of August. She needed that type of grit and fortitude to open the car door and walk up the long driveway and ring the Daggett's doorbell. Today did not differ from the previous three-thousand-six-hundred-and-fifty days since the accident in front of this house, but over the years the moat surrounding the ranch grew ever wider. However, this morning, she felt frustrated enough to swim with the alligators. Images of the ruined dinner last night flashed in her mind. She fell asleep on the couch and waking at the crack of dawn, found James had already left. A growing sense of panic made her call and wake up Kendra and see if she could locate the video and pictures. After another hour, her fingers felt arthritic from checking multiple social media sites expecting the big reveal, but found nothing. Then the walls of the house felt like a vice. She grabbed her coat and keys and came here for comfort.

Filling her lungs, she eased herself out of the car with the same slow motion precision astronauts use when performing a space-walk. She made her way slowly until the road met the driveway. Taking another deep breath, she ignored the multiple alarms ringing in her ears and began the ascent.

Despite a brisk breeze, it was a mild February morning with the sun bright in a cloudless sky. The birds chirped loudly, grateful for an easy winter day with spring only a month away despite the joy-kill groundhog prediction. The beauty of God's creation alone should have eased the trek, but she found her eyes glued to the pavement. When William called her out on this strange habit of looking at the ground, she thought it a teenage exaggeration and said she feared black ice. But after watching herself for a few days, she discovered he was right and could not reason why. *Maybe it was to avoid an ugly glare from a townie or trying to shrink and keep from being noticed.*

Continuing up the driveway, she noticed the moving landscape beneath her feet; sand and pebbles and small stones, some showing dings and scrapes from being trampled by feet and cars and snowplows. *Everything is always colliding in this ever-spinning world,* she thought as her legs felt like they were getting shorter and her breathing became labored.

When she reached the bottom of the front stairs, she alternated between exhaustion and anticipation, an odd couple on this overdue mission. Six brick steps remained between her and the doorbell, and she wished she asked Sean or Kendra to do this for her.

She pushed the thought away and climbed one stair before the door suddenly opened. *The summit was coming down to her! Maybe it is better to look up from time to time,* she thought.

A thin gray-haired woman of about seventy appeared behind the glass storm door and eyed her with a look of curiosity.

Cassie climbed another step as the woman opened the door.

"Mrs. Daggett?" she asked.

The woman did not reply, but she pushed on. "Hi. I'm Cassie MacLean."

"I know who you are," the woman responded and pointed at the street. "You've been sitting in the front of our house for years."

The acknowledgement almost blew her back to the driveway with all the injured rocks, but she held onto the black iron railing and simply nodded in reply. She never sensed being watched when she came during the day, but at night sometimes the front lantern would come on and she wondered if they would call the police. They never did.

"When you first showed up, we ran your plate and then put two and two together." Mrs. Daggett eyed her like she was a time traveler. "Marty bet me you would never ring our doorbell, but I thought otherwise." She glanced at the snow on the front lawn. "I predicted it would be winter given the history here."

New Hampshire in January is tough enough, never mind the anniversary of all this. Little wonder I'm on Zoloft, she thought and rolled out a smile. "Well, looks like you won."

"Yeah," the woman replied and paused for a moment. "It's a shame I'll have to take a raincheck on the back rub he owes me. My husband passed last year."

"I'm sorry," she said mechanically while thinking she lost another witness.

The widow opened the door wide. "I have a fresh pot of coffee on. C'mon in."

She climbed the remaining stairs and stepping on a mat in the tiled foyer, slipped off her shoes.

"Bless you, my dear," the elderly lady remarked. "It's a wonder there's not a skylight in here from my head exploding when family and friends march right into the living room with snow and mud caked shoes."

"My son does the same thing no matter how much I plead. It's May before I get rid of all the sand."

The host pointed at a microfiber sofa in the corner. "Make yourself comfortable and I'll get us that coffee."

"Thank-you," she replied and made her way across the comfy looking room. On the way, she stopped at a wedding picture hanging on the wall of the Daggett's. The bride's blonde hair was pinned up high, and her husband's sideburns journeyed south of his ears. She figured they were married back in the sixties. On a side table she eyed an 8x10 framed photo of Mrs. Daggett holding a baby dressed in pink.

Before her eyes could explore more, the hostess came in carrying a silver tray with two coffee mugs, a small container of cream, and a bowl of sugar.

"I have blueberry muffins baking in the oven. If you can stay a bit, they are worth the wait."

She sniffed the air. "They smell delicious but coffee is more than generous, thank-you." Her mouth felt dry. After taking a sip of the high-test brew, she added a heavy dose of cream.

"Please call me Pam," Mrs. Daggett said watching. "Marty was an electrician and started his days before sunrise. He liked his coffee really strong so it would zap him awake."

"Given how I've been dragging myself into the office lately, I should buy a gallon of this from you." She took another taste and compared the burn in her throat to a shot of whiskey. "How long have you lived here?"

"Twenty-seven years. We were happy with our house in Methuen, but fell in love with this dead-end street and the woods out back. It's funny though. We used to go on vacation every summer in Maine and take hikes looking for wildlife but see more in our backyard— deer, foxes, coyotes, turkeys, and even a bobcat."

"All the development around here is really squeezing their habitat," she replied continuing the small talk. Growing up, her father sprayed starter fluid in the air duct of their classic lawnmower after the winter, and it would roar alive after one pull of the starter rope. She took another sip of coffee hoping for the same effect.

The woman's green eyes reminded her of the pine trees standing like sentries around the tragic spot. "Your kindness is very touching," she began and looked at her coffee and thought how a little cream changed not only the complexion but softened the bitterness. "I have to confess your generosity differs greatly from others in town."

Mrs. Daggett leaned forward and looked her in the eye. "I've learned not to believe everything you read in the paper or the gossip from family and friends." She finished the astonishing statement not with the usual look of pity, but understanding.

"That's very kind of you. Let me say right up front, I honestly can't reconcile what happened that night. My Mom is a good woman and to do something like—" She stopped and took a deep breath. Even after ten years, she had difficulty talking about the tragedy. "Leave the scene of a terrible accident and plow into a pole?" She shrugged. "That's not the woman that brought me up."

Mrs. Daggett frowned at her coffee.

"You don't agree?"

She bit her lip for a moment before looking up. "No matter what she did, I understand she's still your mother. What I question, and didn't mean to broadcast on my face was her blood alcohol level. She was more than a little buzzed. I doubt whether blitzed covers it sufficiently."

This lady is no pushover, she thought and wrapped her hands around the mug taking in its warmth. "I'll admit my mother had an issue, but never drove impaired. Never."

Pam nodded as the frown slowly relaxed.

She pointed at the picture window facing the street. "When I first started coming here, it wasn't to think about that night. Heaven knows I can't escape it, and even if I could, there's plenty of people around town to make sure I never do. No, I came here to remember Mom fully alive instead of seeing her in suspended animation."

"Marty and I disagreed about the reason behind your visits. He thought you felt your mother's presence here and maybe wanted to put a flower arrangement in front of the pole like you see in fatal accidents. I said that was ridiculous since your mother was still alive and it would be pretty insensitive given the loss of life on the bridge. No, I thought you came here to try to figure out what happened and maybe ask us about what we saw. As the years passed, I figured the wounds were so deep you were paralyzed."

Cassie cleared her throat and realized again how her family dominated many a dinner conversation for years. "Yes, I wanted to ask what happened."

Pam sat back on the couch. "Then why didn't you?"

"I leaned on my father. He said other than calling 911, you saw nothing. He also claims you made it clear you didn't want to get caught up in the media circus."

"I don't remember ever talking with him, but yes, we avoided the reporters and didn't answer the door or the phone for quite a while. That said, we held nothing back from the police."

She took another taste of the coffee and thought of Dad shoveling applesauce laced with-who-knows-what into her mother. An unexpected smile bubbled up. "I'm sure you've read she's awake. I consider it a miracle, even if she faces a long road ahead."

Mrs. Daggett nodded. "Yes, I heard the news. How wonderful."

"It also motivated me to go back through the police reports on my own. "So, you didn't see the accident?"

Mrs. Daggett fingered the handle on her mug. "No, but from the sound I thought a plane crashed out front. Marty couldn't remember what he had for breakfast, never mind ten years ago, so you're lucky I'm sitting here instead of him. I remember waking up after midnight, which felt later because we went to bed early since Marty got up at four in the morning. I'm a light sleeper. A mosquito in the next room would wake me, never mind a car slamming into a pole out front."

"Did your husband hear it too?"

"No, he snores like a diesel truck."

"What happened after you heard the crash?"

"I jumped up and looked out the window. There was a lot of smoke rising and it curled around the tilted utility pole. The pine trees blocked seeing anything else. I immediately called 911."

"Did you go outside?"

Pam shook her head and took another sip of coffee.

She glanced at the picture of the woman holding her granddaughter. *She's clearly a very kind woman, yet someone crashes into a pole outside her house and she just calls it in and what? Goes back to bed?*

Her eyes wandered next to the framed wedding picture. "What about Marty? Did he go out to see what happened?"

Pam hesitated a long moment before nodding. "Yes, and I've always felt bad I didn't go with him. Don't get me wrong. Marty was a wonderful husband and provided for me and our two sons. But he shunned getting involved in other people's business."

"Other people's business? There was a terrible accident on a dead-end street."

"Exactly! We argued about it for a few minutes. He wanted me to come back to bed, but I'm no pushover. I finally ran to the closet and threw on my coat. Marty said don't be stupid and wait for the police! But I was worried someone might be lying in the street in the cold. My husband yelled a few choice words, before he went out in his flannel pj's and slippers. He made it to the end of the driveway, before a cruiser came flying down the street. A few minutes later he came back inside."

"What did he see?"

"A man standing by the car crying. As he walked toward him, a policeman yelled and told him to go back inside because a power line was down."

She thought about the timeline review with Sean. "There was no mention of downed wires. Did the electric company show up?"

"I can't answer that. We went back to bed not long after. I didn't sleep a wink for the rest of the night. Can't say the same for Marty."

"Any idea how long it took for the ambulance or another cruiser to arrive?"

"When there's an accident like that, every second seems like a year, so it's hard to say, especially now."

Cassie sighed.

"If Marty were sitting here, I would refill your mug, bring in those blueberry muffins and talk about something happier."

She had nothing left to offer.

"But," she said and hesitated like she was working on convincing herself, "that's how my dear late husband rolled. I would have stamped "mind your own business," on his gravestone if it wasn't my final resting place too. There's something else that's bothered me about that night."

She could think of a few pithy sayings for her father's stone too. "What do you mean?"

"Well, the next morning after Marty left for work, I was standing at the kitchen sink doing the breakfast dishes as the sun came up and noticed footprints in the snow that went across the backyard. Normally given the deer and other critters, they would have been lost in the animal traffic, but we had some fresh snow a few days before and they stuck out. Later that morning, I walked out and found the tracks went from the accident scene, up our side yard, across the back and into the woods."

"Did you tell anyone?"

"I told Marty. He went out and looked and said it was probably some kid taking a shortcut. I thought that was rubbish. The footprints were pretty large, and the woods were full of picker bushes which is a shortcut to nowhere but a good hiding place. He thought maybe the police were checking out the area after the accident. We were good sparring partners, and I told him he was missing the big picture. Everyone and everything they needed was inside that car except maybe who was driving. Police are busy enough without taking a winter stroll to nowhere."

"Did you tell the police?"

She shook her head. "Mister Mind-Your-Own-Business, had to have his way and we stuck by our initial statement that we only heard the crash and called it in." She laughed and looked at the ceiling. "Marty, you still owe me that back rub, even if it's going to be rough."

CHAPTER TWENTY-NINE

FINDING HER FATHER'S BMW SUV parked behind the family Jeep, made her think life alternated between wandering in the desert and performing in a three-ring circus. The next hour looked destined for a matinee show under the big top. That James was home this early was concerning, along with the fact her workaholic father was not at the office or home waiting hand and foot on the buxom blonde. More troubling though, she could count on one hand the number of times James and her father had been alone. Her role as peacekeeper kept any belligerence from going nuclear when Dad played interrogator, and James provided one-word answers if he replied at all. On more than one occasion, she interceded and held his hand tightly before he could flip off his father-in-law. Taking it all in, she also noticed a large tv truck parked across the street and two men were inspecting the dish satellite. It would be a shame if there were any technical issues that might prevent broadcasting the free-for-all that might spill out of the house any moment.

Exiting the car, the third ring performance suddenly launched when her phone announced Ray was calling. Caesar might have said, "divide and conquer," but the knives eventually teamed up to make its point.

She took a deep breath and answered the call. "Hi Ray."

"Why was the project review meeting rescheduled?" he barked.

Cassie winced. Her boss was polite to a fault and skipping hello was like seeing the water recede before the tsunami hit. She thought everything was under control when his stellar assistant Terry, who choreographed everything on Ray's calendar, said she would buy her another day, and he would not notice. Clearly, he was monitoring her performance.

"Yes, but we're on for tomorrow," she said quickly hoping to put out the fire.

"What's the delay?" he spit back. A couple months ago, he would have prefaced the question by asking if someone on the team wasn't pulling their weight or what milestones were at risk of slipping. That he didn't, meant he considered her the problem.

"The revised financials came in late. I want to sanity check them before the meeting."

She thought she heard him sigh. "I don't have to tell you again how senior management is watching, and we can't afford any missteps. How about I swing by your office and we grab lunch and review your concerns?"

The saliva in her mouth disappeared, and she saw a huge wave on the horizon. "I'm sorry, I can't."

"Why not?" he shot back.

"I had an appointment and took an early lunch." She looked at the BMW and Jeep in front of her and glanced back at the tv truck. The satellite dish was pivoting so it looked like the glitch had been resolved.

"Stop by my office in an hour," Ray said quickly before the phone went dead. He never hung up on her before and hoped she didn't hear him say goodbye or the signal was lost. Checking her watch, she calculated she could dedicate only ten minutes to the vortex on the other side of the front door before heading back to the office.

Halfway up the sidewalk, the door swung open, and her father came rushing out minus a coat. His arms were spinning like a pinwheel and his face the color of a beet.

"Have you lost your mind?" he yelled, nearly tripping down the stairs. "I have a good mind to disown you!"

The words blew through her abdomen so fast she fought the urge to check her midsection for the entrance wound. "You disowned me and Mom when you moved in with you-know-who."

He held up his left hand and pointed at the gold band. "I'm still married to your mother!"

"Why the woman you sleep with permits that is one of the great mysteries in life."

She braced for a slap across the face and surprised when it did not arrive. As a girl, such a display of insolence would have resulted in Dad removing his belt.

He pointed back at the house. "Better take the plank out of your eye daughter, before giving advice on marriage."

Her throat tightened as she pictured both James and Ray with smoke pouring out of their ears. "Look, I don't have time for this."

"Then can I get on your calendar because you never pick up the phone!"

"I had a crazy morning and had my phone on silent. Why is every call of yours urgent?"

"How would you categorize it? You told that holy roller I'm poisoning your mother!" he yelled back.

"I never said that."

"No? Then why can't I feed her anything but the mush they give me and someone has to sit and watch while I feed my wife? To think I pay the bill for this level of disrespect! What's next? Being frisked before they let me in?"

"No one is accusing you of anything, Dad. They are worried Mom has regressed a bit and has been sleeping a lot."

"So, you think I'm drugging her?" He came an inch from her face and she could smell the black coffee he chugged all day long.

She held her breath and returned the stare. If this was one of those superhero movies, one of them would have melted.

"Say it to my face, instead of using that nurse that should be wearing a nun's habit given all the mumbo-jumbo she says over your mother."

She would not betray the nutty roommate that was turning out to be a saving grace. She stood on tippy-toes and returned the fire. "Julie didn't accuse you of anything. If she thought you were dosing Mom with something, you wouldn't be standing here, but talking to me through bars."

"She doesn't have to say anything to my face, but you would have to be a turnip like your mother not to figure it out."

Before she could recall her hand, she slapped him hard across the face.

Her father looked stunned and the surroundings took on a weird yellowish tint.

"I deserved that," he said in a whisper. "Forgive me for referring to your mother like that. My anger gets hot sometimes and you're good at stoking the fire."

She did not answer and concentrated on her stinging hand.

"I told Julie to drop dead and get your mom tested," he continued.

"In that order?"

He cocked his head and thought for a second. "Well, if Julie is six feet under there's no need for a test unless you can't be trusted either."

She stepped back in the ring and pointed at the man she once adored. "Get off Julie's back. She's been a better daughter than I could ever pretend to be the way she feeds, bathes and yes, prays for her. If you would just stop and notice the way Mom looks at her, you would understand." She looked up at the cloudy sky and wished the clouds would let go and wash some of the filth off their souls. "As far as your meltdown over the prayers, Mom had more faith in a coma than we could ever match." She thought about the trips to the virtual world and how her piety continued even there. "I'm sure she's storming heaven on our behalf even now. Talk about two impossible cases."

"Well, you better hope she's praying for you, because your hubby is on the warpath."

She didn't have to ask why.

"I never understood what you saw in a nerd allergic to barbers and wears flip-flops in January. He may have tidied up his appearance over the years, but he's still the same awkward geek that avoids me. The way he paced around the house after I arrived, I could tell something was wrong and when I brought up your name, he started mumbling and throwing things around. Then I found out my grandson is holed up in his room and refuses to come down to see the man that bought him a car! Some gratitude! You all deserve one another."

She heard enough and started for the house, but stopped and considered whether to deal with the office crisis first.

"Nice way to box me in," her father said pointing at his vehicle. "How do you expect me to leave?"

She started toward the Honda, but he held up his hand. "Don't bother, because I've learned by now how to maneuver around my little girl." He started down the sidewalk and then stopped and turned around. "Your mother is being transferred tomorrow." He looked her up and down and laughed. "If you want to dress her up one more time in silly space goggles, better do it before lunch." He shook his head. "And the nurses have *me* under surveillance?"

"Did James tell you that?" she asked, hoping he did not read it online or see it on tv.

"Yes, Jimmy told me all about it. It's the first time he ever put two sentences together in front of me," he said walking away.

Cassie did not wait to see if her father found freedom before she bolted for the house. Downstairs seemed ghostly quiet and stopping to listen, she heard movement upstairs.

When she reached the bedroom, James was stuffing underwear in a gym bag. It looked like a familiar scene from a hundred gut-wrenching movies she watched. Words escaped her.

Her husband slammed the bureau drawer shut and opened the next one down and began rifling through a stack of t-shirts.

"Look, I'm really sorry."

"Save your breath, Cassie. I don't have time or the stomach for this right now." He moved quickly to the closet and grabbed a pair of jeans off a hanger. "I told Brad what happened. We're going to work all night and get the product launched before the market opens tomorrow."

"Can you pull that off?"

"We have no choice," he mumbled.

That was the sort of curt reply that upset her father. Dad enjoyed color commentary because he envisioned a struggle of wills over most things. "I have a friend at the *Tribune* trying to find out where the video and pictures are being sold."

He glanced at her and shook his head. "I didn't think you had any friends, never mind one that works at a newspaper."

The acidic comment found the same hole her father made. She wrapped her arms around her stomach trying to hold the rest of her intestines in. "That's not fair!"

James pointed at her. "Fair is not putting me in this situation or ruining our family with twisted theories."

"But they're real. If you had time, I would explain."

He stopped and looked at her with the same disdain he used whenever they talked about the open wound ruining their marriage. "I've been waiting ten years for you to explain why you rolled a big ass stone across the opening to your heart. Neither of us were in that damn car, but might as well have been because we've taken the ride with your folks. Now Mom is semi-awake, and you're putting everything at risk— us, William, and all we worked for. There's no other way to say how bad that sucks."

She was too stunned to cry and watched James move to the bathroom and throw some things in a shaving bag. The clock on the nightstand caught her attention. She should be driving to the office by now.

"Why are you taking a shaving bag?" she half whispered.

"If I don't get canned, I'm going to spend some time with my brother. I haven't seen him since Christmas."

"And commute from Vermont?"

"I hope that's a problem I have tomorrow."

He stormed past her, and she listened to the heavy footsteps on the stairs and then the front door being slammed. She knew she should run after him, but collapsed on the bed and closed her eyes.

The tears were still coming when she felt a hand on her shoulder. Looking up she found her son, his eyes glassy and wearing the same lost look as her.

CHAPTER THIRTY

A FAMILY ROOM is anything but that when you're sitting alone in the dark and nursing a glass of wine. After James stormed out of the house and her tears subsided, she drove to the office expecting another tongue lashing. Instead, her manager's fatherly instincts kicked in after he took one look at her. Ray said nothing about her puffy eyes and shaky voice. Instead, he calmly explained his expectations for the project review meeting and promised to remove any roadblocks.

She sought refuge in the dark an hour ago and tried keeping her mind blank while sipping the Cabernet. The strategy worked mostly because she was exhausted. As her eyelids grew heavy, she hoped sleep would gift a deep nothingness instead of assembling a series of troubling dreams trying to make sense of it all. Just as the couch gave way to a long dark tunnel, a bright light overhead called her back. Opening her eyes, she found William standing by the wall switch studying her. He liked to borrow his father's sweatshirts, and tonight he was a Warrior from Merrimack College. Though the two men in her life shared some of the same mannerisms, her son's approach was more direct than James. Discounting the teenage angst which drove her nuts, he had an innate gentleness that sometimes surprised her.

"Why are you sitting in the dark?" he asked.

She sat up and rubbed her eyes, still over-faced from him comforting her earlier. "It's been a long day, and I'm closing my eyes for a bit. I didn't hear you come in."

"Tim's mom dropped me off." He eyed the glass of wine on the table. "I had dinner over there. Can I get you something?"

"That's kind of you, but no."

"How are you doing?" he asked.

"I'm fine."

He walked across the room, and sat down next to her on the couch. "It drives me nuts when people say that when in fact they're dying inside."

She let out a small laugh. "You could probably do a whole comedy routine on things people say to hide behind. But I think you're old enough to know most people don't want to know the real answer. It's like saying good morning. A common courtesy but really nothing more than those pop chips your dad likes that are nothing but flavored air."

"But I'm your son, not someone you work with so that's a cop out!" He looked her in the eye. "Let me ask again. How are you?"

"Miserable," she spit out. "You were upstairs earlier and know why."

"Well, you've had us on pins and needles."

"What are you talking about?"

"Normally Dad and I steer clear of you when your smile goes underground for more than a few days. Lately, you do nothing but frown, like it's chiseled in granite."

"You woke me up to tell me this?" She rubbed her forehead. "Your father and I are going through a rough patch, that's all. I have been consumed with …" She stopped and shook her head.

"You're not telling me anything new, because I live here, remember? Between his work and your obsession with your mother—"

She held up her hand interrupting him. "Why do you always call her my mother instead of Nana?"

He shrugged. "Probably because I was so young when she did what she did and then went into a coma. I don't know the woman and honestly have a hard time wanting to be related to her. Calling her your mother instead of my grandmother keeps her at arms-length."

"Understood, but obsessed is the wrong word to describe how I feel about her. It's more a feeling of being utterly overwhelmed, like I went over the falls with her in a wooden barrel and we've been stuck underwater until now. I'm just trying to get us to shore."

"See! There you go again. You didn't go over the falls with your mother. She did that herself and sadly, took many souls with her."

The image was jarring, and she put her arm around him. William tried pulling away, and she held on. "I know you and your dad have been waiting for me to surface. The three of us are too ashamed to call the tragedy reckless murder. Instead, we've become masters of euphemisms, calling it a tragedy or the unspeakable troubles, and using crass shorthand by saying she mowed down a bunch of folks. More often than not, I just use vague references and that's enough for people to fill in the blanks."

She grabbed her son's hand. "You hate people hiding their feelings? Sometimes, the non-answer is better than saying, I can't face another day where my drunk mother killed five, critically injured others, and nearly took out my father."

He sat back on the cushion like he needed support. "This is the woman you prefer to us?"

She took a deep breath. "Is that why my nickname is Dad?"

His cheeks got red. "Why did he tell you that?"

"People share things they shouldn't when upset. Denial, anger, and depression have defined me. But there are too many secrets in this family and that's why we had the argument today. What if I told you I used the headsets and went into a VR session with your grandmother and found out what really happened? Just like everyone mimics each other saying 'good morning!' or 'how are you?' and not expecting a reply, what if I heard my mother say she's innocent?"

He bolted up straight. "That sounds like a sci-fi movie. Did this really happen?"

She couldn't contain her smile. "I believe everything we know has been slanted."

He jumped up. "I don't understand. How?"

"I'm not sure yet, and keeping my hopes in check because I don't know how this will play out." She wrapped her arms around him. "I can't say more, except I love you to the moon and back for checking in on me."

He held on. "You can't give me half an answer like that. It will drive me nuts."

She pulled back and laughed. "I see you had to insert 'drive' into the conversation. Please give me some credit for talking your father into letting you keep that pocket rocket."

His eyes beamed. "Yeah, I saw your prints all over that."

They looked at each other for a moment like they had a new understanding. "I'd ask if you wanted to take another trip into VR, but it's gotten me into a bunch of trouble already."

He nodded. "Though it would be cool to come along and see Nana talk."

She smiled, and handed him the remote. "Pick out a movie and I'll get us some popcorn."

CHAPTER THIRTY-ONE

CASSIE THOUGHT, *painful days like this you just have to power through*. She entered her mother's room and encountered Julie emptying a closet while Rose watched from a wheelchair. The nurse glanced her way and gave a simple nod before returning to the task.

"Hey Mom!" She said as cheerfully as she could muster and gave her a peck on the cheek. She stepped back and studied her mother's outfit which she purchased before the sleeping saga. The navy-blue cotton sweater hung loose but at least hid her painfully thin arms. The khaki pants looked okay, but it was hard to say without her standing up, and that goal still in the future.

Rose studied her with a lopsided smile which made her look like she suffered a stroke, but the facial muscles had simply atrophied over the years. Given everything, Cassie wondered why hers hadn't too.

She pointed at two white plastic bags on the bed which held the remnants from a ten-year residency. "I remember helping you clean out Grammy's room after she passed. We picked out a few things to donate and threw the rest away. For the longest time, I kept a pair of her trademark white sneakers in my closet so I would remember her every day." She looked at the bags remembering the exercise. "But looking at Grammy's corkboard filled with pictures of family, friends, and a half dozen cats all named Furry, we became a mess. I still have it and worry who will want it when I'm gone? Your grandson .... well, he travels light and keeps everything in the cloud." She let out a snicker. "Maybe I'll have James bury it with me."

Julie walked over with a flannel nightgown and placed it in a bag.

She noticed how puffy the nurse's eyes looked and touched her arm. "Before you started here, this room looked pretty sterile. Can I pack you up too?"

Julie fished a tissue out of her pocket and blew her nose. "I try to make this a home for everyone."

"You sure do and were a lifesaver for Mom," she said and looked at the empty shelves. "Because of the coma, I didn't think of decorating the room with pictures." Her eyes narrowed on their own as she heard herself lie, because it was the resentment that kept the room sterile. A sharp pain rolled across her breastbone knowing her mother was innocent, despite all the questions that remained. She thought about the pictures she should have decorated the room with. There were dozens of framed photos of her and William and James that would have been easy additions, but what about her father? Maybe she should have pinned up their wedding picture as a reminder for him.

Her mother watched her with a look of curiosity. Thank goodness they were not in VR where thoughts were laid bare. It felt surreal seeing her sitting up, and she knelt down beside her. "I should have been here a lot more so you could feel the love." She squeezed her hand as an internal voice mocked her. *What a crock. You hated her more than loved her for what she did. You dreaded stopping by this prison.*

Retreating from the self-disgust, she looked away. Suddenly, she felt a light touch on her arm and found her mother scanning her face. "Love ... you," she stuttered.

Julie stood overhead. "It's good to see her talking again," she commented. "I find it mighty interesting she's not taking any more afternoon naps."

"Is my father still coming for lunch?"

"I was off the last two days so you'll have to check the register. But if he did, Rosa or Ana monitored any feeding." She glanced quickly toward the hall. "Is he stopping in before the transfer?"

"Predicting what he will do is like forecasting New England weather, but I think he will pass. It wouldn't surprise me if he's waiting up north since cold and blustery are his calling cards." She rubbed her mother's shoulder. "Is the transfer still on for one o'clock?"

Julie smiled at Rose. "Yes, and it's a wheelchair van so you can enjoy the ride. The beauty of the White Mountains always takes my breath away."

"I wish I could follow the van, but I'm on a short leash at work." She reached in her coat pocket and pulled out a small wrapped box and handed it to the nurse. "There's no way I can ever thank you properly." She looked at her mother who was following every word.

Tears welled up in Julie's eyes as she unwrapped the box and found a gold guardian angel necklace.

"It's beautiful," she whispered.

Cassie pulled her in for a tight hug. "I am eternally grateful. You truly have been a guardian angel for my mother."

"It's been easy because I love her." She bent down and gave Rose a long hug. "I hope you don't mind if I come up and visit."

"I would be hurt if you didn't," Cassie replied. "We consider you extended family now." The nurse let out a short laugh. "That's kind, but I think your father would have another view! I'll check with you before I come up so I don't upset him."

"I think it's safe to say you can pick any day of the week and won't run into him," she replied rolling her eyes.

Julie embraced her mother. "In the meantime, I'll keep praying this miracle continues." She stood up and looked at Cassie. "By the way, I saw the story about the headsets on the news last night. The reporter speculated you and your mom were playing some type of virtual reality game." She looked at the guardian angel necklace. "I don't understand the technology, but to be honest I have a lot of questions about what you were trying to accomplish."

She sighed. The hoodlums bypassed the local press and pitched their treasure trove to a Boston television station which aired the story. This morning three tv trucks arrived in front of her house before breakfast. William acted as a decoy and walked out to the garage so she could slip out the back door and cut through a neighbor's yard. She ended up taking an Uber to the office and called another one to come here. Who knew what waited when she got back to the office?

"The media loves a mystery. Between us, I used the headsets to talk with my mother. I know it sounds preposterous, but in the virtual world she's her old self."

Julie pointed at the miraculous medal around Rose's neck. "Not with faith. The doctors are still puzzled why the woman woke up and is improving. There's clearly something happening here beyond the rational dimension."

Cassie looked out the window at the fat snowflakes gently parachuting to earth. "Walking in from the car, the snow frosted my head and shoulders, and I thought how appropriate since I've felt like the ice queen for some time." She glanced at her mother. "Compared to her, I was baptized in ice which doesn't purify anything."

Julie pointed at her head. "But you're dry now. A warm heart will do that."

Madelyn came floating into the room holding a Styrofoam cup and came rushing toward her.

"I can't thank you enough for paying the receptionist to pick me up a coffee when she goes out to lunch."

Cassie smiled and nodded. Ann had a serious addiction to Dunkin Donut coffee and jumped at the chance to get a free cup, as long as she brought one back for Madelyn. Money well spent, and allowed her alone time with her mother. "Don't mention it."

Rose chimed in with a long groan that sounded like gibberish.

Julie looked puzzled. "I'm sorry Rose, I don't understand what you're saying."

Madelyn retrieved a magazine from a cubby next to her bed and headed toward the hall. "She's asking for a mirror."

Rose nodded and Julie shook her head. "Madelyn never ceases to amaze me. I'll get a mirror and be right back." She followed the interpreter out of the room.

A moment later, Cassie heard heavy footsteps approaching and thought either Madelyn was relocating her celebrity gossip club, or news cameras were ambushing them again.

Instead, James and William came rushing into the room.

Her husband had no coat and wore the same jeans and sweatshirt from yesterday's fight at the house. The stubble on his face together with the wild hair made it apparent he had not slept. William imitated his father— no coat and uncombed hair too. He held a familiar looking box.

William stopped short and stared at the woman in the wheelchair. Her husband offered a sheepish smile and gave her a quick peck on the cheek.

"What's this all about?" she asked.

Her husband ignored the question and knelt down beside the wheelchair. "Hi Rose! So nice to see you."

Cassie motioned to her son, and he shuffled over beside her.

Rose moved her eyes from James to her grandson and gifted them with a crooked smile.

In Hollywood, this would be a tender moment, but the air felt staged instead of authentic. "It's been a long time since you saw these two characters," she offered as a fill in. "One of them has grown up."

James shot her his infamous 'are you serious?' look. "Can we talk in the hall for a minute?"

She gave her mother a fake smile. "If you hear any crying in the hall, it won't be from me."

CHAPTER THIRTY-TWO

THE HALL SMELLED of rubbing alcohol, stale popcorn and a hint of urine. James leaned against the cement block wall, while William looked around like they were in a tough neighborhood and might be mugged any second.

"Why are you here?" she asked wanting to drill him deeper into the cement. "You haven't visited my mother since they deposited her here." She fingered the worn bandage on her right hand remembering the police escort the ambulance received.

"I'll explain why, but want to acknowledge our son first. He made me see things differently."

She pivoted to William. "Speak!"

"I said we should support what you're trying to accomplish," her son answered quickly. "Given the stakes, we should use the headsets and find out what happened. Bottom line—"

"We should support you," James said finishing the confession. "I apologize for going ballistic yesterday."

William held up the box. "We brought the launched product so you can talk to Nana before they move her."

He's referring to her as Nana, she thought and looked back at James. "After arguing about this for years, our son strings together a few magic words and you have an epiphany?" She scanned his face because he stunk at poker. "What's really going on here?"

"What do you want me to say? That more than hearing, I finally listened?" He looked away for a second before returning. "As genuine as my apology is, I'll admit we're here for another reason too. Promise me you will keep an open mind."

"Says the guy with tunnel vision."

He grabbed her injured hand. "Look, the last twenty-four hours have been so intense I'm on the verge of being a babbling idiot. Things were already hot but went super nova after the tv piece about your mom aired last night. Brad burst into my office and peeled the paint off the walls with obscenities. Before he canned me, the venture capital firm that owns a majority stake in the company called. Their CEO saw things differently, and thought the possibility of our technology expanding beyond entertainment into the medical arena could be a multiplier for the upcoming IPO."

She pulled her hand away and folded her arms. "What an incredible idea! I wish I thought of that."

He hung his head. "Guilty as charged, but it saved my butt. Now I've been tasked with fast tracking this application. Brad's a snake and must have realized the opportunity to increase the value of his stock options, though he tried covering up his greed by saying I would be promoted if it works. The office is a madhouse with the launch, but he asked me to verify what you accomplished."

"Shareholder value trumps everything as usual." She took a deep breath. "I don't know if I should be mad or pity you. Are you too blind or exhausted? You're being used!"

James opened his mouth but no words came out.

She pointed at their son. "If William makes you see things differently, then you better have another session or two and hash it out."

"I know how this looks, but I'm being honest," James said waving his arms like he was trying to get her attention. "If I'm exhausted, it's from jousting with you." He pointed at his mother-in-law's room. "We've been fighting for so long over this that our lances have no blunt ends left. I want it to end before we stab each other."

She looked down the hall and saw Halle sprinting through a congregation of residents, her long tanned legs moving effortlessly dodging wheelchairs and walkers. None of the old men noticed her. She shook her head and the repeating image disappeared. James was right, they had suffered a major disconnect and much of it her fault. She wondered if he was confessing something else in code regarding his co-worker.

"When I came home looking for you, William confronted me," he continued. "You might think it's us boys against you, but he's in your corner." He touched her cheek. "I am too if you'd let me."

The words were filling her ears too fast, and she sought refuge by hugging her son. He pulled back quickly, embarrassed by public affection in an empty hall.

"This is what you hoped for," he said with his lower lip trembling. "Stop standing alone in the dark looking for a way out. We have the flashlights."

"I need time to think it over."

"But we don't have time," her husband added.

"Translation: you don't have time. Admit it, you want to go back and wow your bosses and get another promotion so you can spend even less time at home." The image of Halle stood a few feet away, licking her lips and holding a bottle of Dom Perignon and two champagne glasses.

"We can wait until later this week, but aren't they moving her today?" he countered.

William stepped forward. "C'mon Mom! You said you want to clear Nana and here we are. Don't blow the chance!"

She left them and walked to the window at the end of the corridor. The snow had stopped and the sky and the ground were a white canvas, waiting for an artist to add color, texture and meaning. She heard her mother whisper, "Carpe diem."

She walked back to her family. "Okay, but under one condition."

They nodded in unison.

She addressed James. "The initial session will only be my mother and I. That way, I can keep her calm and explain how the technology can help many people. Then I'll transfer the headset to you."

"Sounds like a plan," he replied and grabbing the box from William, they all rushed back into the room. Rose smiled watching the parade usher in. They congregated around her bed and James quickly unboxed the headsets.

She noticed the new headsets were black with purple stripes running along the temples. "They look different," she commented.

James held up one. "You've been playing with the beta version. VISION2020 is the product launched this morning. We have preorders for ten million units, but when gamers get a load of what these babies can do, we will sell that amount weekly."

After slipping on the headset, she fired it up and out of the blackness, the sky lightened and she watched a sunrise. Strangely, none of the option screens appeared.

"This is weird, nothing's working," she said and slid the headset off.

"That's impossible!" her husband said. He grabbed the headset out of her hand and slid it on. "All the units go through extensive diagnostics after assembly." His fingers worked the controller. "Okay, I'm in settings. What's the password for the network in here?"

"Password?" She glanced at the confused look on her mother's face and felt like she was looking in the mirror. "What are you talking about?"

Her son rolled his eyes. "The Wi-Fi password, Mom! At home it's ittybittyspiderman22."

She bit her lip as the silence lengthened and James continued fiddling with the controller. Pins and needles crisscrossed her chest, and the fear was palatable but could not say why. "I can go ask Julie. She left to get a mirror for Mom and must have gotten distracted."

James ripped off the headset and gave his wife a strange look. "I don't get this. How many times did you use it in here?"

The pins and needles morphed into hives and her throat suddenly felt on fire.

"Cassie!" her husband called. "How often?"

"Getting privacy in here isn't easy, so just a few times." She avoided her husband's stare and focused on the steel railing of her mother's bed. *I won't let him intimidate me with his tech mojo,* she thought.

"Tell me what you did after booting up the system."

"I figured out how to skip the intro of watching a sunrise or the full moon rising and selected a landscape. The forest and beach were spectacular, but I think Mom's favorite was the Chapel of the Holy Cross in Sedona built into the red rock."

"Chapel of what?" James asked. "That location is not in the beta version or the launched product." He rubbed the back of his neck and thought. "Our lab had different prototypes. Which units did you use?"

"The ones you brought home on Thanksgiving."

His eyes darted back and forth before zeroing in on her. "Are you sure? They were gray with black pinstripes on the side."

She shrugged. "I don't remember the pinstripes. They were the ones you found in the hall that ended our romantic dinner."

He pulled on his chin. "They were an earlier version, but minus any downloaded content because of the risk. So, without an internet connection all you would see would be the installed intro." He looked at her. "Nothing else would work."

She read his expression and held up a bandaged fist. "If you value those lovely front teeth, don't give me that pity look and think I made this all up!"

He sighed and rubbed his bloodshot eyes. "I'm just trying to make sense of this." He took a deep breath like he was about to give up his ghost. "Making something up isn't the same as wishing it so."

Before she could lunge at him, William stepped between them. "Instead of fighting, let's try connecting and see what happens."

As if on cue, Julie came in holding a small makeup mirror, and seeing the looks on their faces stopped short.

Cassie was too dumbstruck for introductions. She wanted to grab the mirror out Julie's hand and take a good look at herself. *Who would I see? A looney-tune?*

"What's the password for the Wi-Fi in here?" James asked in a strained tone.

Uncharacteristically, Julie initially ignored the question and walked over to the wheelchair. "The router is in the reading room on the first floor, so the signal is pretty weak up here if you can find it at all," she replied holding up the mirror for Rose. "In the renovation plans for next year, they plan on extending the network to all the rooms. That will allow us to automate a lot of our records."

Cassie felt the air get sucked out of her lungs, and she grabbed for a mobile tray to steady herself.

"Humor me. What's the password?" James repeated.

"Stairway to heaven and it's one word," Julie replied with a laugh. "We have an IT guy that thinks he's funny."

James did not crack a smile and slid the headset back on, as his fingers worked the controller. He began walking around the room. "There's no signal up here so it's just loading the sunrise loop."

"How about we try down the hall," William suggested.

James slid off the headset and shook his head. "I think we're done here."

"No, we're only just beginning," she replied and looked at her mom, wishing she would stand up and explain the places they visited and the things they discussed. But apparently, she imagined that too.

CHAPTER THIRTY-THREE

THE TWO CIGARETTE BUTTS standing somewhat tilted in the thick clam dip, reminded her of the headstands she nailed in a neighbor's pool as a nine-year-old. But what surprised her more, were the red lipstick stains on the filters, since this type of display was usually the work of the macho crew who would do anything for a laugh. Must be one of their biker chick girlfriends, she thought. Tired of psychoanalyzing the work further, her eyes surveyed the carnage from the company celebration which embraced her father's motto of "intensity to the max." Bottles of wine, whiskey, vodka and tequila circled a crushed box of Dom Perignon on the bar, while on the dining room table, the abandoned remnants of a king's feast grew cold.

Walking along the mahogany table, she glanced at a dozen lobsters boiled to death and the bloody juices from slabs of tenderloin. She thought how life is not only fragile but sometimes snuffed out for the garbage pail. Taking a deep breath, she let her eyes wander to the green-bean casserole.

"How I miss green this time of year," she whispered to herself, figuring that's why the color of life is so prominent at Christmas. But now January's trinity of white, black and gray reigned, and no amount of Valentine hearts in the weeks ahead would shorten this annual Lenten season without color.

Hearing a familiar laugh, Cassie looked toward the adjoining room and found an older version of herself. Her mother looked elegant in a cobalt blue dress that complimented strawberry blonde locks and conversed with someone out of view. For the first time in years, she looked not only happy, but hopeful as if discovering some internal reservoir. Cassie glanced back at the bar and the empty liquor bottles that revved up the ego of her dad and two dozen others. If there were a monitor for loose tongues and back slapping laughs, it would redline now. It made her look again at her mother's flute of ginger ale, which was too far away to gauge its carbonation, too far away to notice any shade of caramel coloring from a nip or two. Taking a sip of her white wine, she could hear the snake tempting her mom with the same selfish logic used in Eden. "You should lead this party. After all, you kept Charles' head screwed on when he thought the company would go bankrupt before winning this contract. Without you, he would be lost. A little splash of something from the bar is your right. Feel a little warmth tonight, and be free! You can go back on the wagon tomorrow… or the day after that."

Rose must have heard her thoughts because she suddenly stopped talking and looked her way. Their eyes locked and all her doubts about her mother's sobriety disappeared as they rested in each other's gaze.

Suddenly, the thud of something hitting the wall behind her broke the moment. Turning around, she watched her father stumble into the dining room.

"Are you okay, Charles," Uncle Phil asked following close behind her dad.

"Yeah, but when did you add this stupid wall? Get Carl in here now, and he can tear it down in ten minutes."

"What are you talking about? The bones of this house haven't changed in thirty years," his partner replied and shot her a "help me!" look.

"Hey Dad!" she called rushing to his side and pointing at the leftover feast. "Can I make you up a plate? I haven't seen you eat a thing tonight."

Her father gifted her with a look like she was a mangy dog he patted every once in a while. The juxtaposition with her mother's loving gaze made her take a sip of wine, and wonder if he ever noticed how time had changed how she looked at him. As a little girl, he would bring her to work sites, and she would marvel at all the earth-moving machines. She would hold her breath so not to miss a single syllable as her hero explained the function of each. But in time, the same snake of Eden made her question authority. Exiting the innocence of youth, she uncovered a father whose ego grew larger with the more sand he moved.

"Listen to your daughter," Phil added. "If you don't get something in your stomach to wick up all the whiskey, you'll be bumping into walls for the next week." He picked up a plate from a side table. "What can I get you?"

Charles eyed the food for half a second. "A large serving of the new industrial park in town, but go light on the negotiations because it gives me heartburn."

Phil nodded. "You got it. In the meantime, how about some beef tenderloin and a baked potato?"

Charles shook his head. "Too much chewing. I've limited myself to a liquid diet tonight." He pointed at all the liquor. "I see we have vino groupies, but where is my bottle of Jameson hiding? I started singing, 'When Irish Eyes are Smiling' a couple hours ago and still have a verse or two in me."

Phil pointed at a barrel in the corner of the room full of empty beer cans. "We take recycling seriously, and I think your empty is in there." He turned around and opening a cabinet door, pulled out a fresh fifth of the Irish whiskey. He handed the bottle to his partner. "Promise me, you won't call three hours from now when you can't get your head out of the toilet."

Her father grabbed two glasses from the bar and poured two-fingers of whiskey and handed one to Phil. "We're partners," he said with a bit of a slur, "which means we share the pain so I expect you to be kneeling next to me expelling your guts too." He raised his glass high. "Now bottoms up or I'll whip you good before I tear out that misplaced wall myself."

She watched knowing Phil always kowtowed to her father. After they downed their drinks, her father staggered toward her as Phil exited stage left into the kitchen. The smell of whiskey, cigars and sweat arrived first. He held the bottle of whiskey up to her face. "Honey, your old man made it. How about you toast me?"

She wrestled the bottle away from him and placed it on a table behind her. "I've lost count of how many drinks you've had. I don't know how you're still vertical."

He studied her for a moment while his brain buffered the words, then grabbed her arm and steadied himself. "That's what the bankers said when our subcontractors went on strike, but they misjudged this stubborn S.O.B." He looked around. "How come we're alone? Where did everyone go?"

She listened and noticed the sudden quietness too. "It's getting late and nobody has your stamina." She glanced toward the living room and saw her mother stacking plates.

"What's she doing?" he spit out in a whisper.

She thought he must be talking about someone else, but the familiar look of disdain on his face said it all. "That's what everyone loves about Mom, she always pitches in and helps. Besides, Phil might be a whiz with spreadsheets, but as far as housekeeping goes, he's lost with Ellie out of town."

"Stop making excuses for her," he slurred. "It's time my wife kicks it up a notch."

Drunk or not, she could not let this go unchallenged. "What do you mean by that?"

"Well for starters she's married to me – " he began, then hesitated trying to remember the point. "Since I'm somebody now, she should stand next to me instead of playing busboy."

She moved to block his view of the cleanup operation. "Sounds like you want a trophy wife, but since you want her at your beck and call why not get a dog instead?" She pointed at the array of liquor. "This whole night has been about you. I didn't hear you recognize her even once. No, you've droned on about the sacrifices you made, and the 24/7 effort by the construction crew to come in on time and under budget.

Who worked double shifts when you barely made payroll and brought your dinner to the office?"

"Next, you will tell me you're measuring her for a halo." He looked away. "Just don't ask me to sign the petition for canonization."

She put the wine glass down and grabbed the bottle of Jameson off the table. Maybe it was not lady like to take a swig, but neither was the woman who stood the spent cigarettes in the dip. The burn felt good.

Her father nodded in agreement.

She pointed at him. "That shot was medicinal given the poison rolling off your tongue. We all have our faults and weaknesses. Have you given any thought how Mom put herself at risk tonight for you? She's only been in recovery for a few months."

He waved her off. "There you go again taking her side. I earned tonight's celebration."

"I thought you were drinking top shelf?" she replied pointing at his chest, "not guzzling piss-poor-me."

His eyes narrowed which she knew meant the launch sequence for a slap. Phil suddenly shuffled into the room and redirected the drunk man.

"Where have you been, buddy?" Charles asked way too loud.

"Just saying goodnight to the Lawton's." Phil scanned the dining room like it was artwork he did not understand, and rubbed his face with stubby fingers. "All I know is I'm not dealing with this mess tonight. I'm sure it will all be here in the morning." For reasons only known to him, he thought the comment funny, and breaking out in laughter slumped on the hardwood floor.

She rushed over and helped him up. "Are you okay, Uncle?"

He looked at the hardwood floor. "Yeah. I have to lie down, but preferably someplace softer."

Her father staggered over and bear-hugged his partner. Seconds later, Phil's knee buckled and they toppled together like wooden blocks in a Jenga game.

They laughed like hyenas before Phil crawled to the doorway and pulled himself up. Charles looked content to sit on the floor.

"Let's bring the party down to my new ground level office. Grab the bottle of Jameson!" he said waving at Phil.

Her mother entered the room carrying a serving tray stacked with glasses and plates. Rose eyed the two men and shook her head.

"Time to get you home, Charles," she said.

"What a buzz killer," her husband replied.

She helped her mother and it took both of them to get her father off the floor and into his coat. In the process, Dad alternated between singing, 'When Irish Eyes are Smiling' to questioning their love for him. Phil stood by and silently watched the show and his sole contribution amounted to opening the back door of the sedan so Charles could crawl in. After refusing the seat belt, he toppled sideways on the leather seat and passed out.

Closing the car door, she found Phil looking like a lost dog so she escorted him back inside and deposited him in a leather recliner. When she made it back outside, she found her mother standing at the front of the Mercedes staring at the car keys.

"What's the matter, Mom?"

"I have trouble seeing at night. Would you mind driving?"

She took the keys out of her hand. "I've had a couple glasses of wine, but I think I sweated it out getting Dad in the car. You can be my co-pilot."

Starting out, she noticed the roads were slick from the days melt and without cloud cover, the temperatures were in the mid-teens. She drove cautiously, as the vehicle felt unfamiliar and nothing like her Honda which responded like an extension of herself. Making her even more anxious, none of the approaching cars dimmed their high beams no matter how many times she flicked hers on and off. With each passing car, the glare of the lights caused momentary blindness, leaving her uncertain where she was in relationship to the road. In quick order, she became increasingly dizzy and her mouth feeling full of cotton. It made her wonder if the excessive blood alcohol level in her father's bloodstream was being transferred to her.

Without warning, the car felt like it was gaining speed even though the speedometer remained at a steady thirty miles an hour.

"Something's wrong!" she said in an urgent whisper afraid of waking her father and having him want to drive. Gripping the steering wheel, she glanced over at her mother and found her slumped in the seat asleep.

Another vehicle approached and even from a good distance, its LED high-intensity headlights seared her eyes. The size and position of the blinding orbs made her conclude it must be a good-sized truck. She desperately blinked her high beams on and off, but the truck did not respond – if anything the lights got brighter and it felt akin to staring at the sun. An inner voice told her to pull over and let the dragon pass, but frustration got the better part of her.

"Screw you!" she yelled and stomped on the gas pedal hoping to race past the blinding monster. The Mercedes responded effortlessly and shot forward past the tractor trailer truck onto a small bridge. In the next instant, the rear end of the car felt like it wanted to run away on its own.

She knew from years of driving how bridges freeze first, and the best action when hitting black ice is not to slam on the brakes. But her foot was no longer tethered to her brain, and she pumped them furiously. The car began sledding sideways, and her eyes emerged from the momentary blindness to see multiple dark figures on the bridge. There were too many to count and worse, too late to react – except to scream. The right fender of the car hit one and then another, their bodies making a terrible thud as the car acted like a break ball in a game of pool. A shadow rolled across the hood, and a millisecond later, the agonized face of a woman appeared on the windshield. Before she could react, the car zigzagged in the opposite direction and found more targets. A couple went airborne over the railing.

The wheels suddenly found dry pavement and raced on. Her mother and father were yelling at her to pull over and stop. But her hands were glued to the steering wheel, and she could not command her foot to let up on the gas.

The car rocketed down Lawrence Road and then took a sudden right. No high beams were needed to see the approaching utility pole. Yet, no matter how much she turned the wheel or pumped the brakes, the dark sentry remained straight ahead.

The sound of a loud knock on the side window made her think her father was pretty upset she totaled his black beauty. Opening her eyes, she was surprised by daylight and the untouched utility pole in front of the car. Blinking hard, she looked to her left and found Pam Daggett standing on the other side of the window dressed in a heavy cotton robe. The sky behind her was a shade of rosy pink.

Meanwhile, the nightmare would not let go and played on… her father weeping looking at Mom's bashed in head. The smell of smoke, cold leather, and blood filled her nostrils.

The air temperature outside the car matched the interior, and she shivered sitting in the refrigerator. Staggering out of the car, she glanced at her feet hoping to see ruby slippers so she could click them three times to go home.

Mrs. Daggett began rubbing both her arms trying to restore blood flow. "My goodness woman, have you lost your mind? I got up to go to the bathroom in the middle of the night and noticed you sitting out here. When I saw you were still here this morning, I thought you either froze to death or …" She glanced at the back of the car and the exhaust, "made a terrible mistake that you can't take back."

"I'm sorry for the worry," she mumbled and worked to keep her teeth apart so they would not rattle. The knots at the base of her neck were in full revolt and she massaged them with her frozen fingers. "I must have fallen asleep. Wow! I'm mighty stiff."

Mrs. Daggett pulled the neck of her robe around her neck. "If we stay out here much longer, we'll both be stiffs. As much as I miss Marty, I don't want to see him today." She grabbed her arm. "Come in and have some coffee and a blueberry muffin."

That would sure beat going home and having James and William alternate between sulking and asking if I lost my mind, but I have to face the inevitable, she thought. "Thanks, but I really have to get going."

The reply was met with a worrisome look. "What on earth made you sit out here all night?"

What on earth, indeed! She shrugged reliving yesterday. *Pity and disgust fought for control on her husband's face, but William just looked embarrassed. They left without saying goodbye, and she drove in a trance to the project review meeting. She found a full conference room, and became an observer as an emotionless part of her went line by line through the milestones with a precision and coldness never employed before. Her colleague's expressions asked, "who is this?" Ray was all smiles afterwards, never realizing it was an imposter. The real her remained with a headset on revisiting the past, or imagining it.*

Getting back in the Honda, she reached under the seat and took out the near empty pint of brandy she drank while questioning her sanity. There was a generous shot left and she downed it to fight off hypothermia.

Starting the car, she waved goodbye to Mrs. Daggett who watched with a look of amazement mixed with concern.

"Everyone thinks I'm crazy," she said making a U-turn. "Killer dreams or not, those sessions with Mom put me in the driver's seat, where I should have been all along." She slammed on her brakes in front of the cursed utility pole, and flipped it the bird.

CHAPTER THIRTY-FOUR

IT DID NOT TAKE A DETECTIVE to figure out James did not come home last night. The missing cereal bowl in the sink said it all. Over the years, she gifted him with hearing loss while questioning why he refused to deposit dishes, bowls, glasses or silverware in the dishwasher. No matter the volume or the cuss words employed, for some inexplicable reason, James made this a hill to die on. Before she wandered through the rest of the house, she checked her phone again hoping for at least a curt text message, but her husband maintained cellular silence. She wished she could track his phone and see if he slept anywhere other than the office, but shook her head refusing to go there.

Upstairs confirmed James did not swing by even for a nap. She considered calling her brother-in-law to check, but that would raise some uncomfortable questions. Looking in William's room, she found an unmade bed and a bath towel on the floor, which defined his line in the sand. She presumed he went to school, though she seldom checked his room in order to keep her blood pressure from spiking. For all she knew, it might have looked like this for the past week.

Her phone suddenly buzzed, and she took a deep breath expecting James had consumed enough caffeine and aspirin to begin a long-winded sermon. Instead, an unknown number appeared on the screen. Normally, she would not answer and let it go to voicemail, but given how little these days made sense, she broke the standard operating procedure.

"Hello?" she said preparing to hang up if someone was selling an extended warranty on the Audi they no longer owned.

"Hey Cassie, its Kendra. I'm in the area. Can I swing by for a few minutes?"

She planned on taking a hot shower to loosen the stubborn knots in her neck while sending the remnants of the nightmare down the drain. "I'm running late for work. We can meet later if that's okay."

"I only need five minutes," the reporter replied pushing back.

She rolled her eyes. "Okay."

"Good. I'll be there shortly," she replied and hung up.

"Couldn't she just have told me over the phone?" she mumbled.

Switching into overdrive, she took a quick shower and no sooner threw on some jeans and a sweatshirt when the doorbell rang. After running down the stairs with her hair wrapped in a towel, she opened the front door to find Kendra holding two cups of coffee. Thankfully, the tv trucks were gone.

The reporter looked her up and down. "Is that what they call business casual at your company?" She handed her a tall Styrofoam cup. "Decaf."

Cassie frowned. "That word is not in my vocabulary."

"It is now because you won't need any additional stimulant after this drive by visit."

"That sounds like the leading line of my life story." She led Kendra into the kitchen and waited for her to sit down at the round oak table. "I take it you wanted to gauge my reaction or afraid I might go mad if you told me the news on the phone. Which is it?"

Kendra let the question hang, clearly enjoying the moment. "I've been busy meeting other deadlines and apologize if things felt like they've been in limbo since we met."

"Limbo? That's been my address for so long I'm thinking of running for mayor."

The reporter smiled. "I've found in working on any story, mapping relationships is key. That's what I started doing with your mother's case."

She took a sip of the coffee and it curled her lips. "Yuck! What's in this?"

Kendra looked at the coffee and winced. "I remembered how you liked extra cream and three sugars. Don't tell me your tastes grew up too?"

"James would say no because I still have a serious sweet tooth, but I take my coffee black now. But I'm touched you remembered." She pushed the cup aside. "But why map the relationships from that night? The dead don't talk, but their families sure do. I've heard almost everything."

Kendra shook her head. "No, I mean taking a look at all the players that responded to the accident: police, doctors, nurses."

By habit, she reached for the cup and took a sip of the coffee and ignored the sweetness. "Enlighten me on your findings."

"Well, for starters, there's the officer that responded to the scene after your parents hit the utility pole."

All this buildup for ground we've already covered? She took a deep breath. "Yeah, Brian Dowd. He works for my father and doesn't want to talk about it."

"Did he say how he ended up working for him?"

"The usual vanilla answer that he needed a career change and then worked his way up." She recalled his eyes undressing her. "He's a pig and doesn't try to hide it. You would think having a young daughter would make him think differently. Poor thing had two bone marrow transplants."

Kendra's eyes narrowed. "Who?"

"His eleven-year-old daughter, Savannah."

"That's impossible," Kendra replied and took a sip of coffee.

"My family thinks I imagine most things these days, but Dowd showed me a photo of his daughter in pig tails and braces."

"It's not you I'm questioning, Cassie. Brian Dowd is divorced and has no children from my background check."

"What?" The image of the heartsick dad flashed in her mind and she recalled the long wait in the lobby. "We talked about his daughter more than anything else. Made me feel like slime for asking about the accident."

"Good tactic, but that's not the half of it. Your dad's partner had a twin brother that died in a boating accident in his early twenties. Were you aware?"

"No."

"Well, besides his wife he left an infant son. Want to guess his name?"

The lack of sleep made the question run around her head before the connections were made. She grabbed Kendra's coffee and took a sip of the dark brew. "Phil is like family and I thought I knew everything about him. Are you saying, I'm not the only one that calls him uncle?"

Kendra nodded.

"Maybe that's the string we pull on and everything unravels?"

She shrugged. "Like I said, I'm just looking at relationships at this point."

They both sat quietly for a moment before she looked at the digital clock on the microwave and moaned. "I have to get going or I'll be pouring coffee in some fast-food joint next time we talk."

The high school friend reached across the table and lightly touched her arm. "There's one more thing. Your father's girlfriend—"

Cassie cut the air. "We don't say her name in this house."

Kendra smiled. "Understood. She's a nurse, right?"

"Yeah, so what?"

The reporter bit her lip for a second. "I have a good source that tells me the name that shall not be spoken was working in the ER that night."

Her response began in her right arm and as she punched the air, she caught the sixteen ounces of sugar-sweet coffee and sent it flying across the table and splattering on the hardwood floor.

Kendra eyed the mess and jumped up like she had seen enough and began walking backwards toward the door.

"All these puzzle pieces point to a massive coverup!" she said on the way to the counter to retrieve a roll of paper towels. The pitiful looks James shot her for years came to mind. *Meanwhile, Dad is scared and slipping sleeping pills to keep his wife silent,* she thought.

Kendra eyed the roll of paper towels like she wanted to help but dared come no closer. "Do you remember our earth science class?" she asked.

"Sure. We made a good team. I toyed with a shovel but you were like a possessed miner swinging that pickaxe."

Cassie began wiping up the mess. "I've never been afraid of getting my hands dirty."

CHAPTER THIRTY-FIVE

IT TOOK EVERY OUNCE OF SELF-CONTROL and discipline not to call her father on the way to work, and the main reason came down to fearing what she would say. Instead, she fumed over Kendra's bombshell and wondered if this was the tip of the mammoth iceberg.

She no sooner got to her office, and booted up her computer when her iPhone buzzed and displayed Jackson Long Term Care. She quickly said hello hoping this was just a courtesy call after her mother's transfer.

"Ms. MacLean?" a formal sounding woman inquired.

"Yes," she replied and looked out the window at the tiny red buds on the branches of a maple tree.

"This is Marlene Pickett. I'm the administrator here and look forward meeting you." She hesitated and cleared her throat. "Actually, that will be today when you pick up your son."

She jumped to her feet. "What?"

Her phone buzzed with another incoming call and the display read Salem High School. "Can you hold for a minute?" she asked before waiting for a reply.

"Hello," she said expecting the voice on the other end of the phone would wield a verbal sickle and take out her knees. It was going to hurt, and she tensed every muscle.

"Yes, this is Tricia Vale from Salem High. We're calling to check-in on William. He skipped his last two classes yesterday and wasn't in home room this morning when attendance was taken."

The melt down at the nursing home beat her ears. *When William arrived with James, it did not occur to me it was early afternoon and too early for him to be out of school. Apparently, neither did James as he was too consumed with the product launch and her screwup.*

"Thank you for the call," she said launching into self-preservation mode. "We had a family emergency yesterday, and in the heat of the moment, I texted William and my husband picked him up. I apologize for not following protocol." She winced feeling like a teenager again and about to get detention.

"Well, this is quite unusual," the woman replied. "I'm afraid—"

Afraid? She has no clue what that means, she thought. "Look, I'm on a critical call right now," she said interrupting. "My son will be back in school tomorrow. *Even if he's bleeding from the ears,* she wanted to add.

She hung up and reconnected with the nursing home administrator.

"Sorry for the delay. Let's start again. You said my son is there?"

"Yes. He came to visit his grandmother which of course is fine—"

"But your facility is a hundred-and-twenty-five miles away and he doesn't drive," she said interrupting, "not to mention this is a school day."

"I agree." An awkward silence followed.

She sat down to turn her computer off. "I apologize. I shouldn't be taking this out on you."

The woman sighed. "I have two teenagers, so I understand. I hate to raise your blood pressure any more than it is, but we're also concerned about an incident."

"Incident?" Nothing good ever follows that non-descriptive word. *Did he give jelly donuts to a diabetic or feed peanuts to someone highly allergic?*

"One of the staff found William trying to put some weird looking goggles on your mother. She became quite agitated."

She looked out the window again and thought she saw the maple buds shrink. *I thought if I could get inside Mom's head, I could fix everything. Now William is trying to save me and prove I wasn't dreaming. What have I started?*

"Hello, are you still there?"

She grabbed her throat which felt like it was closing. "Where is my son now?"

The administrator laughed. "In the dining room, enjoying his third breakfast."

"Well, he better eat up because he will be on bread and water for the next month." She glanced at her watch. "I'm leaving now and will be there in about two-and-a-half hours."

***

The long-term care facility was a renovated nineteenth century inn, situated in the heart of Jackson, New Hampshire, a picturesque town in the White Mountains. Cassie admired how the front of the building had a wrap-around porch, and across the street a trail for cross country skiing and snowshoeing. She remained beyond angry that her mother was so far away, but the landscape and the fresh air were certainly perfect for recuperation.

William must have been on the lookout because he came running down the front stairs the moment she got out of the car.

She spent the last couple hours excoriating him out loud instead of listening to the radio, but the moment she saw him sprinting toward her with a worried expression on his face, she saw the little boy with a big heart that often jumped before thinking. She hugged him tightly and blinked her eyes hoping to hold back the tears.

"What were you thinking?" she said with her voice breaking.

William stepped back and folded his arms in the cold. "That I could fix things you and Dad can't because instead of putting your heads together, you're too busy bashing each other's in."

The blunt remark made her throat tighten. "Driving up here, I was so angry I could have used a broom instead of a car. Now I realize, I'm the one that needs to apologize." She hugged him tightly. "I'm truly sorry." She asked herself if she could ever apologize like this to James and balked. One-way streets in a marriage do not work.

A cold wind kicked up and she noticed her son shivering. "As usual, I see you're traveling light. Where's your coat?"

He shrugged. "I think it's in the dining room," he replied with a smirk. "The cook says he ran out of eggs and bacon because of me."

"Well, you won't be too popular with the residents if they have to eat cereal for the rest of the week." She put her arm around him, and they started walking toward the building. "How did you get up here?"

"After the circus yesterday with Nana, Dad dropped me off at home and went back to work. I called Dan because he just bought a car and promised him a headset for a day if he'd drive me up here. But the way things turned out, he'll be lucky if I play checkers with him."

She took a deep breath in preparation. "Why?"

"Because his car overheated when we got to Portsmouth." Her son pulled away and walked ahead a few feet before turning around. "Just remember, I could let you think he drove me all the way up here, but I'm sick of the constant spin."

Cassie the mother did not know how to respond, so just nodded.

"He nursed the car to a truck stop. There was a diner there and Dan called his father for help. We ordered some cheeseburgers and a trucker at the next table overheard us talking and offered me a ride the rest of the way."

"What!"

"Ronnie wasn't one of those perverts you read about. He finished tractor-trailer training school last year and lives in Concord."

"I missed the part where we taught you to accept a ride from a stranger."

"Like I said, I didn't have to tell you any of this. Ronnie was headed north and offered me a ride."

"Dan was okay with this?"

William shrugged. "No, he told Ronnie to screw, and I told him to cram it."

She rubbed her forehead. "I'll never forgive myself for putting you in danger like this."

"The trucker was cool. We talked about video games most of the way. When he let me out, I only had to walk a couple miles. It was still dark, but I found a coffee shop and hung out."She shivered from the confession. When they reached the lobby, she led him to the corner of the room and a cast iron radiator to warm up. William held his hands out and yawned.

"Before I try to make good with the administrator, what happened with your grandmother?"

"Nothing really. When I went in and saw Nana, I thought she would remember me from yesterday, but she looked at me like I was a two-headed monster. I fired up the headsets and connected them to the network. But when I tried putting the headset on her, she freaked out. I didn't think she could yell so loud! A nurse came running in ..." He shook his head. "They almost called the cops even after I explained who I was."

"I would too if I were in their shoes and some teenager falls out of the sky with goggles and says he just wants to meet with Nana in a fake world." She laughed at how crazy it sounded.

He yawned in reply.

She noticed his eyelids drooping. "Have you had any sleep?"

William motioned to a leather recliner on the opposite side of the room. "I nodded off for a bit."

"Why don't you shut your eyes while I spend a few minutes with Nana, and then get you paroled from the administrator. It will be good practice when I have to do the same at Salem High tomorrow."

William rushed toward the chair apparently happy to let her fix things. "She's in room twenty-seven on the second floor. I left the headsets on the shelf in the room. Make sure you don't forget them or Dad will be furious."

She sighed. *If James had been home last night none of this would have happened*, she thought. Her conscience immediately kicked back, *the same could be said of you.*

Mom was lying in bed when she entered the room.

"Thought I would pop in for a quick visit," she said and flashed a big smile that felt like the oversized wax teeth she enjoyed as a kid. They were good for a while before you began drooling.

Rose gave her a tight hug as she scanned the room. It looked similar to the previous warehouse in Salem, except this one was located on the north side of the building given the way the afternoon sunlight came in slanted.

Stepping back, she thought Mom looked tired and questioned whether it was from the long ambulance ride or perhaps her father found a way to season her food.

Rose fingered amethyst rosary beads and if she had to guess, they were a parting gift from Julie. *Outclassed again,* she thought and imagined the guardian angel she bought the faith-filled nurse blushing at the latest antics of their family.

She sat on the bed and stroked her mother's arm. "I'm sorry Dad moved you way up here, but maybe the mountain air will do us both some good. It will be tough getting up here during the week, but count on me coming every weekend." *Maybe James would drive up with me and we could use the time to reconnect,* she thought.

Looking around the room for a distraction, she eyed the headsets sitting on a shelf by the coat rack. She glanced back at her mom, who watched her with that crooked smile of hers that filled her with joy and broke her heart.

The headsets were in her hand before she realized it, and she held them up in front of her mother. "Believe me when I say these contraptions scare me too. Actually, I'm wondering if they were manufactured in hell. I realize I've used them because I wanted to connect with the old you. But deeper than the coma you were in, I also see my selfishness. Back in Salem, you're on the wall of shame with some unforgettable characters, and I felt indicted too." She studied the headsets. "I wanted to know why you did what you did, but everything you've told me points in the opposite direction." She paused, feeling like she wanted to crawl behind her mother's eyes and explain. "I feel like I emerged from a coma too and feel ashamed. Guilty or not, you're still my mother, and I love you."

Rose reached for her and they embraced.

When her mother let go, she stood up and faced her. "This time, I'm putting the headset on you because I need to know what's wrong with me."

Rose held still while she adjusted the headset and then donned hers. Her racing heart drowned out the program music after booting up the system. Luckily, William had already connected the system to the network. Just as she went to launch the program, she suddenly hesitated, sensing a fork in the road. One was a brightly lit highway, with glitzy technologies and rational algorithms that would prove whether all the sessions were real. The other option was a narrow footpath through lush vegetation where everything was unscripted, but nothing impossible with the right heart.

She shut off the system, removed their headsets, and laid on the bed next to the woman that gave her life. The two held hands and stared at the same blank ceiling that held nothing but possibilities. Minutes passed, and she felt her eyes grow heavy and soon found herself standing in the middle of a dry riverbed. The sun sat directly overhead in a cloudless sky. Withered vegetation surrounded her along with a few bleached tree skeletons, their nakedness a terrible sight to behold. The intense daylight felt like a hundred-thousand-watt light bulb, forcing her eyes downward to the dried-out pebbles in front of her feet.

A hot sandblasting wind kicked up, and she hid her face in the crook of her arm. When it subsided, she found her mother kneeling beside her, and wearing the same bland nightgown that defined her life for years in a coma.

She crouched down and noticed how her mother's eyes were closed as she clasped the amethyst rosary beads.

"Mom!" she called out in her thoughts.

All she heard in reply were a parade of intercessions. "*Pray for us now and at the hour of our death,*" echoed in her ears.

The wind picked up again, but her mother did not move. She worried a nurse would wander into the room and end this dream.

She tried rousing her mother from her prayers. "Mom, please tell me all the places we visited, and all the conversations we had in the virtual world, were real?"

Rose opened her eyes and gave her a piercing look. "*Forgive those that trespass against us,*" she replied.

Is she referring to my apology or her guilt? Her mother looked blurry in the bright light and sand. "I'm sorry for abandoning you," Cassie whispered.

Rose did not reply and began clawing at the ground. The first few strokes merely swept away light-colored sand and pebbles, but after a few dozen attempts, her mother hit darker clay. Stopping to wipe away the sweat from her brow, she shot her a curious look.

"We condemn ourselves to Hell, and did that when I made the bottle my god. My faith was as dry as this dust. I also learned the door to Hell is locked from the inside, and it's too thick to hear those screaming your name wanting to help." She grabbed her hands. "My beautiful broken daughter, you have lived too long in fear like a leper yelling, 'Unclean! Unclean!' to all that come close."

Rose drove their hands into the dark earth, and they began digging in unison. Cassie felt the gritty silt invade her fingernails, and as the hole deepened, the clay slowly turned moist and then muddy. The progress emboldened her, and the silent marathon continued. The resulting sludge soon covered their arms, and shirts, and spit on their faces. Nearing the point of exhaustion, water began bubbling up and grew into a steady stream.

They stopped and washed their mud encrusted hands, arms and faces in the cool water that smelled of lilacs and roses.

When they were finished, her mother cupped her hands under the growing spring and took a sip. Refreshed, she offered her some.

Cassie drank deeply from her mother's hands and felt something inexplicable inside her shift.

CHAPTER THIRTY-SIX

THE DIRECTORY IN THE HOSPITAL foyer listed the cafeteria on the lower ground floor, but after taking the elevator down a level, she found herself in the catacombs. Walking down a long hallway of painted cement blocks, she wondered about the marketing spin for shunning the word 'cellar' to describe the location. Was it to keep people from feeling claustrophobic? Before thinking it through, the smell of bacon sweetened the stale air and she arrived at the commissary. After purchasing a cup of coffee, she set up camp at a side table, and kept her nerves in check by eavesdropping on the banter between a short-order cook and a couple of men wearing green scrubs. Their conversation receded into the background when she watched an elderly gentleman shuffle in rather aimlessly. He had a shock of white hair that looked like an oversized Q-tip, and apparently did not care a lick about his untucked corduroy shirt. His slow steps ended in front of a cooler holding a selection of fruit juices, soft drinks and water. She wondered about the circumstances that brought him here. *Did his wife take sick in the middle of the night, or did he just kiss her goodbye before surgery? I remember running into the emergency room after Dad called. We both talked at once and a few minutes later not at all.* She sighed studying the lost soul. *But I never ventured down here looking for nourishment. Why would I? The underground reached up and swallowed me whole.*

The old man took a flip phone out of the back pocket of his baggy jeans, and after answering the call shuffled away. *Life is so fragile*, she thought and remembered Marco Island in VR, and pawing through the broken treasures at low tide.

Returning to her coffee, she smirked thinking about the undrinkable concoction Kendra bought her. Her mom used to tease, *"why not have some coffee with your cream and sugar?"* She took a sip and let the bitter brew envelope her tongue and wondered when she grew to prefer this taste.

When her eyes roamed back to the food area, her heart skipped a beat. The woman, or more aptly, "the nurse that would not be named," was paying the young cashier for a yogurt and a bottle of water. *How appropriate*, she thought, *a breakfast of fermented milk and bacteria. The bottle of water represented a placeholder until she decided what she was thirsty for and then would text her Sugar Daddy.* She eyed the nurse's blonde hair pulled back in a tight ponytail and gritted her teeth until they hurt. *She has to count calories to keep that moneymaker figure of hers. It's a shame most of her assets were hiding under green scrubs or she could land a surgeon or an anesthesiologist. Then again, maybe they know she only dates ATM's.*

She took a deep breath and hurried over and positioned herself in the path for the exit. No beast this side of hell would get by her.

The nurse almost ran into her before looking up.

"Cassie?" Her dad's girlfriend exclaimed as her head snapped back like it bounced off a force field. The surprised look immediately turned to worry. "What are you doing here? Is everyone okay?"

She nodded, hating to ambush her like this, but could not think of a better way.

The woman's dark chocolate eyes narrowed, and she gripped the water so tightly the plastic crinkled in protest.

"Do you have a couple minutes?" She pointed at the table and the lonely Styrofoam cup of coffee.

The nurse glanced at the digital clock on the wall. "Sure, but my shift starts in ten minutes."

"I promise this won't take long," she replied and led her to the table.

When her invited guest sat down, the nurse opened the water bottle and took a quick sip. Her mouth felt dry too, but ignored the feeling as her eyes locked onto the plump pink lips her father kissed. *Ugh! They look a lot like Halle's.*

She cleared her throat and the troubling thought. "I'll be brief. As my dad probably told you, I've been reviewing all the details around my mother's accident."

"Yeah, he's mentioned it a couple hundred times," she replied and looked away, "but I never understood why you call it your mother's accident. Your father was in the car too and could have been killed or injured like the others. I also think calling it an accident clouds what really happened. Don't you?"

"What would you prefer I call it? An unfortunate incident?"

"Look, you can twist words into a pretzel but as a nurse working in the ER, I deal with the aftermath of tragedies like these. What went down that night sent five young souls to the morgue and sentenced others to life-long afflictions."

She clenched her fists under the table. "Don't forget it also sentenced my mother to solitary confinement for ten years. Every time I heard a silver alert, I thought of Mom because she was missing too. But hey, that's what she gets for driving drunk. Right? At least Dad recovered nicely! He calls the last ten years his second act."

She tilted her head and shot her a quizzical look. "What's this all about?"

"I want to ask—"

"How's your mother doing?" the nurse asked interrupting. "I read in the paper she woke up?"

Her head jerked back. "Is this a sick joke? Didn't my father mention it?"

She shook her head with gusto. "He gets upset whenever I bring her up." The nurse took another sip of water.

Cassie thought the woman's eyes suddenly looked glassy. "She's making a lot of progress but it's a long road back."

A long-painted red fingernail began peeling the white label on the water bottle. "Let me guess. You're here because you want to know my intentions, or rather, who will Charles choose?"

The bluntness stunned her and she could not even blink.

"I hope he's been clear it's none of your business. I am curious though. You have our address and phone number, yet you ambush me here at work. Why?"

"Point taken. To be honest, I thought surprising you might provide some honesty and prevent you from scripting the answers with my dad."

"Really? Do you think we haven't talked incessantly about this ugly situation? I told him years ago that if he didn't make a commitment, I would leave." She looked at the fat diamond ring on her left hand and smiled.

"My father told me about the ring. He said it was simply a gesture. You can't get engaged to a married man."

"Think what you want, but this is no friendship ring." She stroked the water bottle slowly. "I know how to make your father listen."

She pushed her chair away and studied the nearby counter housing a napkin dispenser, various condiments, and plastic utensils. She was confident she could quickly amputate all the hussy's fingers with a spoon.

The nurse waved to get her attention. "You didn't call me because you might have to say my name on the phone. I understand Charles has been teaching you the pronunciation for some time."

"My problem is I like the name Rachael, but it doesn't convey what I think of you."

"See how easy it rolls off your tongue?" She glanced at her ring. "Don't worry, though. I won't make you call me Mom after Charles and I get married."

A boisterous laugh echoed from someone in the kitchen underscoring the horrible idea.

"Look, I know you despise me so let's get this over with," her nemesis continued. "What's the question that has you sneaking around like a female James Bond?"

"When did you first meet my father?"

The nurse's eyes narrowed. "Are you channeling some junior high dance?" she replied with a sigh. "We met at the chamber of commerce dinner. My boyfriend was a member and we had a stupid argument during the cocktail hour. Roger stormed out and left me to fend for myself. I was starving and stayed for dinner. Your father sat at the same table, and we hit it off. We enjoyed each other's company. We still do."

She nodded. Her father attended every community affair trying to build his network.

"If you're asking if we fooled around before that awful night—" She stopped and pointed at her cup of coffee. "I think you'll need something stronger than that if you want to know more." She glanced back at the clock. "I have to get going."

"Yeah, that reminds me. I understand you were working the night of the accident," she said exaggerating the last word.

"Yes, and I try to forget the carnage." She reached back and started playing with the elastic on her ponytail like it was too tight. "Such an unnecessary waste of life."

"Did you treat my mother?"

"The ER operated like a field hospital in a war zone that evening." She shot her a slight smirk. "You're as bitter as the coffee here. Are you like this all day?"

"I'm surprised my father hasn't told you how I can be like a pit bull and can't let go. Did you treat my mother when they brought her in?"

"You don't get to pick who you help. Your mother presented with serious head injuries. We, meaning the entire team, did what we could to stabilize her before sending her to the OR." She stood up quick. "I really have to go but if you have any questions call me." She pointed at her name tag. "You know my name and your father has my cell number."

Standing, she thought her legs might fold. "Last question. If I pull the hospital report, will I find you managed my mother's care? I'd be really curious to know if it was you or a phlebotomist, that drew her blood for the alcohol analysis."

The nurse opened her mouth wide like she was going to say something and then turned away.

"Don't worry Rachael, you've already said more than enough."

CHAPTER THIRTY-SEVEN

SEEING HER HUSBAND'S JEEP parked behind a police cruiser in the driveway, sucked the air out of her lungs. *The cruiser was here before James arrived?* She hurried into the house, feeling like she was having one of those dreams where your feet refuse to cooperate.

There was an eerie stillness as she burst into the kitchen and found James and Sean seated at the kitchen table.

"Is-everything-okay?" she said in one word while noticing their empty coffee cups.

James spoke first. "Aces, but as usual you look like a ghost is chasing you." With the way he curled his lip, she knew he was still angry and now not happy playing host.

Meanwhile, Sean looked like he wished he was anywhere else. "Most people putter around the house on Saturday mornings, so I was surprised when no one was here when I first arrived."

"Well, we haven't been your typical family for some years," James chimed in. He stood up and walked to the counter and poured himself some more coffee. Halfway back to the table, he looked her way. "Want some?"

She shook her head. The coffee from the hospital continued burning her esophagus and wondered about the reason for this early visit. *Did Sean think James was at work?*

Her husband motioned to Sean. "How about you Detective? Another cup?"

"No, I'm trying to cut back," he replied and shot her a quick glance.

She sat down at the table and noticed James watching her. "Why don't you take your coat off and stay a while?"

"Yeah, good idea," she said and fumbled with the zipper.

"You must feel flustered coming home and finding me chatting it up with your old flame."

"A little, but nothing like how red your face turned at the reunion when I met Sandy." She winked at Sean. "Sandy used to play spin the bottle with him, and said James was unforgettable given his passion for sour cream chips." She looked at James and smiled. "But he's as thick as a brick regarding lessons learned. He tasted like an onion bagel when we first kissed."

The two men laughed and she relaxed a bit.

"Cassie hasn't eaten a bagel since," James said twirling the cup in his hands. "Have to admit, I've enjoyed hearing a few snippets about my wife's wild side from the detective." He shot her a look. "I'd like to meet her sometime."

The last few days ran through her head. "I'll introduce you when we go see my mom. I was thinking how she and Dad used to rent us a cabin in the summer up there. I remember visiting the Old Man in the Mountain." She found her husband's eyes and held on. "Too many freezes and thaws led to its collapse."

"Well, it wasn't for lack of trying," he countered. "I remember reading how they shored it up with cables but the erosion proved too great." James suddenly glanced at the cop, like he forgot he was there. "Sean told me about reviewing the files on the accident. Seems I've been out of the loop."

She shrugged. "No one will ever say you have a memory like an elephant because you can't find your car keys or wallet most days. I don't know how you survive managing a team, because we went over this. As usual, it went in one ear and out the other."

"Be gentle, poor hearing is a congenital thing with men," Sean said with a quick laugh, clearly playing peacemaker. "Just think of the marriages saved with GPS because we don't argue about stopping for directions anymore!"

"That's true," James added, "but there's certain rocky roads Cassie revisits again and again as if the pitch or the location will change."

This feels surreal, fighting a guerilla war while entertaining, she thought while reloading. "What brings you home this morning, honey? Your kid brother wouldn't wash your underwear?"

Her husband's eyebrows arched, a feat she rarely achieved.

The detective moved in his chair. "I stopped by for two reasons. The first is to give you a heads up that we've heard some new chatter about vengeance on your mother."

"Thanks to the *Insight's* barrage of Scud missiles," she replied.

"Just remember this is nothing new. These threats flare up every now and then. In the past, we added extra patrols around the nursing home. Given the change in your mother's residence, we shared the info with the authorities up in Jackson. I just wanted you to know."

"We appreciate it," James said to his coffee.

Sean nodded and turned his attention to her. "I also wanted to tell you I finished my review."

"I thought we agreed I would read the files and seek your counsel if needed?"

"Of course, but you also made it clear you didn't know what you were looking for. I thought I would take another look and see if anything stuck out."

In her peripheral vision, she saw her husband look up at the ceiling.

"I located all the missing photos too," he added with a smirk and glanced at James. "Cassie was pretty hard on me when she found out some had not been uploaded."

"Cassie hard on you? You're kidding me!" James deadpanned.

She ignored the comment. "After all this buildup, please tell me you found something."

"I won't go that far, but will classify it as interesting." He pulled out his iPhone and began swiping through pictures and then stopped.

"Exhibit one," he said holding the phone in front of her. It was a side view of the interior of the Mercedes after it slammed into the pole; airbag deflated, the dashboard split in half and the windshield shattered.

She studied the picture for a long moment before giving up and looking back at Sean. He gazed at her intensely like the way he did in high school whenever he wanted to go parking. She could feel her cheeks getting hot. *What is he doing?*

"See anything?" he asked softly.

She gladly looked at the picture again, knowing she was terrible at finding hidden items in a picture. "Nothing other than a totaled car," she whispered, "and lost lives."

"Look at the position of the driver's seat," the detective suggested.

She obeyed and noticed how it angled back like a recliner. "That's the way my dad drives. Head back, one arm on the wheel, the other drinking coffee or texting someone. Heaven help anyone that cuts him off."

"Understood, but take a gander at the driver's seat and notice the distance to the gas pedal and brake."

She stared at the picture. "It looks pretty far away, but maybe it's just the angle?"

"I thought so too." He swiped the phone a few more times and showed her a different image that did not take in the windshield. "I remember your mom being about five foot two?"

"Yeah, about that. Why?"

James suddenly leaned in and looked too. "Because the position of the seat is for someone my size," he said matter of fact.

She looked at her husband and for the first time in ten years saw doubt on his face. It must have given him a sudden headache because he rubbed his temple.

"Does this prove anything?" she whispered.

"I'm sorry, but no," Sean replied.

She jumped to her feet. "Why not?"

"Think about it. Maybe in extracting your mother from the driver's seat, they changed the position. The officer at the scene—"

"Dowd!" she interrupted.

He nodded. "Yes, Officer Dowd wrote in the report your father tried to rouse his wife before help arrived. So, maybe he moved the seat. But that still doesn't explain my biggest question."

"Which is?" she asked.

"The controls are electric and after slamming into the pole, did they still work?"

The three sat in silence thinking through the scenarios. "Can I scroll through the pictures," she asked?

"Sure, I uploaded all of them," he said, handing her the iPhone. She scanned through a dozen photos of bent steel, broken glass, bloodstains and empty nip bottles. The final picture was a shot taken from the back seat highlighting the shattered windshield and broken center console. Her eyes focused on a small space under the radio where you could store sunglasses or a wallet. She used her fingers and expanded the frame.

"See something?" the detective asked.

Cassie filled her lungs through her nose and worked on keeping a calm demeanor. Her mother's words of a near-death experience echoed in her ears. "*Everything is jumbled. A motherly voice is telling me it's not my time, that I have to leave the warm embracing light and go back to the cold and pain. In the background, I hear Charles crying, and Phil is trying to calm him down.*"

"Cassie?" Sean asked again.

"All I see is devastation," she replied, while thinking of pawing through the broken shells again at Marco Island.

CHAPTER THIRTY-EIGHT

THE SHINY BLACK GRANITE GRAVESTONE would never blend in with its gray neighbors. Neither would the man kneeling beside it, retrieving rotted leaves hiding behind a three-gallon pot of winter jasmine. At Ellie's funeral, the widower said he selected the high gloss finish hoping to frustrate Mother Nature's eternal kiss that muted everything. The poetic comment was typical of Uncle, but she knew if pushed, he would admit the black granite symbolized a hole that could never be filled, and the white cursive lettering of Ellie's name a testament to her angelic nature.

Standing a few plots away on the frozen grass, she could see Phil's lips moving, perhaps in prayer or conversation, or maybe a combination of both. She did not want to ambush him, because she had to slice him open meticulously for this autopsy. Since Mom's resurrection on Thanksgiving, the pendulum swung wildly between hope and doubt. But after Sean let her review the accident pictures, her spirit went deeper than all the graves at Pine Grove cemetery, to a place hotter than molten matter. Her anger would never cool into igneous rock.

She looked up at the swollen sky, its color matching the gray headstones. Showers were in the forecast for later in the day which would erase the remaining patches of snow. But no monsoon this side of hell could extinguish the fire she was about to light. Peals of lightning and the sharp crack of thunder beat her insides.

"Cassie?" a voice called out.

She found Phil facing her, his hands on his hips.

Walking over to join him proved slow, the cement might have left her heart but not her legs that plodded forward on the soggy ground.

"This is an odd place to run into you," Phil said trying to sound chipper but the way he scanned her and then the road, it looked anything but.

"Well, I stopped by the house and your next-door neighbor yelled over that I just missed you. He said I might find you here."

"I can't hide anything from Tim," he said shaking his head. "Ellie shredded our mail because she thought he went through our trash out of boredom. But it's no secret I come here a few times a week. It gets me out of the house, and I catch Ellie up on all the news." He pointed at the yellow grass with a work-gloved hand. "I'm tired of winter and can't wait to get my hands in the dirt again. I know it's early, but thought I could begin the spring cleanup."

His voice sounded unsteady, and that was understandable the way their last visit ended. The red down jacket hung on him like it was a size too big, and his hair still looked wild, but at least the cold air painted some color on his cheeks. Last time she saw him, his complexion reminded her of a yellow legal pad, and it looked the same today. Scanning his face, she noticed a faint smudge in the middle of his forehead.

"I see you're still a good Catholic boy and got your ashes today," she said pointing at his head.

He brushed off the top of the gravestone. "Not sure about good, but *dust thou art and dust you shall return*."

Well, before that happens, I need some answers, she thought.

"So, what's so important you had to track me down?" Phil asked quickly.

Cassie felt a shiver travel up her spine. "Every winter, I watch icicles form along the edge of my roof. Drip by drip some get so big, I'm afraid they will decapitate someone, so I knock them down, and they shatter or stab at the snow." She let the comment hang for a moment and scanned the cemetery. "But you never see icicles on any of these headstones. It makes me realize nothing else can be added or subtracted from their lives. Everything has been said and done." She leaned in. "But our stories are still being written. Lies are like icicles and can grow to dangerous lengths. Truth seeks to knock them down before they hurt the innocent."

Phil cocked his head listening. "Normally, I would tease you that's pretty deep for a Wednesday afternoon, but it makes me think of the weeks Ellie spent in hospice. We talked a lot about the past, and neither of us colored where we fell short." He looked away. "We shed some tears. I couldn't love her more."

How touching but is he playing me? she wondered. "I grew up calling you Uncle because you were like a member of the family. You and Dad were practically brothers growing up on the same street, going to the same schools, hanging out with the same gang, even dating the same girls."

Phil laughed. "Some called us Thing One and Thing Two. He had his eyes on Ellie, but I asked her out first."

She smiled. "Dad says he only told me ten percent of your adventures."

"Yeah, the rated G material."

"I can't let my mind go there," she said with a knowing smirk. "But it's crazy to think of the years you spent together in grammar and high school, and then college. I would think after being glued to one another for so long you would want a break, but then went into business together. It makes me question why you—"

"Yes, we've been like brothers," he interrupted. "What's going on here? Are we recording *This is Your Life*?"

Don't let him distract you, she thought. "Even after that horrible January night and all the chaos that followed, you didn't abandon my father."

Phil took off his glove and wiped one eye.

Say it! the voice inside screamed. "Given all that, I don't understand how you could betray our family."

"Betray? Are you kidding me?" He looked down at the ground. "We're not going there again. I had heartburn for a week after your last visit."

She pointed at his head. "You went to church today. Why?"

"You know why! It's the beginning of Lent."

"You may think I'm a heathen, but Mom drilled the details into me. Lent is forty days of prayer, fasting and almsgiving to prepare for Christ's passion and resurrection."

"You're reminding me of this because?"

"It's sacrilegious having a cross imprinted on your head like a devout believer, while for ten years you've let my mother carry the cross for your crimes."

He stepped back too quick and almost tripped on the pot of winter jasmine. "How dare you stand on sacred ground and make an insane accusation!"

"No, it's more like how can you stand on that saintly woman's grave and continue to lie? It's a wonder the ground doesn't open up and take you to the ninth ring of hell where all the traitors congregate." She pointed at the white cursive lettering honoring Ellie. "If I had a say, your name would be written in black."

"He shook a skinny fist peppered with liver spots at her. "You think you're scaring me? If you remember any of your father's stories, fear was afraid of us, because we were the storm! What are you blaming me for?"

"After you put my father in the back seat, you told my mother you would drive them home. It was you that hit all those people and then plowed into the pole."

Phil leaned against the gravestone for balance. "Then what? My ghost flew home? I know you like sci-fi movies but no one in Hollywood would buy this script. What makes you think I'm some mass murderer?"

"Because I saw your keys in the console of the Mercedes."

He fell silent, and his right eye twitched a couple times. "What keys?"

"When James and I were in Ireland a dozen years ago on vacation, I came across a keychain with the Walsh family crest and gave it to you at Christmas. That's how I know the keys were yours. Plus, you're almost as tall as my dad and the driver's seat was set for you not my five-foot-two mother. The only question I have is whether your nephew watched you transfer my mother into the driver's seat or he helped you? Either way, afterwards you took off through the snow and hid. I don't know how you looked my father in the eyes after that." She pointed at the grave. "Did Ellie know?"

Phil bent over and sobbed into his jacket. When he caught his breath, he waved her away. "You have it all wrong. Get out of here!" he screamed.

She stood her ground for her mother and watched the traitor stumble away through the silent residents.

CHAPTER THIRTY-NINE

HER IPHONE STARTED BLOWING UP an hour after the showdown at the cemetery, as her father left a half-dozen messages demanding she call him back immediately. She ignored the command so he could simmer in his own juices while she concentrated on getting lost in spreadsheets, word documents and Gantt charts.

Three hours flew by before she left the office. Driving home, she noticed the bright headlights of the approaching cars, they pulled on her eyes and reminded her of the nightmare of being blinded and hitting all those people. After the hundredth car passed, she suddenly realized the high beams in the dream illuminated what she did not want to see.

Making a U-turn, she headed for her father's house, and strangely the traffic thinned like this was the proper route, and the headlights of approaching cars no longer bothered her.

The condominium she avoided for years was a corner unit at the end of a long winding road that cut through the woods and gave the impression of being in the mountains. But the country vibe immediately disappeared the moment she got out of the car and heard the hum of the highway a mile away.

A police siren screamed in the distance as she made her way up the short brick walk and pressed the doorbell.

The approaching footsteps rattled the storm door before it opened, and seconds later her father stared at her from the other side of the glass. By the way his head jerked back, she knew he was stunned. It also made her question whether he would let her in. Seconds passed and she watched the chest of his black t-shirt rise and fall.

Finally, the door opened.

They were too much like each other and neither said a word. She followed him down a narrow hall, feeling like a stranger in her father's house. She never darkened his door before, and the reason for this visit amplified the feeling.

Entering the living room, her eyes took in a leather couch, large screen tv, and a gas fireplace. The glass coffee and side tables had a modern vibe, unlike the country taste her mother preferred.

She looked toward the hall which led to the kitchen. "Are you alone?"

"Who are you referring to?"

"I'm not playing your sick game tonight," she countered. Looking at his muscular arms, she wondered when his live-in would make him tattoo her name on his bicep just to piss her off. But this was not the hill to die on tonight.

"Fine. Is Rachel home?" she asked.

He flashed a smug smile because he kept score on everything. "No. She needs some alone time after you attacked her at the hospital. Rachael has a friend in Miami and is warming her bones while trying to forget both of us for a few days."

"Both of us? Don't tell me there's trouble in paradise?"

He pointed at her. "She thinks I didn't raise you right, for doing something so hurtful. We had words, and I got upset and took a five-mile run before calling you. Of course, you never answer, no matter how many times I try."

"Well, here I am, visiting your humble abode after all these years." She looked around. "I still can't believe you sold the house."

"Well, I didn't need so much space."

"Not to mention it would be weird if Rachael slept in Mom's bed."

"I see you remember her name when you want to hurt me." He retreated and sat down at the far end of the couch next to a glass table that displayed a framed picture of father and daughter in the front seat of the Yankee Cannonball at Canobie Lake Amusement Park. She was ten years old at the time and snuggled in the crook of his beefy arm. Mom refused joining them and took the picture before they slowly inched up a long wooden hill. *It feels like we've been on that ride ever since, and Mom's missed all the harrowing hills and dips. Now we may come off the track before reaching the station.*

She no sooner sat down, when her father got up and headed for the kitchen. Moments later, he returned with a couple of long neck bottles of IPA and handed her one.

He quickly drained a quarter of the bottle. "Why don't you answer the phone when I call?"

"Why don't you tell me the truth when I ask?" she replied with her own volley. She glanced again at the picture and remembered how much she adored him back then. He could do no wrong, and it triggered a pang in her throat. She took a swig of the IPA to sedate it.

"Phil called me an hour ago," he barked on his way back to the far end of the couch. "What was your New Year's resolution? See how many people will take a restraining order out on you this year?" He took a long pull on his beer. "From what I can tell the other day, your husband is pretty fed up too." He shot her one of his classic sarcastic grins. "If he throws you out, you can always stay here with us. We have an extra room and Rachael would love someone to try her fancy recipes out on."

The buckshot pushed her deep into the couch, and she glanced at the mantle and found a black and white pencil sketch of herself when she was seven. "You have it backwards, Dad.

With Rachael on the prowl in South Beach, I better hurry and order that pull-out couch James and I have been eyeing."

Her father hung his head. "That's the first thing you've said in quite a while I agree with. Given the grief she gets from you, I wouldn't blame her if she looked for a warmer climate and less complications." He held the cold bottle to his forehead. "You're nothing but a migraine sometimes."

The words extinguished any remaining threat of tears. "Did Phil say anything special you'd like to share?"

"I wouldn't use the word special to describe it. Showing up at Ellie's grave and asking more questions? That's unconscionable! You should be ashamed of yourself. He's grieving and a mighty sick man too."

"Sick with guilt," she replied.

"I promised not to say anything, but want to give you some heartburn. Phil has pancreatic cancer. He found out a few weeks after losing Ellie. My guess is he was so focused on her battle, he ignored all the symptoms." He shook his head. "It's stage four, and he refuses chemo. Makes me wonder if he just wants to get it over with and join his wife."

She looked at the beer, wanting to trade the rest for something stronger as she felt both empathy for the horrible disease, and dread he would take the secret to the grave. "That's terrible," she got out.

Her father slammed the bottle hard enough on the glass table to shatter it. "This ends now! Leave him alone."

"Fine. I'll take what I know to the police."

"There you go again! This is the crazy talk your husband can't stand. When are you going to let this fantasy go? I don't know if you need a shrink or a priest. Maybe holier-than-thou Julie knows someone that can cure both mind and soul."

"Until recently, I would see my doctor, and he would increase the meds that dulls everything. But I think the police would be more interested than a doctor, shrink, or priest in hearing Mom didn't drive that night."

He sighed. "So that's why you're here? Make a grand entrance and accuse me of being behind the wheel after hounding poor Phil?"

"I was headed in that direction until the other day, but no."

Her father sat back on the couch, and eyed her with suspicion. "Wow, what a relief! Now I can sleep tonight."

"Or maybe never again, because Uncle Phil drove the car."

"Why would you say that?" he asked softly.

She paused, expecting his reaction to produce a mushroom cloud over Salem. The soft words were strangely peculiar. "A combination of things, really. The photos of the car show the seat position too far back for Mom to reach the pedals. I also spoke with the neighbor who called in the accident after you and Mom hit the pole. She says she found footsteps in the snow the next day from the accident scene, which went through her yard and ended in the woods out back. But what struck me was a picture of the car with Phil's keys in the console. I know they're his, because I bought him the key ring in Ireland."

Her father sat silent for a long moment, and then got up and came over and sat down next to her. "Remember that silly game we played when you were young? You would name some object, and we would suddenly see it everywhere. One time you picked an owl, and when one took up residence in a pine tree in the backyard, you freaked out thinking it was hunting you. What I'm saying, is you're seeing connections between random things. For example, your mother liked her SUV because she could sit up high and see everything going on around her. She hated the Mercedes, and whenever she drove it— which was rare, she would sit on the edge of the seat. Given the number of first responders trying to extract her from the car, I'm surprised they didn't take an axe to the seat frame. As far as footsteps in the snow," he stopped mid-sentence to think for a moment, "I know from working construction that when you have to take a leak, you do what you have to do. One of the cops were probably juiced up from all the coffee working the midnight shift, and went into the woods to relieve himself. Did the neighbor notice any footsteps returning?"

"I think you're missing the point. She saw —"

"Footsteps ten years ago. Give me a break!" he said interrupting. As far as the keys, what does that prove? Phil and I were partners and saw each other more than our families. We were constantly in each other's car. He probably left the spare set there."

"I'm not one of your lackeys that has to nod and accept your bull. I suppose hiring Uncle Phil's nephew is a coincidence too? What about your sweet Rachael? Is it a coincidence she took care of Mom in the ER?"

Her father's cheeks suddenly turned purple like he was holding his breath.

She pointed at the framed rollercoaster picture. I remember you screamed at the top of your lungs because you thought we were plummeting to death, so for you to sit here calmly and explain this all away makes me know this is a coverup."

"I'd be happy to yell and raise the roof if you prefer?"

"Or, you can be straight with your daughter. If not, I promise as sure as I'm sitting here, I'll call Sean when I get home. I'm sure you remember my high school sweetheart? He still laughs about how you would sneak out and bang on the hood of his car if I spent too long saying goodnight. Sean's a detective now, and I asked him to review everything. He's suspicious about all these random connections. I haven't told him about Phil's keys or Rachael tending to Mom. Makes me think he will want to chat with you."

"I'll take my chances. In the meantime, I'll stop by and see the Chief. He always welcomes me. Last year, my company donated money for a new cruiser."

The smug look on his face confirmed what she already knew. There was no damming piece of evidence that would change his mind.

Her father drained the rest of his beer like he was through with her too. She needed a bigger weapon. *There's no way to fight his lies except with one as big,* she thought.

"I was hoping to convince you to level with me without bringing Mom into this."

He put the spent bottle down. "What are you talking about now?'

"Your applesauce sleep therapy scared not only me but your wife too."

"Are you really going to sit here in my house and accuse me of—"

"She told me Phil drove that night," she blurted out.

He jumped to his feet like a cattle prod kissed him in the butt. "Liar!"

She catapulted off the couch, and concentrated ten years of frustration by driving her finger into his barrel chest. "No, I'm broadcasting the truth! The mountain air cleared out the cobwebs, and she remembered a few key things about that night. I know the memories are real because they mirror what you told me. Mom won't tell you because she thinks you're covering for Phil. She's afraid what you would do if she came clean."

He eyed her and bit his lip. "She can barely talk never mind recount what happened ten years ago!"

"Which to her is the day before yesterday." She thought back on their first virtual reality session. *What can I say that would be vague enough but believable?* "She told me how she hurt her right hand trying to open the passenger door after the car slammed into the people on the bridge."

Her father came inches from her face and stared into her eyes like he was checking every corner of her soul. "You're making this up! She remembers nothing," he whispered.

She matched his intensity and stared back. "You can tell me the truth here and now, or wait until there's a knock on your door tomorrow," she said standing on tippy-toes. "In the meantime, I'll have Mom talk to Sean. Maybe you should call Rachael and have her arrange a bushel of Florida oranges be sent to the prison in Concord."

CHAPTER FORTY

SHE WATCHED HER FATHER'S BROAD SHOULDERS collapse before he shuffled down the hall. Minutes passed, and she heard cabinet doors opening and closing, and then he reappeared with a fifth of Jameson and two glasses. He poured a good two fingers in each glass and handed her one.

"Better drink up, because you will not like what I'm about to tell you."

She sat down and took a sip of the whiskey. It did nothing to calm her racing heart.

Her father joined her on the couch and addressed the glass. "The biggest mistake is mine because we shouldn't have had the party at Phil's house to begin with. No house party, no accident. Sure, we won a major contract that put our company on the map, but my best friend and partner was also dealing with Ellie's cancer and worried sick about it. It was selfish of me to push for the celebration. When Ellie decided on visiting her sister between treatments, I talked Phil into planning a celebration because I thought it would recharge his batteries." He rubbed his forehead, and took a deep breath. "At first, he refused saying he was spent, but I don't take no for an answer. Phil soon caved and agreed to host the party." He looked up to see if she was paying attention. "It turned out to be a fantastic celebration, but Phil took my advice a little too much to heart. He's always been a lightweight with alcohol and tried keeping up with me shot for shot."

She looked at the dark elixir that fueled the nightmare and placed the glass on the table. "Skip to the end. Did Phil drive?"

He looked away which confirmed it.

The admission made her dizzy, and she thought she might throw up. "Why would Mom let him drive given his condition?"

"I've asked myself that question every day for the past ten years. All I can figure is some people get loud when they're trashed, and others get super quiet. But you have to understand, Phil is a different breed. When he has too much to drink, he goes mute and that's the calm before the storm. After another drink or two, the needle on his compass goes nuts, and you wouldn't recognize the mild-mannered guy we all love. Little wonder back in college his nickname was Jekyll. Bottom line, your mother gave the keys to a quiet man and somewhere along the way Hyde took over." He took a gulp of the whiskey and put the glass down next to hers. "After he hit all the people on the bridge, your mother began screaming which woke me up."

She braced herself. "But you were drunk."

"Yet sober enough to know we were in trouble. I can still see your mother waving her arms at him, begging him to pull over, and Phil screaming his life was ruined. He must have been going ninety down Lawrence Road trying to run away from all the bloodshed. I didn't have my seatbelt on, and every time I sat up and pleaded with him to stop, the car would swerve and back down I'd go."

"Knowing every cruiser in town would look for him, he flew down a side street to hide and didn't realize it was a dead end. The police report says there were no skid marks so he was probably looking in the rearview mirror and never saw the pole," she said completing the story.

Her father nodded. "After the crash, my head hurt a lot. I smelled smoke and antifreeze and thought the car might catch on fire any second. Before I could move, Phil opened the door and pulled me out. We stumbled around to the passenger side and found your mother. Her head was a bloody mess and I couldn't find a pulse, but with brain fog from drinking and the concussion it's little wonder."

"Did Phil help you?"

"Are you kidding me? He was wailing so loud, I thought he might have a stroke. We both thought if she wasn't dead, it was seconds away."

"So, you moved a dying woman?" she asked as hot tears streamed down her cheeks.

He looked down at the floor and pulled on his hair with both hands. "I was crying and Phil continued howling. The sight of Rose knocked the drunkenness out of him. Ellie was in the fight of her life with cancer and needed her husband. He begged me to put Rose in the driver's seat. I remember swinging for his face and telling him to go to hell. Then Phil stumbled over and felt for a pulse on your mother, and then said she was gone. I fell to my knees, and Phil cried Ellie would be dead too without him."

She wiped her face on her sleeve. "Based on that sad but senseless logic you moved her?"

"Look, I was still buzzed and my head was ringing. All I knew was my wife was dead, and I loved my best friend and Ellie. I knew we only had a couple minutes before the police arrived, and I made a horrible decision."

"Horrible doesn't come close. The man wipes out all those people and then kills your wife and my mother and you give him a pass?" She jumped up and went over to the picture of her and her father on the rollercoaster and threw it on the floor and stomped on it. The sound of glass breaking said it all.

Her father watched silently until she was finished. "It haunts me every day. If I could go back—" He stopped and bit his lip. "I think part of me felt like I owed him."

Cassie's temples began pulsating. "Owed him?"

He got up and began pacing around the room. "When Phil and I were fifteen we thought we were invincible and did some stupid things. Sometimes, another neighborhood kid named Rick would hang around with us. He was a couple years younger and had a chip on his shoulder to compensate. Raging testosterone and cheap beer meant we were always competing to be king of the hill. Some of the contests were stupid like sticking our tongues to a flagpole like they did in *Christmas Story*, or borrowing our parent's car even though we were too young to drive." He picked up her glass and took a sip. "Life doesn't care if you're naïve, the consequences are the same if you play a game of chicken with a train."

"What do you mean?"

"It was a Friday in December, and we skipped school and bummed a ride to Haverhill. The sun was MIA, and we had just polished off a twelve pack of Bud when Rick saw the freight train approaching a good half mile away. He jumped up on the track and dared us to play chicken. Phil and I stumbled on to the track and stood next to him. I took the middle position which for obvious reasons is insane. I was fed up with the little punk and wanted to see him piss his pants. The train came toward us with its horn blaring, but Rick kept calling me a coward. Anger outweighed fear, and I would have stayed on that track and been runover if Phil hadn't grabbed me at the last second. The wind from the train blew us down an embankment and into some picker bushes."

"Okay, so you ended up with another tall tale and grateful to your best friend."

"That's not the end of the story. Phil and I ran for a mile before we stopped. Rick— or what was left of him was splattered across fifty feet of track." He sat down and buried his head in his hands and began crying in great sobs. "That kid was just trying to fit in."

She watched with no desire of providing comfort. "Did Mom know about this?"

He shook his head. "Not something to share on a first date or any day after."

Cassie waited for him to stop crying, and then got on her knees and grabbed his chin. "Look at me Dad. I don't get it. Mom didn't die that night, and you still let her take the blame."

He pulled away. "What does she know? She's been in a coma and left me to fight the mob."

"You?"

"Our entire family of course. I would have gone bankrupt if Phil hadn't helped."

"You mean paid you off," she replied and moved back to the couch. "If you owed your friend so much you should have gotten in the driver's seat before the police came."

He nodded his head like he never considered it. "I had no time to think, and I was trying to protect…"

"Your friend and business partner. I take it Officer Dowd figured things out when he arrived?"

"Given everything, it was a very lucky break. We just finished moving your mom into the driver's seat, when we saw the blue lights. Any other cop and this would have unraveled quickly. Phil and Brian yelled at each other a lot before more flashing lights arrived."

"Then you and Phil paid him off by hiring him."

"That's too simple an explanation."

"Really? Tell me how does Rachael figure into this grand scheme?"

He looked at her like it was odd to hear her say her name. "You already hate me enough so why say more?"

"Because the floor is gone, there's no light in this pit, and I'm sinking fast in the mud. Tell me, were you seeing her before the accident?"

He looked away.

"I'll take that as a yes. I don't want to hear how needy you were because Mom was making love to her wine. Rachael was on duty that night. What did she do to help you?"

"Kept Rose alive."

"I don't see your girlfriend as Mother Teresa's twin sister. Anything else?"

He closed his eyes and shook his head. "I didn't ask and don't want to know."

"Ah, ignorance is bliss and provides plausible deniability." Her mind shifted into the project management role and the questions kept coming. "Yes or no. Did you see Mom have anything to drink at the party?"

"No, but I wasn't with her all night. She could have snuck a few."

"The people I've talked with said she acted fine. No one saw her drink anything but ginger ale. How do you square the fact Mom's blood came back three times over the legal limit?"

He pulled on his lip.

"Did Rachael take a blood sample from you and submit it as Mom's?"

"No, and why would she? I wasn't driving."

"Neither was Mom! If you ask me, the blood sample came from either you or Phil."

"Like I said, the sample didn't come from me …and Phil was hiding in the woods.

"Anything else you'd like to get off your chest? Maybe how you were drugging Mom to keep her asleep?"

He got in her face, and she could smell the whiskey mixing with his cologne. "I may be guilty of a lot of things, but I didn't medicate my wife. I have enough guilt for ten lifetimes so you don't have to pile on any additional charges."

"If I were the executioner, I would put you and Phil in the electric chair for a few volts, then hang you until you turned blue, before letting the firing squad finish you off. Have you given any thought about the five people that died, and all the injured? Everyone thinks Mom is the daughter of the devil. How do you intend to make this right?"

"I don't know what to say. I can't turn Phil in, especially now that he's sick."

She heard Phil squawking in her ears. "Because you two are like brothers and would do anything for each other. But let's be honest, they would arrest you too."

"All I can say is I'm sorry."

"You're apologizing to the wrong person. Last time I looked there's quite a line."

"Take the emotion out of it for a second, will you? Your mother is improving but she still suffered brain damage. This will never go to trial, and if it did, we would have to come clean."

"That's easy for Phil. He will be dead."

He nodded too fast, and she realized he was trying to sell her on remaining silent.

"But until that day, we have to keep this secret. Think of the lives it would ruin," he continued.

Her mother's crooked smile came into her thoughts. "I am."

CHAPTER FORTY-ONE

SHE SURVEYED the box of tissues perched on her stomach and the half dozen paper balls scattered across the floor. An angry spring from the ten-year-old couch knifed her in the back again but did not stop the perpetual mental loop of her father's confession.

James sat on the couch cradling her feet in his lap and gently rubbing them. From time to time, he would stop the massage and give her a quick glance, but mercifully remained silent. She recalled being eight months pregnant with William, and how her feet and ankles looked like they had been grafted from an elephant. James worked on them every night hoping to provide some relief. It helped little, but she felt like he was in her corner. Tonight, felt the same. She made it home before the Jericho walls came tumbling down, and she collapsed in his arms and relayed what her father said in fits and starts.

She closed her eyes and concentrated on the tenderness of her husband's hands. Unlike her father and grandfather who worked construction and counted calluses as marks of pride, his hands were soft as velvet. *Maybe that's why Dad didn't like James even after Mom pointed out his many admirable qualities*, she thought. Opening her eyes slightly, she studied his tired expression and realized once again how he pushed himself just as hard as the carpenters, electricians, and plumbers her father employed. When she took the time to observe him working rather than bark dinner was getting cold, or they were late for some engagement, she would sense how his mind and hands became one with a PC board or computer. Different than blue-collar work, but the end results were the same when it becomes the number one priority and results in silent nights between husband and wife. She understood how the demands of a career can momentarily leapfrog family plans and schedules, but the last year felt different, like they shared an address but lived independently.

James ran his hand along the front of her right foot and slowly up her ankle and massaged her calf muscle. Suddenly, Halle was sitting on the other side of him, and placed her long tanned leg on his lap. *Which would he choose?*

She bolted upright.

He cocked his head and stared at her like he did when analyzing something he did not understand. "If it helps any, I can rub your back instead."

She stretched her arms to the ceiling trying to find the edge of his microscope slide. "Thanks, but I'll take a hot bath instead."

"You should eat something first."

She shook her head in reply.

James stood up, and she could not remember the last time he looked this concerned for her. She thought the reservoir was tapped out but a few new tears welled up.

He heard the sniffles and sat back down. "I can make you a sandwich or call in something. Just name it."

How about Halle's head on a platter," a funny voice inside recommended. "Maybe later," she replied instead. "I feel nauseous right now."

"Good. That gives me time to deliver the Molotov cocktails to your father."

"That's just what we need, more press."

"Don't worry, I intend to sue the *Insight* for harassment too." His eyes bore into hers, and she looked away.

253

He touched her arm. "You need time to process everything, but any idea what you'll do?"

"For now, open a bottle of wine because the sight of IPA or whiskey would make me hurl."

James let out a short laugh. "You and your one-liners. We could go on the road, and I'd be your set-up man."

"Beats selling your soul to make a buck."

"Maybe you're right," he replied and slowly nodded. "I got the product launched on time and under budget. It's not fair they moved the goal line on me."

Any other day, she would have pounced but did not have the energy. "What's the latest on the medical application?"

"They tried it on a few stroke victims, and it didn't go well." He shrugged. "Which means little without further testing and analysis. Maybe a few software tweaks will do the trick. If not, a re-engineering project will be required to determine feasibility. It's disappointing after what you experienced with your mother even if it …" He stopped mid-sentence. "Sorry. This isn't the night to go there."

She grabbed his hand and longed for the days when they sat and just talked. Back then, the tv was the only thing in the house feeling lonely. "Look, I can't explain what happened when I used those headsets on my mother. I know the Mister Spock inside you will consider nothing like telepathy, or divine intervention, or anything that isn't hardware married to software. All I know, is if she didn't tell me what happened, I would never have re-examined everything and uncovered this mess."

His mouth began moving and then stopped as he reconsidered how to reply. "I always thought we'd both feel right at home living in Missouri because it's the 'Show-Me' State. I'm familiar with the literature on telepathy, as our developers used some of the known studies in developing the algorithm. But your experience goes way beyond that and leaves me wondering if you've taken a sip of your mother's Kool-Aid in categorizing this as a miracle."

"Whenever I confronted Mom about unexplained things growing up, she would counter *that faith is the realization of what is hoped for and evidence of things not seen*. Faith is an integral part of Mom, and when she tried passing it on to me, I balked. Still, I can't shake the feeling that something bigger than us is at play here. I mean for her to wake up after all these years, and then in the weirdest way help me discover the truth?" She thought for a moment. "It sure wasn't my prayers. Maybe Julie's faithfulness unlocked something."

He squeezed her hand. "I'll file it under unexplained. But now that we know the truth, I owe you an apology. I regret sorry only comes in one size. If it weren't for your tenacity—" His voice broke and he looked away.

She closed her eyes because the end did not justify the means. James would never condone that she lied to her father to trick him into telling the truth.

"Resentment is a terrible thing," James suddenly added.

She half heard the comment because she was picturing her father and Phil hurriedly transferring the severely injured woman into the driver's seat. After so much death and destruction, this should have made the earth shiver and open up and swallow them. She opened her eyes and studied her fingers intertwined with her husband's. Touching yes, but weakened by bitterness.

"I have an unbiased perspective on the damage that's been done to us," she offered softly.

"I know you may have trouble believing me with all the rocks we've hurled at each other, but I do love you."

The words shredded her throat. "I love you too," she replied hoarsely.

He squeezed her hand. "There were many days I felt resentful and questioned our future. I understand now the wounds in our marriage were not self-inflicted. It makes me regret the things I said and furious at—"

She kissed him softly before he cursed her father and adopted uncle.

"Well," he said looking at her with wet eyes she did not recognize. "This coverup has to be exposed for what it is."

"The truth will rock the town!"

"No more than the lies already told. If I were in your shoes, I would have dropped a dime on Daddy and his BFF."

"That's because you haven't seen your father in twenty years," she replied.

"Divorce does that sometimes."

"Well, I'd trade you today. I'll never understand how my father lives with himself."

"Don't ask me," he countered. "I never understood the guy."

She looked at his wedding band of gold. Besides keeping the lie secret, she also left out the part about her father's affair with Rachael. It felt too close.

Her iPhone buzzed on the couch, and she gasped. It was her father.

"Do you want me to answer it?" James asked reaching for the phone. "I think you've had enough of him for multiple lifetimes. I've been in the bullpen warming up for this and ready to bring some heat."

It's rare for James to suit up like a knight, but I'm a lot stronger than he gives me credit for. She picked up the phone and answered. "I have nothing left to say to you."

"It's over," her father slurred apparently not concerned with the dismissal.

Ah, the first of many casualties to come. Cassie pictured Rachael strutting along a nude beach in Miami, flipping her blonde hair at some muscle head with a spray-on tan. A real cougar if there ever was one.

"Can't say I'm sorry to see her go. Maybe you should think about joining my boycott club and never refer to her by name again."

The line went quiet for a few seconds. "You're jumping to conclusions like always. I should marry Rachael just to hear you call her Mom."

"But you'd have to divorce your wife first. Then I could refer to Rachael as my evil stepmother or the hundred other names I have in mind."

"Whatever. I don't have time for this because I need your help. Phil just called me, and says he's on the way to the police station."

"Why? Did he run over someone else?"

"Not funny, Cassie! Look—"

"I hope he's going there to request protective custody," she said interrupting, "because I intend on haunting you and Phil until you do what's right."

"Did you call him on the way home? Is that why he's turning himself in?"

"No. I was so discombobulated I could hardly drive."

"Then exactly what did you say at the cemetery that made him come forward after all these years? Did you tell him your mother remembered he was driving?"

Be careful, she thought. "No, but maybe he defrosted his conscience enough, and thought he should confess now or risk the consequences on the other side. Mom believes in seeking mercy this side of the grave, and I know he wants to spend eternity with Ellie." She bit her lip thinking how her father was probably pacing around the condo with a fifth in one hand doing damage control, instead of being on his knees begging for forgiveness. If his shadow ever darkened a church, it would be to inquire how big a check he needed to write for absolution.

"I told him to wait until morning and let me come over and discuss it, but he refused," her father continued.

"That's because he knows you're a bully and will twist his arm."

"So, I'm supposed to sit back and let him destroy what's left of his life?"

"Give me a break! This is about you protecting you."

"Hear me out. Like I said, what good will it do? It changes nothing."

"Except clear your wife and my mother!" Cassie glanced at James sitting on the couch. He looked like he was watching a horror movie. "Phil's turning himself in," she mouthed and put the phone on speaker.

"Your mother's reputation has been trashed but so hasn't ours. Phil coming forward won't change that. Everyone in that car is complicit. Like I keep saying, your mother's better off in La-la land where the law can't touch her."

"I'm hanging up now," she said.

"Sure, go ahead. I could have dialed a random number and received more sympathy than what I'm getting from my daughter."

"And while you're making random calls, if you come across a real father type, someone that does what's right no matter how the chips fall instead of framing a woman he vowed to love and cherish, let me know. Maybe he'd like to adopt me too. It would be an easy gig."

"Shut your mouth."

"Mom said more than once she hoped you would take the road to Damascus."

He snickered. "I told her while I waited for Jesus to show up and knock me off my horse, I would build a few strip malls and make a couple bucks. I can't believe you're treating me like this."

She closed her eyes. The reel of what her father and uncle did started playing again.

"Look," her father continued in a measured tone. "Phil is sick, and it's coloring his judgment. Maybe you have a point.

He's afraid he won't be around and wants to make things right. He promised not to involve me and will stick by the story I was unconscious when he moved your mother."

"How can he? You were his partner in crime."

"Stop it!" he yelled, cutting her off. "You can put on your black robe, and judge me some other day. Right now, I'm calling as your father and asking you to get hold of your detective buddy, have him explain the ramifications to Phil before he signs any confession. If you ask me, all he would have to do is tell Phil they don't sell bottled water in the prison commissary and he will have second thoughts."

"I'm thinking you must have finished the whiskey, because you're out of your mind if you think I will do that."

"I'm asking you to put family first."

"I am!"

"What if I hadn't told you what happened? Would you be standing by me now?"

The lie she told resurfaced, and she took a deep breath. "But Mom told me who was driving. All I know is you should have clobbered Phil when he tried moving her."

"Then I will go down to the station myself and help Phil."

"Sure, why not add a DUI and another count of obstruction of justice to your rap sheet?"

He hung up.

James shot her a weird look. "Why didn't you tell me your mother remembered Phil was driving?"

"It's complicated," was all she could reply.

CHAPTER FORTY-TWO

THE PROJECT REVIEW MEETING droned on with the usual grenades exchanged between Sales and Marketing regarding customer needs. Instead of attempting to find kernels of agreement from both camps, she asked Ron, the financial analyst, to provide an update on the R&D spend. Ron no sooner introduced the first PowerPoint slide, when she noticed a few people in the back of the conference room whispering. A minute later, the virus spread and a half-dozen colleagues were glancing at their iPhones and then at her.

A colleague suddenly tapped her on the arm and directed her toward the conference room door, where Ray stood and motioned for her to step out.

Her manager wore his emotions on his sleeve, and it did not take a degree in psychology to read his mood. Ray paced when anxious, rubbed his beer belly if hungry, and growled on the rare occasion someone pissed him off. But this morning, his pouting lips displayed pity, and the last time he unrolled that wrinkled expression, it was because the summer intern had a kidney stone attack during a department dinner.

"What's up?" she asked and stood next to the cement wall in case she needed support.

"Is the meeting almost over?" He looked past her into the conference room.

She glanced back, and everyone was looking their way.

"Almost," she replied, returning to face him. "Just reviewing the project spend."

He nodded. "I see we have an audience. Let's go talk in my office."

Cassie hesitated, wondering if she should retrieve her laptop and project files, but did not want to add any more drama to the moment. Her colleague Cheryl would safeguard them.

They did not talk on the way to his office, and when they got there, he closed the door. This was never a good sign, though he was not the type of manager to pull her out of a meeting and fire her. He would do that professionally and without fanfare.

"Look, this is none of my business," he began, "but I wanted to give you some space because the internet is blowing up this morning."

She nodded. "I assume it's because my father's business partner came forward and admitted he was behind the wheel and not my mother."

Ray sat back in his leather chair. "So, you know?"

"My father told me last night." She worked on keeping a neutral face, though her eyes said enough from not sleeping a wink.

Her manager's expression softened. *So, this is how a real father acts*, she thought.

"I can't believe you came in this morning," he said leaning toward her.

"I didn't think I had a choice given—"

"I'm not that much of an ogre," he said interrupting.

"No, and you have been very understanding given all my absences."

He sighed. "I strive to be fair with everyone on the team. That said, we've worked together for several years and I respect— no, admire, the way you handle yourself despite what you've been through."

"I appreciate that."

"It's truly remarkable, and I doubt I would have handled it with as much grace." He pushed his leather chair back, and looked out the window which featured a meadow of yellow grass. "Many people are going to owe you and your family an apology." He looked back at her and shook his head. "Cases like this is why I'm against capital punishment."

She nodded in reply, still wondering if her mother had come out of the coma while Ellie was still alive, if Phil would have come forward. Her father would not have, too mesmerized by the buxom blonde.

Ray leaned forward in his chair. "You need to take some time off and deal with the consequences of all this."

"Thanks, but I'm fine."

The fatherly concern disappeared and the mid-level manager returned. "Unfortunately, this is more than an ask. We can't turn this place into a soap opera, with tv crews outside. Senior management will flip their lids."

"Okay, then let me work from home."

He sighed. "I applaud the work ethic but you'd be a distraction to your colleagues. Did you see the way they were watching you when you left the room? I don't want you taking vacation time so let's classify the next couple weeks as …"

"Collateral damage," she said filling in the blank.

CHAPTER FORTY-THREE

THE BRISK MARCH WIND made the long hike to the end of the employee parking lot feel like she was wrestling with Mother Nature and losing badly. She no sooner unlocked the car door when her iPhone buzzed, and she saw it was Sean.

She let it ring a few times before answering in order to catch her breath. When she said hello, Sean was already talking. "I had yesterday off and didn't hear the news until this morning."

"She did not respond before he was off to the races again. "You sound flat, Cassie! How are you? I bet flabbergasted doesn't cover it."

"You got all that from hello?" she replied. "Yeah, I feel shellshocked."

"Me too, especially since you thought your father was the guilty one."

Guilty? she repeated the word in her thoughts and pictured her father helping his friend like an evil Simon move Mom into the driver's seat. "I've spent a lot of time in the last twelve hours thinking about accountability."

"I can't imagine what you think now of your adopted uncle."

She rubbed her head, contrasting how Phil tended to a sick spouse, while Dad lived it up and turned on the crocodile tears when threatened. It made her feel nauseous. "No, you can't."

"I understand he's pretty sick, and that's why he came forward."

"That and I saw his keys in the Mercedes."

"What are you talking about?"

"I should have said something the other morning, when you stopped by the house and showed us pictures from the scene. I saw his keys in the car's console and figured he was involved."

The line went silent for a long moment. "I don't understand. How did you know they were his?"

"Because I bought the keychain for him," she replied matter of fact. Her head throbbed and though she owed him an explanation, she did not want to disclose everything yet, especially the lie she used as a crowbar to unseal the ugly truth.

"You sound exhausted, but must be relieved your father wasn't responsible."

She bit her lip to not say more and rounded the mental wagons. *I need time to think through what I should do.*

Sean picked up on the pause. "Look, this call is both personal and official. Phil won't sign the statement until he talks to you. I know this is quite unusual, but with all the media attention this is getting, the Chief wants to button things up fast."

"How did the news get out? Some disgruntled cop at the station?"

"You don't know?"

"Know what?" she asked and thought about exiting the car and standing in the brisk wind so some of the stress could be blown off her.

"Your father went on cable news this morning, and said Phil told him the truth a couple days ago. He claims he had suspicions for years but with Phil fighting a terminal disease, he convinced him to confess."

She opened the car door in case she got sick. "He took credit for all this?"

"Yeah. He said it was a great day for justice, and for his critically injured wife who had been the target of so much hate.

Then he donned a halo by saying he would pray for his friend who caused so much death and suffering."

"Pray? He considers that the ultimate four-letter word."

"Pretty epic, isn't it? It makes me wonder why he went public. Maybe trying to get ahead of the frenzy and cement future business? All I know is a couple more interviews like that and the selectmen will put his statue on the state line. I can see it now: welcome to Salem, New Hampshire— home of Saint Charles."

"I'd rather see his mug next to the word surreal in the dictionary."

"So, what should I tell the Chief? It's no issue if you don't want to do this."

"I'm on my way," she replied, hoping Dad would be there too so she could take them both out at the knees.

"The tv crews are out front, so come around back," he advised.

***

Ironically, the designated meeting room ended up being the same one she and Sean used to review the accident files. Cassie looked through the door and saw Phil seated at the table with his hands folded. He must have gotten a haircut before he turned himself in, because the wild white locks were now short and tamed. He wore a crisp white button-down shirt, tan khakis and his signature loafers. He looked like a colleague from work, except Phil's complexion was the color of a manila envelope.

Phil looked up when she entered the room and gifted her a weak smile.

She took a seat opposite the man she once called Uncle and searched his face. Besides the jaundice, the skin looked so strangely tight that if he were a conceited man, she would think he had BOTOX injections. *How did he escape the worry lines of guilt? Then again, how did Dad?*

"Thank-you for coming," he began softly.

"Says the gutless monster. I'm here so you will autograph the horror story for the police. After that, you can rot in hell," she blurted out in a hoarse voice.

He looked down at his folded hands and nodded. "I deserve that, Cassie. Believe it or not, there's nothing you or anyone else can say that will match what I've already said to myself."

"Is that supposed to make me feel better?"

Phil sat back in the chair and looked at the textured ceiling, as if waiting for the acrid smoke from the insults to clear a bit before continuing.

"Why did you want to see me? Didn't I say enough at the cemetery?"

The prisoner continued gazing at the ceiling. "I know everything will be chaos for a while, and the fake news will make the rounds touting unnamed sources, so I want you to hear this from me. I'm truly sorry."

She heard enough and got up to leave, when suddenly she recalled her father's halting confession and questioned how much he twisted the details into a shield of self-preservation. She sat back down.

"My father told me everything," she began. "Basically, Ellie was staying with her sister, so you hosted the company celebration, got blitzed, and then went haywire driving my parent's home. Seems you have a history where too much booze makes you crazy."

"That sounds like your dad barking in bullet format, but the truth is a bit more nuanced."

"How so?"

"Facts aside, I question who took advantage of the situation."

"I will not defend my father, but he went along with your plan to frame my mother because he owed you."

"Owed me?" Phil asked.

"Yeah, because you pulled him off the train tracks before he got run over like the other kid."

Phil screwed up his face. "Your father would make a dangerous historian."

She stared at the pine table between them and smelled stale coffee and some sickening cologne. Phil must have spritzed all his clothes, thinking it would have to last until the embalmer came calling.

"Look I'm not getting into ancient history," Phil said sounding exhausted. "Like you know, I love him like a brother and would do anything for him. When some big contracts were canceled because of the publicity, I helped him out financially so he could make payroll."

"I know that."

"We were still struggling, and Ellie needed me, so he offered to buy my half of the business. It was all hush-hush and I stayed on part-time because I needed the health insurance." He thought for a moment and looked away, like he needed a moment to consult the script. "But given everything, if the situation were reversed, I would not have taken advantage of him and paid pennies on the dollar for the business I helped build."

"You're sitting here facing multiple counts of vehicular homicide and want to review the business arrangement with my father? Are you for real?"

"Just trying to give you the full perspective."

"Well, how about concentrating how you and your partner in crime framed my mother?"

He nodded. "We didn't think she would live. I was afraid if we didn't do something drastic, neither would Ellie."

"How about the stain on my mother and our family?"

"Charles knew the price."

"Yeah, thirty pieces of silver and payback for the freight train. Tell me did your wife know?"

"That's why I'm sitting here, because you reminded me at the cemetery of promises made. Like I said, when Ellie was in hospice, we talked about the past, and neither of us colored where we fell short." His eyes filled. "Confessing to the world is nothing compared with the pain I saw on her face. Ellie was so upset, she refused to let go until I promised on making things right."

"But you didn't."

"I was a coward for months. Every time I went to her grave, she beat me about the ears, and I kept promising to come clean once I got my affairs squared away. The cancer put an exclamation point on that. When your mother woke up, I was terrified Rose would point the finger at me. That's why your dad and I pulled a few strings, and had my cousin Madelyn move into her room to monitor things. She was supposed to be an advanced warning system."

"She was a plant! Are you kidding me?"

"No, but it was a bust. Madelyn fell in love with Rose and told us to leave her out of it."

"Level with me. Did my dad feed my mom applesauce laced with sleeping pills?"

"What are you talking about?"

She waved him away.

He let out a long sigh, and they sat in silence for a moment. "I simply want to apologize for everything."

"What do you want from me? Forgiveness? I'm at the end of a very long line, the people you killed, all the injured, what you did to my mother. I doubt there would be any ashes left for me to forgive after that bonfire."

"Perhaps. But I'm begging you to keep quiet about your dad's involvement."

"Why? He's on tv throwing you under the bus and taking credit for everything."

"He's doing that to recover what your family has lost."

She looked at him sideways. "Are you telling me the truth or did he put you up to this?"

Phil shook his head but avoided her eyes.

"My question is who owes who?"

CHAPTER FORTY-FOUR

OPENING THE FRONT DOOR, a bouquet of white and yellow daffodils greeted her. Before she could take in their delicate fragrance, she sucked in her breath realizing who was holding them. In the next instant, her eyes fell from the bell-shaped flowers to the woman's right leg— or where it used to be.

"Good morning Mrs. MacLean," the fiftyish woman with a Dutch-boy haircut said in an overly bright tone. The greeting sounded alien coming from the woman that in every interview sounded like angry peels of thunder.

At a loss for words, or more accurately afraid anything she said would result in a savage beaning with the red clay pot, she simply smiled.

"You may remember me," the woman continued. "I'm Tanya Lagasse."

"Of course, and please call me Cassie," she replied as her smile collapsed in coming face to face with the spokesperson for the dead and the injured. In the first few years after the tragedy, she led weekly rallies outside the nursing home, demanding her mother be moved to a prison hospital. She heard through the grapevine Tanya was on the speed dial whenever the *Insight* wanted to kick the hornet's nest. Last summer, the accident victim made the front page of the paper standing in front of the courthouse and holding up her prosthetic leg.

"These are for your mom, and please call me Tanya." She handed her the plant.

"For my mother?" she asked trying to hide the surprise in her voice. *Did hell freeze over or maybe she thought Mom died and wanted to celebrate?*

"Yes, and I hope she likes them."

"They're absolutely beautiful," she replied and motioned toward the dead grass in the front yard. "It might be spring, but we need some April showers to wake nature up." She looked at the smiling woman and wanted to snap a picture of her, because James would think she imagined this too. "Mom is living in northern New Hampshire now, where winter likes to hang around until May." She put extra emphasis on the word living.

Tanya nodded and continued grinning. Beside admiring her brilliant white teeth, the awkwardness between them grew faster than the coming dandelions.

"Would you like to come in?" she felt compelled to ask.

"Yes, for a few minutes. Thank-you."

She let her in and thought about taking her coat, but hoped for a short visit and headed straight for the living room. She brought along the potted daffodils as a reminder of the olive branch.

"Would you like something to drink?" she offered as they sat down on the couch. "Coffee or tea or a soft drink?"

"No thanks," the unexpected guest spit back like a machine gun. She noticed how the woman sat on the edge of the couch. Her right hand gripped the cushion like a tornado might come through the living room any moment. Out of caution, she planted her feet on the floor in case things went south.

The mystery woman pointed at the coffee table. "I went round and round in my head regarding what to buy. The florist suggested daffodils."

Something inexplicable in her soul told her not to take her eyes off the woman with the flushed face. *Was she nervous or hot from the wool coat?* "They're beautiful," she repeated as a filler.

"I selected them," Tanya began in a matter-of-fact tone, "because they represent rebirth and forgiveness."

She noticed the woman's mouth suddenly trembling. "After a long winter, it's the perfect flower," she replied.

"Maybe so, but my reason centered on rebirth and forgiveness," she repeated. "Life is strange. Remember that old adage, 'never say never?' I would have bet my missing leg on never darkening your door, or talking with you except in a courtroom. But here I am."

"Yes, here you are," she replied with a quick nod.

"I've been mesmerized by the news this week."

Help her through this, so she will leave, she thought. "Haven't we all? I never knew you could feel so many emotions at the same time. Within five minutes I cry, laugh, and sob again. Having my mother awake and found innocent is beyond my wildest dreams."

The woman nodded, and her green eyes became glassy. "I read the article in the *Tribune*. What you and your husband and son have been through really touched me. You came across as a soulful daughter."

"If I have one complaint, it's that I came off looking better than I am. My mother deserved a better daughter than me. I'll never be able to appropriately thank Kendra Jacobsen enough, in reviewing everything about that night and writing a piece from my perspective. I'm also grateful to Detective Phelan."

"I heard the police want to question Brian Dowd?"

She replied with a shrug. Trying to remain the good uncle, Phil protected his nephew in the confession by saying he finished moving Rose before Dowd arrived. Nevertheless, questions remained. *Dowd will probably show the police the pictures of his fake daughter too,* she thought.

"Your father must be devastated his lifelong friend and partner did this to him."

She clenched her jaw and studied the plant. Kendra asked a lot of questions about her father and so had Sean. She got the sense they both knew there was more. What she would do, she still had not decided.

"After hearing the news and reading the piece about you, I wanted to apologize in person." Tanya hesitated and bit her lip for a long moment, trying to regain her composure. "I not only lost a limb that night but my marriage got run over too. After Kurt left me, I would have volunteered to put the noose around your mother's neck, inject the needle, or flip the switch." She touched her artificial leg. "I also deeply regret the anonymous hate letters I mailed you." Taking a deep breath, she pointed at her chest. "It's only by acting on the truth that we can seek forgiveness. I'll admit, there were some dark nights when I sat outside the nursing home with the means to be your mother's executioner."

Her stomach felt like it was in an elevator descending way too fast. *I don't need to hear another confession,* she thought. Her eyes scanned the wool coat for any weapons she might be packing.

"I've done a lot of thinking," Tanya continued, "and believe justice cannot be denied, even if it takes time. It's one thing to lose a limb, but more tragic when you lose part of what's in here," she said pointing at her heart again. "Anger, sadness, bitterness, resentment leads not only to hardening of the arteries, but a sepsis of the spirit."

Cassie drank in the pained words. "I went through the same emotions even though I wasn't on the bridge that night. I kept my husband and son at arm's length, and though Mom was in a coma, she felt my alienation too. Kendra captured it beautifully in the article by saying some scars never show up on an x-ray. It changed who I am, but also taught me over the last few months to use my head but follow my heart. If I follow my mom's lead, I'll find my soul too."

"I'm sure there's been some strain with your father."

"Sure," she replied wanting to roll her eyes. "There's still a lot to work through."

"The article said little about him."

She shrugged. "Like I said, there's no shortage of pain to work through."

"Coming back to your mother, I think of her like one of these daffodils, beautiful and innocent. But I wonder why she let that man drive the car."

The U-turn was so rapid she felt the whiplash. "Excuse me?"

"Why did she get in the car if her husband and his partner were blitzed?"

"Mom is getting better and hopefully will remember what happened that night. From what I know, Phil Walsh did not appear under the influence."

"Well, even if she's guilty of bad judgement, she's paid a terrible price. The misplaced hatred bothers me most." Tanya's words were sharp like broken pieces of glass. "I would like to ask her forgiveness when she's well enough to see me. In the meantime, I seek yours."

Her internal bells continued ringing, and she could not put a finger on why. She looked at the clock on the wall and calculated William would not be home for hours yet.

"Cassie?"

She looked back, and Tanya was watching her intently. "My mind is all over the place these days. You don't need my forgiveness. I understand you were coming from a place of intense pain. I'm sure my mother would agree too."

"I tried to see your father."

She moved up on the seat. Tanya was a good thirty pounds heavier than her but she could outrun her to the door. "Oh?"

"I stopped by his office this morning, and they said he wasn't in, but I think he didn't want to see me."

"He's in the field a lot," she replied. *Why do I still cover for him?*

"I want to speak with him about that night, and also the conflicted feelings I have for Phil Walsh."

"I get conflicted! I called the man Uncle my entire life."

"Let me explain," Tanya continued. I never made a lot of money working as a cashier in one retail store after another. After I lost my leg, I couldn't work much because of the pain and was about to get evicted when an anonymous donor started sending me a thousand-dollar money order every month."

"A thousand bucks? For how long?"

"Every first of the month for ten years." Tanya said flatly.

"You didn't know from who?"

"I do now. Phil Walsh turned out to be my benefactor."

"What?" Her eyes bulged.

"It was a mystery until six months ago. Phil mistakenly put an address label on the envelope. I figure he must have been doing bills and got things mixed up."

The air went dead for a moment. "He must have felt guilty and wanted to make amends," she thought out loud.

"Maybe, though it's like emptying the sea one drop at a time. When I first learned who my benefactor was, I thought he was being a good Samaritan. After he confessed, it got me thinking maybe your father knew too."

"All we can go by is what he put in his statement and—"

"Yes, and that gets your father off the hook, doesn't it?" Tanya interrupted. "They could send me millions and it would not make things right." She took a deep breath.

"As they say, you can forgive without forgetting," she offered even if terrible at taking her own advice.

"Perhaps. You are very kind to sit here and listen to my trespasses and recognize they come from a place that does not seek vengeance... but only justice. But if Phil Walsh threw himself on the grenade to save his buddy? Well, I would have a serious problem with that."

How big a problem she did not want to explore.

CHAPTER FORTY-FIVE

AFTER NAVIGATING A FEW CORRIDORS, Cassie finally located the door leading to the courtyard on the west side of the long-term care facility. The small brick patio was shielded by a six-foot white vinyl fence, which kept out the spring wind and wild critters, except for one philanderer. She stood behind the glass door and watched her mother and father interact. It felt like one of those silent movie clips where body language says it all. Dad wore jeans and a blue pull over sweater and looked at ease in a plastic Adirondack chair. Mom's shoulder-length strawberry-blonde hair was swept back and highlighted a complexion that never needed makeup, but also revealed a bit of shyness with her husband. She wore the colors of spring— a peach ruffle short sleeve top, white jeans and a windbreaker folded over the arm of the wheelchair. A little more progress and she could upgrade to a walker.

A small voice whispered it was wrong to spy. *"Can't you leave me alone for a minute?"* she replied to the ever-present critic which missed nothing. *"I just want to imagine the way things were – no, rather how they should have been. I want to see him look at her like he used to, even if she was taken for granted."* Suddenly, Dad leaned over, and he and Mom were face to face and continued for a few minutes in deep conversation. At the end, Mom grabbed Dad's hand and they kissed.

When her father stood, and fished his iPhone out of his pant pocket, she opened the door.

Her mother saw her first and waved. "Hi Cassie!" she said in a strong voice.

"Sounding good, Mom!" she replied and bent over and gave her a kiss on the cheek. "I can't believe the rapid progress you're making up here."

She turned to greet her father who looked up from the phone and simply nodded.

She returned a half-hearted wave.

"No kiss for Dad?" her mother asked.

They both looked at each other, and neither one moved. She broke the awkward moment by pulling over another plastic chair.

"I didn't know you were coming," she directed toward her father.

He flashed his pearly whites and looked around. "It's Sunday, so I figured why not drive up and enjoy a bit of paradise."

"Why? Because you're afraid you may never get to experience the real thing?" The question slipped out before she could stop it.

Her father took a deep breath before looking at Rose. "With all your mother's heaven points, I'm sure she can gift me some."

"I don't know if Saint Peter will validate your ticket because the vow is until death do you part. But then again, you ignored in sickness and in health too."

Her father came at her, but Rose reached out and caught him by the arm. "Why can't you two get along?"

"I'm sorry, Mom. I came up to see you and shouldn't be picking a fight." She glanced at her father who was breathing heavily through his nose.

"Did you get my message?" she asked her father trying to start again. "They have an opening at Northeast Rehab. Bringing

Mom back to Salem would allow us to visit more than on weekends."

"Why would anyone want to leave?" he asked looking around at the private mountain refuge.

"I agree she's making a lot of progress here, but she's tapping out their capabilities and needs a different level of rehab." She looked at Mom for support. "Tell him how we've talked about this."

Rose nodded and looked at her husband. "It would get me closer to home."

Her father rolled his eyes. "You two are ganging up on me like the old days. I'm on board, but my daughter can deal with the transfer hassle."

"Okay, it's settled then. I'll get the ball rolling tomorrow morning," she replied with a genuine smile.

"I just want to go home," Rose added.

She glared at her father. *When is he going to tell her the house has been sold and he's living with what's her name?*

Her father read her thoughts and looked at his watch. "It's quite a haul from here to Logan, so I have to get on the road."

Rose rubbed his hand. "Where are you going?"

"Miami. I have some business to take care of."

"I bet you do," Cassie said under her breath.

He gave his wife a quick peck on the cheek. "I'm thrilled with the progress you're making and glad we talked. You've given me a lot to think about. By the time I get back, I expect you'll be walking."

Cassie smiled. "Then she will run circles around us like she used to." She rubbed her mother's arm. "I'm going to walk Dad out to his car. When I come back, we can talk about what you want for dinner."

"The same thing I wanted for breakfast and lunch. Chocolate!" Rose said with a wink.

The reply was unexpected and made her laugh. She held onto the good humor as she silently followed her father through the building. When they got through the front entrance, he spun around and pointed a finger at her.

"What were you doing back there?"

"I could ask you the same question. Acting like a husband until your mistress summons you?"

"That's uncalled for. Can you at least acknowledge how complicated things are?"

"Seems pretty simple to me. While your wife was in storage you screwed around."

He cut the air with his right hand. "That's quite enough! Rachael took a leave of absence from her job and is staying in Miami for a while. I'm headed there this evening to end it so I can take care of my wife and your mother."

She felt her legs lose their feeling, and wanted to grab hold of her father, but fell back a few steps instead. "Are you serious?"

"Someday, I hope you can cut me some slack as my intentions have always been good. Your mother will never be the same woman I married, but the core of her remains. That's enough for me."

She tried to reconcile the words with the sick look on his face.

"What about Rachael?"

He snickered. "Funny, how you remember her name now? Rachael doesn't need all this drama."

"Why? Because she's afraid Phil will spill more about her role?"

He looked up at the sky and exhaled. "Do you ever run out of bullets?"

"I'm sure Phil could write a tell-all book if he wanted us to know more."

"More like a very short story, with the time he has left." He shook his head. "What do you think? You're his confessor now?" He began walking away and looked back. "I'll be in touch."

She made her way back to the courtyard and found Mom waiting in the same position. The spring day was still unusually warm, but she noticed a sudden coolness in this spot like the area was in its own microenvironment. It reminded her of the long winter journey she fought through.

"Do you remember the headsets I use to bring when I came to visit? she asked.

Her mother nodded.

"How about the beautiful places we visited and the wonderful talks we had while wearing them?"

Her face clouded over. "Sometimes I think so." She hesitated for a moment. "But I question if you planted the idea in my head." She grabbed her hand. "But thankfully, the most important things are ingrained. Maybe, it's a blessing some monsters fade away."

"At least your long-term memory is solid."

"I used to pride myself on being a walking … uh …. uh." Her face contorted.

"Encyclopedia," she offered.

Her mother moaned. "It's so frustrating when I can't find the word. It's like my tongue gets lost."

"I understand, but you're still a miracle woman."

"Your father said the same thing. He kept asking…." She stopped and shook her head.

"About what?" she asked, sensing it was not a missing word that froze her mother's tongue. Her parent's intense conversation, which she spied behind the glass door came to mind, along with the big lie she told her father. *Maybe he was scared Mom remembered him moving her into the driver's seat. He should be more afraid I'll tell Mom, which I will do when she's stronger!*

Rose remained silent, and her eyes began twitching which happened when she felt stressed about something. Her breathing quickened.

She shot her a reassuring smile. "It's okay, Mom. What do you want for dinner? I'm sure we can find something chocolate for dessert."

Her mother took a deep breath and exhaled. "He kept asking … if I remembered who drove home that night? He was more intense than you asking about the headsets. He kept pressing."

Her mind reeled. *Why would he ask who drove? To check up on his daughter's claim that she remembered? But why push for confirmation, when his best buddy confessed! The meeting in the hospital with Rachael came roaring back. She claimed they were engaged, but now Dad is suddenly dumping her and coming home like a prodigal husband, minus the regret and repentance.*

She rubbed her mother's arm. "I warned you he might bring this up." It was her turn to take a deep breath.

Rose nodded and draped the windbreaker over her knees. "We had issues back then, and I suspected he was messing around," she confessed as her voice trailed off. Her mother thought for a long moment and pouted. "I still have enough of my brain intact to realize he gave up on me. I'm sure there's someone else in the picture now." She looked at her daughter for confirmation.

Tears began building, and Cassie held her breath hoping to keep them from falling. "I can't go there with you, and I shouldn't. You need to ask Dad." She retrieved a tissue from her pocket and dabbed her eyes.

Her mother looked away, not pleased with the reply. "That's okay, daughter… I handled it."

"I'm so sorry, Mom." *This is all on me!* she thought.

"He went on and on about how he must have been dead to the world because he hated Phil's driving …. how Phil took drivers ed on the Dodgems at Canobie Lake Park and between that and the booze … hit all those poor people." She took a deep breath. "He said he convinced Phil to turn himself in."

The police report came to mind, and how Dad made sure his version of the story was captured.

"I told him I have flashes about that night, and remembered things differently than what's been reported." A sly smile appeared on her mother's face. "No matter how much he pushed, I left it at that and watched his face change. Fifteen minutes later, he said he would bring me home. He promises to take care of me."

"Why would you say that? You told me you don't remember much about that night!"

"I don't. But when I married your father, it was for life. I don't know who I'm competing with, but I play for keeps." She slowly shook her head. "Charles is a puffer fish when threatened. I can't say how, but I think Phil got stung."

CHAPTER FORTY-SIX

THE NURSE ESCORTED HER into the dimly lit room and pointed at the shell of a man asleep under a thin white blanket.

"He's on morphine, so he may not respond." She checked his pulse and gifted her with a warm smile. "If you need anything, I'll be down the hall."

"Thank you," she replied and waited for her to leave before coming alongside the hospital bed. The dying man's mouth was open wide, and she could smell the sourness of cancer."

She squeezed his clammy hand. "Uncle Phil? It's me, Cassie."

The words did not reach the space between this world and the next. She waited another minute, conflicted between employing a rougher approach or leaving. The thought of her father stocking up on applesauce for the homecoming, broke the impasse and she rubbed his shoulder gently.

She was about to give up when his eyes suddenly popped open; ink wells sinking into white bone.

Phil flexed his mouth open and shut. His lips looked like dry parchment paper. On a nearby tray, she spied a tall plastic cup of water and a long paper straw. She grabbed it and held the straw up to his mouth. He took a small sip and swished it around his mouth before swallowing.

He studied her face for a long moment. "Is that really you, Cassie?"

She leaned over and got close to his face. "Yes."

"With the drugs, I see many people." He pointed at the end of the bed. "Ellie was here a while ago holding the baby we lost when she miscarried."

Cassie noticed the tall shadows on the wall created from the light in the hall. That did not help matters.

"I might be high as a kite but I remember the last time we talked," he mumbled.

She searched his taut jaundiced face. "Including the lines my father fed you to memorize? I've spent years working on a thousand-piece puzzle with most of the pieces missing."

He licked his dry lips and closed his eyes.

She touched his cheek. "Stay with me Uncle."

He obeyed and gave her a small smile. "I always loved when you called me that. If I had a daughter, I would want her to be like you ..." He began drifting off.

She rubbed his hand. "I don't know why I accept anything at face value anymore. I did some digging through old newspaper files, and read about three stupid kids playing chicken with a train in Haverhill."

Phil opened his eyes, and it felt like he was looking through her. "Poor Ricky." He glanced at the end of the bed like he expected to see the dead teenager any second. "He's going to give me hell."

"You told me you took off after he got hit."

"We did, but I was never as tough as Charles and spilled the beans when I got home."

She nodded. "You got the rest backwards too. You didn't save my father, he saved you."

Phil turned his head away.

She went to the other side of the bed and leaned over. "You felt like you owed him. Right?"

He sighed and shook his head. "Best friends don't keep a ledger, but that doesn't mean we didn't compete. That day, I was determined to have more courage than both of them. If Charles hadn't pulled me off …" He put his thin hand to his mouth. "I'd be buried next to Ricky."

"Who drove the car the night of the hit and run?"

"I did."

"You have that story backwards too. My father drove."

He shook his head violently.

"Look. I know the type of man you are. Drunk or not, leaving the scene of an accident isn't in your DNA. Tell me what happened so I can remember a true uncle."

Phil's hand trembled as he rubbed his forehead. "Like I keep telling you...I drove."

She sensed he was tottering. "I know the story you spun at the police station was to protect my dad. Truth seeks the light." She pointed at the bottom of the bed. "Tell Ellie what happened."

Her father's life-long friend took a deep breath, and let it out like he had been underwater for years. "I drove for a bit … but I was exhausted … buzzed … and almost took out three mailboxes. So, I pulled over," he explained.

"Then what?"

"Charles woke up and said he wanted to drive."

"What did my mother say?"

"She told him he was drunk. Charles laughed and said it takes a drunk to know one. It made her cry, and she opened her purse and held up a nip of whiskey. She said she was tempted all night but had not taken a drop."

"Why did you side with my father?"

"I didn't! He got out of the car, and yanked me out. When he jumped in the driver's seat, Rose pleaded with him to let her drive. While they argued, I jumped in the back seat as the car took off. Then the doors to hell opened."

"After hitting the people on the bridge and slamming into the pole, he reminded you of your debt."

Phil looked at the end of the bed and said nothing.

"But your nephew arrived before you finished moving my mother. Brian helped with the coverup for a price. But the guilt was overwhelming, and you started sending money to Tanya every month."

Phil squinted. "How do you know that?"

"You included an address return label on the envelope last year."

He sighed and remained quiet for a long minute. "She was always in the news and so angry. I saw the hurt." He gulped a mouthful of air. "I told Charles about the payments and it ended our partnership."

She kissed him on the cheek. "But why confess to something you never did?"

"Because I'm not innocent. My life is over but Charles and Rose can have a new start."

Tears welled up in her eyes. "But sacrificing yourself doesn't give them a new start. It just adds more air to the balloon of lies that's about to pop." She took a deep breath and then kissed him softly on the forehead. "I still love you, Uncle."

He touched her cheek. "That's all I ever wanted. I pray not to be judged too harshly."

She held his hand until he drifted off to sleep. When the nurse reappeared, she exited the room and made it to the bathroom before throwing up the little she had in her stomach.

When she reached her car, she dialed Sean.

"I was hoping to hear from the super sleuth," he said in a thick voice, like she woke him up.

"Did you ever follow up on my mom's blood test?"

"Her alcohol level was three times over the limit. I haven't received the report yet on who drew the blood."

"I just visited Phil."

"I didn't see that one coming!"

"What if he confessed to something he didn't do?" she asked. Her mother and Phil appeared in her mind and coalesced around her father. "*He was more intense than you asking about the headsets. He kept pressing,*" her mother's voice echoed. "*He went on and on about how he must have been dead to the world because he hated Phil's driving ... how Phil took drivers ed on the Dodgems at Canobie Lake Park and between that and the booze ... hit all those poor people... I told him I have flashes about that night and remembered things differently. Fifteen minutes later, he said he would bring me home.*"

Phil chimed in from his deathbed. "*I'm not innocent. My life is over but Charles and Rose can have a new start.*"

Her heart skipped, realizing the coward was intent on saving his skin. "What if Phil confessed to something he didn't do?" she half-whispered.

"I'd say he was crazy. His name is mud forever," Sean said.

"Or dying and wants to protect a brother?"

"Did he admit that?"

She bit her lip.

Sean exhaled. "I'll take that as a yes, but even if he recanted his statement, who would believe him? He's in hospice on a morphine drip. Your father wouldn't even need a lawyer. No DA would touch it."

"That won't happen as Phil will take it to the grave. All that's left is my mother's memory if she ever recovers it."

"Like I said when you started down this path, you'll end up losing one of them. Phil Walsh is trying to prevent that."

"So, the man that killed and injured all those people goes scot-free?" She shook her head. "He thinks his penance is babysitting his wife, until he can figure out a way to get back with the bleached blonde."

"Your family would make a terrific reality tv series."

She sighed. "Unless I make him realize Miami is as close as he can get to New Hampshire without getting severely sunburned."

Hanging up she thought of the old saying, *keep your friends close, but your enemies closer*, and dialed the *Insight*.

CHAPTER FORTY-SEVEN

PULLING INTO THE PARKING LOT to meet James for lunch, she spied him sitting opposite Halle at a picnic table in front of the two-story brick building. Fate intervened, and she located a perfect parking space for spying. She sat mesmerized watching her husband continually slice the air while Halle sat with her head slightly bowed.

Her thoughts raced regarding the possibilities for this matinee. Work related? A lover's quarrel? Nothing was resolved when her iPhone buzzed, and though she hated the distraction, she answered.

"Phil is in hospice," she offered as a greeting to her father.

Yes, very sad. Hope he goes quick and doesn't suffer long."

"Will you go see him?"

The line went quiet. "Probably not. We've said our goodbyes."

When you were rehearsing his lines? she wanted to ask.

"Got back from Miami late last night and I'm racing to the office," he continued. "Have you read the *Insight* today?"

"I can see you're real broken up about Phil. You must feel conflicted how his confession made you a rock star."

"Don't try to get inside my head again."

But I already am, she thought.

"You didn't answer me. Did you see the *Insight*?"

"Why would I want to read that rag?" she replied with as much disgust as she could muster.

"Because the rest of Salem does, and I've gotten a dozen text messages. The front page has a huge splash that says Phil and I had a secret pact, and he confessed when his cancer became terminal. They accuse me of being behind the wheel that night. There's even a quote from Ellie's sister Jan, saying the night of the party, Phil called late to comfort his wife. He said he felt miserable hosting a bunch of drunks while Ellie was so sick."

I never thought of talking to Jan before visiting Phil in hospice, she thought.

"I'm meeting with my lawyer this afternoon and will sue them for slander!" her father barked.

She watched Halle stand up, and her husband follow. "They've been after Mom for ten years and wanted to hang Phil after his confession," she said bluntly. "Now he's dying, and they don't want the story to end because it sells papers. Your hate mail will triple."

"I'm numb to the threats. But the article says they have a very good source. Some of the details make me think so too."

"Maybe Phil said something?"

"He already said all there is to say. In the past, the *Insight's* rants were just a dump of gossip and conspiracies. But this time they pretended to be a real paper, and included photos of the car, and the position of the driver's seat. The paper claims it fits my frame better than Phil's. It also mentioned that Rachael was on duty that night. Funny, how it all sounds like you!"

She watched James hold out his hand, and Halle pulled him in for a light hug.

"Are you listening to me? Are you the source?" her father asked.

"Why would I do that? Phil's confessed. Everything is innuendo unless it isn't."

"What does that mean?"

"Are you really surprised the *Insight* would think coverup? Think about it. Phil stays quiet for ten years, let's Mom take the fall and then confesses on his way to the grave." She sighed. "I still believe truth stays above ground."

"What are you, some dime store philosopher?"

"No, but in this crazy world where many embrace fake news and conspiracies, this could influence your plans. Maybe you should work from Florida until things die down."

"There you go again, trying to drill into my head. All I'm saying, is none of this would have happened if you hadn't got under Phil's skin. That's why he spilled the beans instead of letting things be."

"Are you saying that with a straight face? I can't get my son to make his bed, but you think I uttered some magic words and your best friend confessed? I still find it curious he took responsibility for everything. Despite the stench, he worked on scrubbing his soul clean while you continue hiding in the muck."

"You're unbelievable!"

"The gossip around town is how Phil made our family whole again, but you're still with what's her name."

"I don't care what people think! It's over with Rachael."

"For how long? A few months? I'm sure that will cost you. She may want a bigger friendship ring."

"I expected that, but you'll see. Your mother and I will rebuild our lives."

"That should give the *Insight* material for years. So, how did the Florida girl take the news?"

"For the third time, stay out of my head."

"When we celebrate the coming home party for Mom, I'll show you a new product James worked on. One spin around the block with those headsets is all I need."

"So, you can feed the *Insight* more trash?"

"I'll have to read the article, though I understand their conclusion. You can dress yourself up as a victim, but it clashes with the truth."

"I have a meeting and enough of your insolence for today." The line went dead.

"Next batter up!" she muttered, and got out of the car and walked toward the fighting duo.

James eyed her first and rushed over. "I thought you were coming at noon?"

She shrugged and looked past him at Halle, who stood glaring at her with arms crossed. "You said your schedule was tight, so I got here a few minutes early." She pointed at the picnic table. "I was finishing a call in the car, and from what I saw thought you might need rescuing," she added in a low voice.

His cheeks grew red as Halle approached. Cassie took in her jeans and skin tight white t-shirt, and knew this outfit would replace the running getup in future nightmares.

They sized each other up for a moment and James noticed. "Cassie, you remember Halle?" The line was delivered so perfectly, he could have a career as an actor.

"Of course," she replied, matching his feat. "You two must run hot to be out here without coats."

James pointed to a lightweight jacket on top of the picnic table. "After the winter we've had, fifty degrees feels like July." He glanced at his colleague. "We're headed out to lunch and can pick this up later."

Halle's eyes narrowed and remained silent.

"Okay, let's go," James said pulling her away.

"Can we take your car?" she asked. "I'm running on empty."

"We can get some gas on the way."

"Why can't we take the Jeep?" she asked.

"Because the keys are in my office."

"Well, hurry and get them. Halle will keep me company."

James hesitated for a second before running toward the front entrance.

"You have plenty of gas, don't you?" Halle asked.

"Filled the tank last night," she replied.

Halle cocked her head. "What's this all about?"

"I'm curious to know your play here?"

"Play?"

"I think that defines it. You could get any guy in a fifty-mile radius but appear to have a crush on your middle-aged manager."

"Of course, this is from all your observations and what else? Stealing my diary or hearing your husband talk in his sleep?" She let out a short snicker. "I hate crushing your plans of having him sleep on the couch tonight, but I was in a long-term relationship which ended badly a week ago. James met with me out here so the team doesn't hear me getting grief for calling out so much."

She almost winced thinking of her own absences. "Sorry for you, but happy for your ex."

Halle licked her full lips. "Now that I'm free, you make me see how I could fall for someone like your husband. He's handsome and a genius in what we're doing here. After a couple beers, he's quite the flirt too."

She thought of her mom. "I know you make slick games here, but with James, I play for keeps."

"You say that," she replied, flipping her hair back, "but from what I've seen, you treat him like a kid brother if you notice him at all." She glanced at the entrance to the building. "Believe me, if I wanted him, he would take me out for long-lunches by next week." She smiled. "For now, his managerial attention is fun enough."

Cassie looked her in the eye and returned the smile. "Go ahead and bring your 'A' game, but be careful. James and I have been married since you were in kindergarten. He listens to me.

I'm sure with a little persuasion, he would have you transferred to the repair depot. I'm sure you'd enjoy tracking all the nuts and screws."

They continued staring at each other as James came running out.

"Are we all set?"

Cassie nodded and gave her husband a kiss on the lips.

He looked astonished.

She smiled at Halle. "Enjoyed our little chat."

"You're a real hoot, Gassie."

They were halfway to the Jeep, when James groaned. "Why would she mess with your name like that?"

She looked at him and they enjoyed a good laugh. The conversation stayed light through lunch, and they were on the way back when her phone rang. Seeing it was Sean, she let it go to voicemail. When he called ten seconds later, she repeated the process, but when it rang a third time, James rolled his eyes and said, "You better answer it."

She pushed the green button. "Sean, I'm tied up. Can I call you back later?"

"Cassie, are you driving?" There was an urgency in his voice which made her heart jump.

"No, James took me to lunch," she replied.

"Good. Something bad just went down at your father's office."

"Huh? He called me an hour ago."

"Things are fluid at the scene. Shots were fired and —"

"Is my father, okay?" she interrupted. "Was he shot?" The questions tumbled out in one long breath.

"He's injured," Sean replied quickly.

She heard a siren in the distance. "How bad is it?"

"Just get to Holy Family hospital."

"Who did this?"

"We have her in custody," he replied. "I have to go."

Tanya's words flashed in her mind. *"Anger, sadness, bitterness, resentment leads not only to hardening of the arteries, but a sepsis of the spirit. If Phil Walsh threw himself on the grenade to save his buddy, I would have a serious problem with that."*

CHAPTER FORTY-EIGHT

CASSIE STOOD IN THE DRIVEWAY looking at the Jeep packed to the hilt with suitcases.

James put his arm around her. "We're only driving two hours north for the weekend, but you're packing like we're headed to the moon."

"Well, I always hope for a flawless mission, but prepare for Apollo 13," she said with a laugh.

James rolled his eyes and smiled at William. "Houston, looks like we have another problem."

She nodded. "As we agreed, after the funeral tomorrow, there will be no soundbites because I'm confiscating both your phones."

James and William looked toward Main Street and the line of tv trucks.

"How am I going to keep track of my friends if I can't check my phone?" William asked for the tenth time today.

"Ask again, and I'll keep it under lock for a week. Your friends will survive with you being off the grid for three days. Plus, if they forget what you look like, I'm sure there will be ample video on tv and social media. We need a family weekend if we're going to survive the next few weeks until this hopefully dies down." She pointed at her mother sitting on a lawn chair in a private corner of the yard, free from prying eyes and cameras.

"Consider your grandmother. She had no electronics for ten years."

"Not true," her son protested. "Nana said her tv droned on for hours every day."

James grabbed her hand. "Maybe if we behave, you'll let us check our email a couple times?"

"You have high hopes."

"The world doesn't stop just because we unplug ourselves." He turned to his son. "Help me get the inflatable kayaks, and we can talk about winning her over."

William was still moping as she wandered over to her mother.

"Why are you smirking?" her mother asked.

She pointed back at the two men in her life. "Because they're hatching a plan to distract me, so they can check their phones this weekend. But I'm one step ahead of them."

"How so?"

"I intend to remove the SIM cards from their phones before we leave." She let out a short laugh. "I'll let them pamper me all weekend and have a good laugh when they find out. We may be in for a long quiet ride home, but that's okay."

"Don't they know by now they can't wear you down? You got your father's tenacity."

"But hopefully not his conscience," she replied and bit her lip.

Her mother slowly stood up and fell into her arms. Their chests rose and fell in unison as they shed more tears.

Taking a step back, Cassie pulled a batch of tissues out of her pant pocket and handed one to her mother.

"Did you sleep any better last night?"

"Not really. I hate taking sleeping pills because they give me terrible dreams and life is tough enough."

Her mother kissed her on the cheek and sat down in the lawn chair. Cassie followed her lead and sat on the spring grass next to a healthy dandelion.

"I just can't stop thinking this is all my fault," she said addressing the flowering weed. "If I hadn't called the *Insight*, Tanya would not have…" The sequence of events repeated again in her mind, and ended on the lifeless shell of her father in the emergency room. "She sat on my couch asking for forgiveness and talking about justice. Then she shoots him in cold blood, acting as both judge and executioner."

Rose let out a deep sigh. *"He causes his sun to rise on the evil and the good and sends rain on the righteous and the unrighteous.* We're in shock trying to make sense of it all. You must remember, the police said Tanya thought of confronting your father at the office once before, but he wasn't there."

"Yes, it was the same day she brought me daffodils."

"So, she had her mind made up long before you called the paper. It was …" Rose's face contorted searching for the word.

"Inevitable?" she offered. "I have a hard time accepting that."

Her mother shrugged. "Then chalk it up to cause and effect."

"Perhaps, but I've come close to taking the headsets down to the funeral home, hoping I can have one last conversation with Dad. Tell him I'm furious, but also heartbroken because he'll always be my father. I still love him no matter the terrible mistakes he made out of fear and selfishness." She looked up at her beautiful mother and felt a stab in her throat. "Unfortunately, the words will come easy because it's how I felt about you for so many years."

Rose sighed. "I appreciate how you sheltered me until I was strong enough, but love you more for finally telling me the truth about that night." Her mother smiled and cupped one hand to her ear. "Listen how the robins, chickadees, and cardinals sing, no matter their losses. All we can do is follow their example, and accept the things we can't change. During those applesauce lunches, your father said more than once it's easy to do the right thing, but knowing what the right thing is …. well, that gets complicated."

"But there's no gray in this black and white picture. That's where he failed."

"And where we won't. We can be the change we want to see in this world." She gently stroked her hair.

"There's been enough pain already to cry the oceans dry, but I've come to realize we shouldn't reserve what needs to be said to our dreams, whether real or virtual," she replied and stood up.

Rose followed and pulled her daughter in for a tight hug. Cassie savored their embrace not virtually, but in the richness of His creation— a beautiful, though sometimes godforsaken place where redemption is possible with enough faith and love.

ACKNOWLEDGEMENTS

THIS STORY IS A COMBINATION of separate threads that came together quite unexpectantly. In high school, I was in the back seat of a car that kissed a bridge wall at a hundred-ten miles an hour. That no one was killed is truly a miracle, and no doubt snuffed out all of my nine lives except this one. I have a lot of regrets about that night and the days afterwards. While I escaped with only a concussion, I've sometimes mused — usually when things go haywire, that maybe this is all a dream and I'm lying in a coma somewhere.

The second thread is the ongoing explosion of virtual reality technology. My son-in-law Michael, is a pioneer in his brave new world and has been very gracious to take me on several tours. Each time I take the Oculus headset off, I'm amazed at the expanding virtual world of the future, realizing its potential for both good and evil.

Weaving this story also required different colored threads of perseverance, love, faith and some of the darker attributes of human nature. In thinking through the tenacity of Cassie, or the faith of Rose, I recalled working at Millipore and sharing the story of Dr. Judah Folkman, a pioneer in the study of angiogenesis, a revolutionary approach of starving cancers by cutting off its blood supply. For years, Dr. Folkman was mocked for this theory, but his persistence paid off and led to life-saving cancer drugs. On a personal scale, but no less incredulous, I have seen instances where the curtain between science and the miraculous blurs. Embracing that outlook makes all the difference.

While working on the final edits of the story, the last thread came suddenly, when I lost my mother. Though heartbroken, I am comforted knowing in God's tender mercy, she is now reunited with my father. When it came to Vincent and Grace Donovan, they did not lead with their heads or hearts, but with their souls. This has given the Donovan clan a different perspective on our parents, and what defines a meaningful and well-lived life. Their impact on both our DNA and conscience is as expansive as the earth and sky— maybe because to build a staircase to heaven, it takes blood, sweat, tears, copious amounts of grace and two inspired guides. While our parents had different approaches, they were in lockstep no matter the time of day, the weather, or the season. The daily ways they demonstrated their love, proves how the earth and sky not only kiss at the horizon, but at every point in between. Faith and family were their oxygen. They represented the ultimate story of two people who fell in love and through incredible self-sacrifice and commitment, lived a Christ-filled life no matter the challenges. They left their six children and spouses, twenty-six grandchildren, seventeen great-grandchildren, and extended family and friends, with a treasure no scale can weigh.

As I have voiced many times, the true reward in sharing these stories are the people I meet, and the feedback received. Bringing a story to its full potential is quite a marathon. No matter how many times I travel this road, I deeply appreciate all the love and support. Special thanks to my wife and best friend Robin, for allowing me to disappear into these fictional dreams. Crafting a story is a joy, it's all the editing that can become mind numbing. Her eagle eye for proofreading kept me sane. The same can be said of my daughters, Heather and Taylor and son-in-law Michael. Their encouragement, insight and creativity are a constant, no matter how busy they are. In particular, I owe Taylor special kudos as she held my feet to the fire to complete this manuscript in record time and read it first. I also have to include a note of love for my grandsons, Nolan and Wesley. They remind me every day, that imagination does not have a shelf-life. I am also blessed with an incredible family and humbled for their continual support. I also want to thank my friends, both old and new in this writing endeavor, in rallying around my previous works. I am especially thankful for being part of the Black Rose Writing family. Their high standards and professionalism are incredible.

I hope you enjoyed this story of the many faces of human nature and the saving grace of perseverance and redemption. I also hope you will post a review, and look forward to hearing from you on my author website: **vincentdonovanbooks.com**.

ABOUT THE AUTHOR

Vincent Donovan, a two-time quarter-finalist in the highly-competitive Amazon Breakthrough Novel Contest, graduated with a B.A in English from Merrimack College and an M.B.A from Rivier University. For over twenty-seven years, Vin worked in various leadership positions in the biopharmaceutical industry. His debut novel *Chasing Mayflies* was a 2017 finalist for the Christian Small Publishers Association Book of the Year Award for General Fiction. His follow-up literary adventures, *A Difficult Crossing* and *Only Dead Leaves Fall* have received rave reviews.

ONLY DEAD
LEAVES FALL

VINCENT DONOVAN

NOTE FROM VINCENT DONOVAN

Word-of-mouth is crucial for any author to succeed. If you enjoyed *Killer Dreams*, please leave a review online—anywhere you are able. Even if it's just a sentence or two. It would make all the difference and would be very much appreciated.

Thanks!
Vincent Donovan

We hope you enjoyed reading this title from:

www.blackrosewriting.com

Subscribe to our mailing list – *The Rosevine* – and receive **FREE** books, daily deals, and stay current with news about upcoming releases and our hottest authors.
Scan the QR code below to sign up.

Already a subscriber? Please accept a sincere thank you for being a fan of Black Rose Writing authors.

View other Black Rose Writing titles at www.blackrosewriting.com/books and use promo code **PRINT** to receive a **20% discount** when purchasing.

www.ingramcontent.com/pod-product-compliance
Lightning Source LLC
Chambersburg PA
CBHW050137120726
47903CB00002B/397